Northwoods Wolfman
Monsters in the Midwest, Book Two

Scott Burtness

FREE Short Story

Get *Five Stars*, a FREE demonic horror comedy short story, when you sign up for **The Paranomedy Pint**, Scott's once-a-month email featuring a great book to read, a fun show to watch, something terrific to drink, and a little paranormal weirdness to enjoy!!

For Liz.

You're the koozie to my beer can.

Contents

It Had to Start Somewhere...

T HE EGG HATCHED, RELEASING the young *Dermacentor variabilis* larva upon an unsuspecting world. Wriggling away from the nest into the surrounding grass, it had no thoughts, no plans, no aspirations. Those were the burdens of more evolved creatures. Only one desire occupied the tiny ganglion of nerves that served as the wood tick's brain. It was time to feed.

Six legs pushing it up a blade of grass, it waited with a spider's patience for its first meal. A field mouse happened by, munching hurriedly on small seeds scattered amidst the brush. The tiny larvae's outstretched limbs snagged its side, and soon it was working its way through the fur to the warm skin beneath.

About four days later, the tick dropped back down to the grassy field. Digesting its meal, the maturing tick molted, sloughing off its skin to reveal an eight-legged nymph. Climbing a fresh blade of grass, it quivered in anticipation of its next host. An unsuspecting ground squirrel passed by, stopped, and scratched, its hind leg a blur of movement. Despite its efforts to dislodge the sudden and unexpected itch, the nymph had already sunk its head in deep. Eight legs gripped, flattening its body tight against flesh as it filled its slowly expanding abdomen with rich, warm blood.

The squirrel carried its parasitic passenger on a haphazard path across the prairie until chemical triggers prompted the tick to drop back to the ground. Saturated with blood, it molted again, growing to its full adult size. The persistent hunger, all it had ever known, pressed it onward. Despite its limited awareness, the tick knew the days were growing shorter, and cooler weather was settling in. Only a few of its siblings would survive the coming cold. To survive, it had to feed.

· · · ● · ● · ● · · ·

The man paused in the clearing, savoring the feel of the setting sun that warmed his brow and the crisp autumn air that cooled it. Searching for an elusive serenity, he stood quietly as the day drew to a close. He hoped that he had trekked far enough into the state park to prevent anyone from getting hurt. Soon, the full moon would come and with it the now-familiar horrors. For a moment, though, he set his worry aside and simply enjoyed the sunset. Lost in his reverie, he didn't feel the wood tick climb his shoe, work its way over his sock, and bite into the skin of his calf.

· · · ● · ● · ● · · ·

Jason and Reggie made their fifth left-turn. While persistence is usually a virtue to be admired, in this case, it has simply made them lost.

When looking at a map, Illinois's Moraine Hills State Park seemed like an old wilderness long tamed. Color-coded paths and helpful sign posts ensured that even the most suburbanized of hikers would safely find their way through the rolling fields, lakes, and wetlands.

What the trail guides and sign posts didn't show was that buried deep inside the orderly arrangement of scenic lookouts and convenient port-o-pots were winding deer trails and coyote runs that could confound even the savviest of Kicapoux trackers. Rather than emerging from their impromptu shortcut through the wooded hills to where their friends waited at the picnic site, Jason and Reggie instead found themselves in an unmarked clearing. Shadows cast by the surrounding trees swelled as the full moon rose. Catching the fading rays of the setting sun, its unnaturally bright silver glow was tinged with hints of orange and red.

"Told you we should've turned left," Reggie deadpanned after a long drag on the mostly smoked joint. The ensuing giggle-fit had the two friends doubled over, tears streaming down their cheeks, when an unexpected voice leapt through the dusk.

"What are you doing here?"

Jason gasped in surprise while Reggie yelped, burped, and laughed in rapid sequence, inducing a sudden and violent case of the hiccups.

"Oh, um. Hic. We, ah, just hic... should'a turned left," Reggie choked out, laughing and trying to take a quick hit between hiccups. Walking toward the stranger through the darkening shadows, Reggie held out the joint in invitation.

"There's a party near the, hic... McHenry Dam, dude. Trade you a toke for, hic... directions."

The stranger shook his head vigorously from side to side and pressed his palms against his eyes.

"*Run*," the man growled, actually *growled* before an arm shot out and a hand grabbed Reggie's neck.

Something between a hiccup and a scream barely made it past Reggie's lips before the stranger's grip cut off any chance of air escaping from his constricting throat. As the hand squeezed, its fingers and knuckles swelled. Nails yellowed and lengthened, sharpening at the tips until they pierced skin and drew blood. Dark, coarse hair sprouted from the back of the hand and crept up the corded muscles of the man's forearm. A series of pops and snaps split the otherwise silent clearing as joints cracked and bones stretched. Cheekbones and brow pushed forward while lips so recently red darkened to a muddy brown. The man's nose turned up. His ears pulled to points. Brown locks of well-groomed hair lost their smooth gloss and curled into a pelt-like nap. Soon, his entire face was covered in coarse fur. Strangest of all, though, were the eyes. Bright, piercing blue with flecks of gold, they stared straight into Reggie's, fully aware of the pain and torment being inflicted.

The metamorphosis from man to beast took less than fifteen seconds. By its end, Reggie's throat had been bloodied and crushed. Finally, the massive, clawed fingers relaxed, and the previously upright Reggie fell bodily to the blood-spattered grass.

Frozen in uncomprehending horror, Jason watched his friend fall lifeless to the dirt. His only lucid thought as the beast grabbed his arms was to wonder why the park ranger hadn't warned them. You'd think a well-tamed state park like this would let people know a werewolf was on the loose.

. . . . ● . ● ● . . .

Jerry was annoyed. His boss had scheduled him for three back-to-back sales calls on the same day, two in eastern Wisconsin and the third all the way down in Illinois. To make matters worse, he'd gotten a speeding ticket trying to make it to the state park on time, only to find that the park's office manager was 'busy.'

"He'll be back soon, though?" Jerry asked, stifling his impatience. "I've got the glossed paper samples he wanted."

And a and a five-hour drive to get home, he grumbled to himself.

Shrugging noncommittally, the girl at the reception desk invited him to wait outside and enjoy the autumn evening. Since there was nowhere to sit inside, Jerry bought a small can of bug spray and headed out to the patio. Muttering about how homicidal mosquitoes and clouds of irate gnats were anything but enjoyable, he soaked himself with the spray, settled into a chair on the patio, and watched the sun slide down the western sky.

When Horace Tulane, the McHenry Dam's office manager and volunteer Park Ranger of the Moraine Hills State Park, finally arrived, the sun had set, the moon had risen, and the gnats had yet to call it a day.

"Sorry," Horace offered. "I would have been back sooner, but some hikers thought they heard a wolf howl. Had to check it out."

Jerry looked worried as he asked, "Did you find one? A wolf, I mean. Are there wolves here?"

"No," Horace replied. "Probably just college kids at the picnic shelter by the dam. They're always sneaking out there after dusk, smoking their dope and making a ruckus. One must've thought it'd be funny to howl at the moon. Rotten kids."

Nodding sympathetically, Jerry flipped open his briefcase and set out samples and brochures. He supposed kids in rural Illinois weren't too different from kids in his hometown of Trappersville, Wisconsin. Nestled in the state's northern woods, just outside the Nicolet National Forest and near the banks of the Wolf River, the small town was a tick-infested, cheese-infused, flannel-clad waiting room for the last train to boredom. Even the summer's spate of murders and whispered claims of an honest-to-god vampire couldn't change the fact that Trappersville was otherwise one-hundred percent Podunk.

Waving away the persistent gnats, Jerry shuffled some brochures around, a clear indication that he was ready to get back on the road. Meanwhile, Horace rifled distractedly through the various samples of paper stock, anxious to head back into the darkening woods and bust some college stoners.

• • • • ● • ● • • • •

The werewolf reveled in the feel of rubbery flesh between his gnashing jaws. Blood-slicked chunks slid down his gullet as he chewed and swallowed the unfortunate hiker, one ripping bite at a time. Engrossed with trying to literally fill himself with humanity, he didn't feel the miniscule parody of his own dark hunger biting deep into his flesh. He didn't hear it when it screamed a tiny wood tick scream, or notice as it rippled and contorted and sprouted coarse hairs all over its arachnid carapace. The resulting abomination bit into its monstrous host with a fierce, unnatural hunger that would only slake with the setting of the full moon.

· · · ● · ● · ● · · ·

Fed up with swatting ineffectually at the cloud of gnats, Jerry reached for his bottle of bug spray. Glancing up, he noticed a man jog out from the trees near the visitor's center. As he squinted into the dusk, he tried to figure out what the guy was wearing. It looked like a sweatshirt and jeans pulled over a gorilla suit.

"Um, Horace?" he managed before the stranger was on them.

Closing the last few yards, the thing Jerry had thought was a man crouched, leapt, and landed directly in front of him. With a high-pitched squeal, Jerry enveloped it in a cloud of DEET before he stumbled backward and knocked his briefcase from the table.

Snarling, the beast turned and leapt again. Briefly backlit by the newly risen full moon, it landed on the roof of the visitor's center, fluidly crouched and leapt a third time, and vanished from sight on the far side. Jerry's mouth worked like a guppy, while Horace's face turned beet red with a tinge of purple around the edges.

"Goddamn stoners!" he yelled, grabbing the radio from his over-stocked utility belt. "Now they're doing the PCP in my woods? No way! Not on my watch, they aren't." Jerry forgotten, Horace hurried inside, urgently calling in to report the hairy, drug-crazed teenager that had just leapt over a building in two bounds.

For his part, Jerry was simply flummoxed by the whole affair. The rational part of his brain kept pinging his eyes, advising them that Horace was right, and they had just seen an unusually hairy teenager on drugs run out of the woods and leap over a building. A perfectly sensible explanation, reasoned Jerry's brain.

Unfortunately, his eyes kept sending a different story back to the brain. They felt quite strongly that it wasn't a teenager at all but a six-foot tall dog appropriately dressed for the early autumn weather and running on two legs instead of four. While his eyes and brain argued, Jerry decided he'd had enough of the Moraine Hills State Park. He gathered up the scattered brochures and samples with shaking hands and returned them to his briefcase. Glancing nervously at the dark woods, he scurried to his car, unaware of the minuscule monstrosity seething with unnatural hunger between brochures and invoices in his briefcase.

• • • • • • • • • •

It was a long drive back to the tiny town of Trappersville, Wisconsin. At least Jerry's boss had agreed to let him work from home the next day. The autumn nights were getting colder, and the furnace was on the fritz.

Just one more reason to hate Wisconsin, thought Jerry. *Sweat all summer and then we freeze.*

He'd called Dallas at That Blows HVAC before leaving on his sales trip, since it was really the only option in town for furnace repair, but regretted it the second Dallas picked up. Jerry could practically smell booze through the phone. The local bowling champ was known by all to be a bit of a drinker, but Jerry hadn't seen him sober in weeks.

A month or so prior, Dallas had supposedly stabbed Jerry's neighbor, Herb Knudsen, with a pool cue at the bowling alley's karaoke bar. When no one could find Herb to confirm Dallas's story, he swore Herb was a vampire who burned right up to nothing after getting stabbed. Other witnesses had differing opinions. A few sheepishly agreed that Dallas was probably right, but most said they couldn't be sure, since a significant amount of alcohol stood between them and a clear recollection of what had transpired. One thing was certain, though. No one had seen Herb since that night.

When the sheriff's department finally searched Herb's rambler in the woods, they turned up a whole slew of dead animals buried in the root cellar, including Jerry's pug. With that discovery, it didn't take much to connect the unassuming line cook to a recent spate of murders. The general consensus was that Herb had killed the animals for practice before upgrading to a tourist, two strippers, and a couple of frat boys. After Dallas confronted him at the karaoke bar, Herb had skipped town for fear of getting caught. Dallas, however, stuck to his story, insisting that he'd saved the whole town from a bloodthirsty monster. Since no one could prove him wrong, he'd crowned himself the Hero of Trappersville and had been soaking in alcohol ever since.

"Better send Pam and the girls to the outlet mall in case he's still drunk tomorrow," Jerry decided as he pulled into his driveway. Sore and tired from a long drive, he groaned his way out of the car and headed inside. Slipping into bed with his wife, he closed his eyes, made an effort not to think of the strange events from earlier that night, and waited for sleep.

Chapter 1

Dallas's alarm clock was a right bastard. A whiny, self-righteous twit. "Don't get mad at me," it buzzed. "Is it *my* fault that you drank a fifth of Wild Turkey?"

He really wanted to come up with a truly devastating response. If the damn thing would just *shut up,* he'd think of a zinger that would put that bleating piece of plastic in its place. But no, the noisy little nuisance wouldn't shut up. It just kept complaining and complaining and complaining…

A hand fumbled out from under the covers and moved across a dark wood nightstand, knocking over a half-empty can of beer and getting tangled up in a pair of fuzzy handcuffs. A second, well-placed grope landed the hand directly on the clock-radio, fingers working to decipher the complex code of a snooze button. The brief moment of quiet was followed by a loud snore.

Dallas flipped onto his side to see what had made the horrible noise. Squinting in the dark and trying to bring his still-drunk eyes into focus, he made out the curve of a shoulder, back, and hip partially covered by zebra print sheets. Closer inspection revealed a nice display of side-boob and dark trusses spread across the pillow. For a moment, Dallas thought a little somethin' somethin' would be just the thing to get his day started, and then the sleeping beauty's mouth opened a little wider and sawed another log.

Yeesh, that girl can snore! he thought as he turned over. *Wait a sec...*

Rolling back toward the girl, he reached out and shook her shoulder.

"Hey. Hey you. Wake up for a sec, would'ya?"

The girl groaned and smacked her lips. First one, then both eyes cracked open to glare blearily at Dallas.

"Wha?" she asked.

"Um, who are you?"

"Fuckyouasshole."

"No, seriously. What's your name again?"

"Mandy." The disgusted glare shut off as the eyes closed again, followed by another long snore.

"Huh. Mandy. Okay then."

Dallas swung his legs out of the bed and dropped his feet to the beer-soaked bedroom carpet. Unfazed by the squishing between his toes, he wobbled upright, staggered toward the bathroom, and started another day.

Mornings were usually like this. In the month or so since he'd killed his best friend, Dallas had done an excellent job of pickling his liver. It wasn't like he'd planned to party and drink all the time. He just didn't want to think about that night, and sex and alcohol made that very reasonable goal much more attainable. Shaking his head to clear away the memories, Dallas made his way downstairs.

Time heals all wounds, he reminded himself. Although in his case, 'time' had been replaced with whiskey and beer. Speaking of which, it was time for breakfast. A glance at the clock reminded him he needed to be quick about it. Jerry's furnace was on the fritz, and Dallas had to save the day.

When he arrived at Jerry's house, Dallas was feeling fine. Jerry seemed a little sick, though. He kept covering his nose and turning his head away.

"Whassa problem, Jimmy? Flu?" he asked.

"Ah, it's Jerry, actually…"

"Whatever. You said the fan's broke?"

"No. I think it's the thermostat. Seems like it doesn't kick on until the temp gets about eight or ten degrees below what we set it at."

"Thermostat? Bullshit. Blower fan. Guaran-frickin-tee."

"But the fan works fine. It's just that,"

"Who's the goddamn furnace guy here?" Dallas snapped. His good mood was slowly giving way to a grinding headache. When Jerry didn't respond, he nodded. "Thought so. Now where's that furnace?"

A few hours later, Dallas had replaced the thermostat, blower fan, filter, electric pilot, and vacuumed out the vent stack. At least, he thought so. While he'd been working, he'd also emptied the flask he kept in his toolbox.

"Guess I got a little carried away," he said with a shrug. "So I guess, I mean. Well, ya know. I'll only charge you for the,"

"Thermostat."

"Right. That, and the,"

"Thermostat," Jerry stated flatly. "I didn't want the other stuff and told you repeatedly not to do it, so I'm not paying. Pam would kill me."

Dallas's blood pressure pushed up a few points, causing a vein to pulse in his forehead. He really needed a drink.

"Shit. Well, you know." Dallas shrugged in resignation. "Tell your friends I did a damn good job, and we'll call it even."

Jerry nodded and turned to find his checkbook. After working his way through the office, bedroom, and kitchen, he returned, looking perplexed.

"Huh. I know it's around here somewhere."

After patting down the pockets of a couple of coats hanging on the wall, Jerry noticed his briefcase sitting on the bench by the door. Leaning over, he flipped the latches and popped it open. After pushing a few miscellaneous brochures out of the way, his hand emerged victorious with a checkbook.

As the two men dickered again over the price of a thermostat with additional free services, neither noticed the small tick climb out of the case, fall to the floor, and wriggle toward its next unsuspecting meal.

Chapter 2

MANDY WAS GONE BY the time Dallas got back from Jerry's. Unfortunately, so was his buzz, and some right unpleasant thoughts were starting to creep in. Pulling open the fridge, he popped the tab on his last Milwaukee's Best and drained it in one long pull, throat working industriously to move the beer from the can to his stomach. Letting out a loud sigh, he eyed the empty can with disappointment. He didn't have any other service calls for the day and figured a trip to Steinknocker's was in order for a real lunch.

After pushing his way inside the local bar, Dallas shouldered past the regulars. He nodded in response to the usual greetings, but did his best to get to the bar without actually engaging anyone.

"That's him!" he heard an unfamiliar voice say in a loud whisper. "Says he killed a vampire."

Dallas pointedly ignored the muted laughter along with the visions that followed closely on its heels. He didn't want to see the inside of Bay City Bowler's karaoke bar, didn't want to see Herb's face as he realized there was a two-foot length of lacquered wood extending from his chest, and he definitely didn't want to see the slow fire burning his best friend from the inside out as Herb turned to ash.

Shifting his gaze to look for Stein, owner and proprietor of Stein-knockers Bar, Dallas's eyes couldn't avoid the framed picture of Helen up on the wall. A decorative vase filled with plastic flowers rested serenely beneath it, surrounded by sympathy cards for Stein. Former waitress at Steinknockers and stripper at Nekked's, Helen had been one of Herb's victims. The full sequence of events was never quite unraveled, but Dallas figured Herb seduced her, turned her into a vampire, and then torched her in the strip club's tanning booth in a vindictive rage when she interfered with his frat-boy dinner. It was so completely 'not Herb' that Dallas had to choke back a harsh laugh.

Hell, seems like the whole summer, Herb was 'not Herb,' he thought.

It made Dallas wonder how well he'd ever known the man he'd considered his best friend since their school days. He missed that friend terribly, but the thing he'd stabbed at Bay City Bowlers, that wasn't Herb. He stopped being Herb when someone, some thing turned him into a goddamn monster. Dallas wished he knew who, so he could bust another pool cue and stab that vampire, too.

Stein made his way over and offered a, "Howdy, Dallas." Noticing the direction of Dallas's gaze, he wiped at an involuntary tear.

"Yeah, she was a gem. A right gem, taken a'fore her time. Never late. Always cashed out even at the end of her shift. Great rack, too," Stein observed with a shaky sigh.

Dallas just nodded as Stein poured two whiskeys and raised one up.

"To Helen," the bartender toasted, eyes moist.

"Helen," Dallas agreed, whiskey burning away his self-doubts.

He'd killed a monster. A goddamn monster. Too late to save Helen, but he'd saved Lois and saved the whole town. He was a hero. A goddamn hero.

Chapter 3

"**Y**OU'RE NEEDED."

The nasally voice cut through the whiskey fog, rousing Dallas from his stupor. Before he could put meaning to the words and identify the speaker, the person was gone.

"Haven't seen him b-before," Stanley commented.

"Stanwee?" Dallas slurred. "Whend'choo get here?"

Stanley had hung around with Dallas and Herb for years. Wiry, fidgety, and a terrible bowler, he had rounded out their backwoods version of the Three Musketeers, or more like Two Musketeers and That Stuttering Guy Who Claimed He Was Abducted by Aliens. Since Herb's death, he'd been Dallas's near-constant drinking companion.

"J-just now," Stanley replied. "Saw you talking to that guy," he said, pointing toward the door.

Dallas's bleary gaze followed Stanley's finger, and he locked eyes with a stranger across the bar. The two considered each other for a moment before the man nodded and walked outside.

With a shrug and a short belch, Dallas returned his attention to Stanley. His friend was scrutinizing a business card, a perplexed look layered on top of the usually perplexed look he wore as a matter of course, making him look especially... Dallas groped for the right word... perplexed.

"Crap on a cracker, Stanley. You looking for the cure for cancer on that thing? Give 'er here and let me help you with the big words."

Swiping the card, he read out loud, "Find us. You're needed."

Dallas borrowed Stanley's perplexed look and tried it on for a moment. He'd heard that before. Recent like. A nasally voice. For some reason, the face of the man he'd just been trading looks with popped back into his mind. The voice he recalled seemed like it would fit the man's face. Gaunt, squinty eyes, straight brown hair slicked back from a dark widow's peak, scraggly hairs making a go at becoming a goatee. Yeah, it could've been that guy, but why was he talking to Dallas? What did they talk about? Why leave the card? A closer look popped the tab on a deeper mystery. Why leave a card telling him to find someone but not leave an address or a number? It was a mystery, pure and simple, and there were few things Dallas hated more than mysteries.

"Guy must have a busted furnace," Dallas reasoned out loud, causing Stanley's head to bob in assent. "Jackass didn't leave a number, though. How the hell am I supposed to help if he didn't leave me a number?"

"Something's on the b-back," Stanley offered, a touch of drama coloring his tone.

Unlike Dallas, Stanley liked mysteries. He had every season of *Murder, She Wrote, Columbo,* and *Veronica Mars,* and took great pleasure in rewatching them and solving the crimes before Angela Lansbury, Peter Falk, or Kristen Bell.

Dallas turned the card over, and sure enough, there was more. *TURN 2 2 AT 2 2 2*

Dallas read the line once, then twice, trying to make it make sense. Sometimes, the right amount of alcohol allowed for just the kind of out-of-the-box thinking a riddle like this might need to solve. Sadly, this wasn't one of those times. This time, the amount of alcohol Dallas had imbibed didn't help him to think around corners, so to speak. It just helped him get more upset in less time. A win from an efficiency standpoint perhaps, but otherwise a complete loss.

"The hell does that mean? Well, I guess the jackass will just have to freeze."

With a grumbled curse, Dallas crumpled the card and dropped it on the bar. Slapping Stanley on the back, he stumbled toward the door and into the gathering night, the strange man and even stranger card already forgotten.

Chapter 4

I T WAS THE SAME dream. Usually with enough whiskey, say, the amount needed to fill a small aquarium, Dallas could keep it at bay. Tonight though, his blood alcohol level must've dropped below point-one-two because here he was, stuck in the dream... no, the nightmare again.

He bounced along on a sea of shoulders while faces beamed up at him, eyes wide and grins stretching ear to ear. The bouncing had a cadence to it, a rhythm. As Dallas bobbed like a ducky in an endless tub, the crowd marched in step and chanted in time.

Ding-dong the vamp is dead. Mean old vamp, wicked vamp. Ding-dong the wicked vamp is dead!

Dallas laughed, whooped, rolled to and fro across the sea of uplifted hands. He closed his eyes and opened them again and now was inside a bathroom. A quick glance around and he recognized it as the school bathroom from eighth grade. Sure as shit, there was Joey O'Connell. The little punk was always bullying the weirdos in school. He had some red-headed kid by the undies, a textbook-perfect wedgie in progress. Dallas knew this day. It was the day he first met Herb and started their life-long friendship. He also knew that for it to be an accurate memory, he should be in a stall making out with Denise Landry, not outside watching events unfold.

That's the thing with nightmares, Dallas thought. *Always getting things mixed up. Scarier that way.*

True enough, the fear was building. Having had this same dream countless times in the past few weeks, he knew full well what happened next but remained powerless to stop it.

Joey laughed, the sound a high-pitched, manic warble that pattered on Dallas's eardrums like BB's on a metal roof. Dallas laughed as well, unable to stop himself. Joey kicked open the door of a bathroom stall, and Dallas sprang out like a jack-in-the-box, busted pool cue in hand. The jagged end slid into Herb's chest, a slight tug the only indication that the chunk of wood was driving through skin, bone, and heart.

Lois screamed, and he pressed his hands to his ears, shouting back in response.

Ding-dong the vamp is dead! Wicked vamp, no good vamp!

He was still screaming as the crowd pulled him limb from limb while Lois wailed and Herb cried, "I love her. I love her. I love her."

Dallas woke with a start, cheek pressed into scratchy shag carpet, and bed sheet wrapped hood-like over his head. Shuddering breaths pulled the sheet into his mouth and blew it out again. Contorting, he managed to bring his feet off the bed and down to the floor where the rest of him had ended up. Wrestling himself clear of the sheet, he gasped and swallowed as his heart rate slowed. The room was mostly dark, lit only by the red numbers of his alarm clock. Squinting, the lines came together well enough to convey that it was one forty-three a.m. As the adrenaline from the nightmare drained away, so did the details. Soon, all that was left was a lingering unease. Shaking his head, he pushed himself back up to the mattress and sat with his elbows on his knees, forehead in his hands. The sudden ring of the phone scared the hell out of him, causing him to jolt upright so quickly that he slid off the edge of the mattress and thunked heavily back to the floor.

"Better be a booty call," he groused.

Another insistent ring was followed by a third before Dallas was able to get to the receiver. He'd barely picked up when Stanley started talking. It must've been something really important, to Stanley at least, because he was talking so fast and stuttering so much that his first few sentences were completely incomprehensible.

"Slow the hell down Stanley! Just... no, you have to slow down." Dallas pulled the phone away from his ear, flipped it upside down, and spoke loudly into the handset.

"I don't know what, 'Burn woo-tu-tu tuh-tu-tu-tu' means. If you want me to understand, talk like a normal person."

Dallas counted to three, flipped the phone back over, and returned it to his ear. Stanley still sputtered and stuttered, but it was a little better than before. Even so, Dallas needed a drink. Whatever had crawled up Stan's butt and injected him with crazy was of lesser concern. Still holding the phone with his shoulder, Dallas fumbled around, looking for one of his many flasks.

"Right. Uh, sure. Okay, a T.V. show. On in a couple of minutes. Yeah, yeah. Channel two at one-fifty-eight. Okey doke, Stan. G'night."

With a long sigh of satisfaction, Dallas slid a still-full flask from the back pocket of a nearby pair of jeans. A quick swig accompanied his hanging up on Stanley.

"I either gotta find a not-crazy friend or change my number," he mumbled to the flask. The flask was an excellent listener as always, but this time it had something to say back. Incredulous, Dallas glared at the back-talking little flask.

"You, too? Well eff off, flasky. I don't know what he was babbling about, but I gotta say, I'm a little surprised you'd immediately take his side."

Dallas cocked his head as if listening to an informed response. Nodding, he returned the flask to his lips and took a long drink.

"Okay. You convinced me. I got nothin' else to do. Might as well watch the tube."

Dallas grabbed the remote and flipped on the bedroom television. The good shit was usually on Showtime or Cinemax this time of night, but he knew Stanley was going to call back right after two o'clock. If he didn't at least pay a little attention to channel two first, Stan would be crushed. Dallas was well-aware of being a little rough around the edges but tried not to be a jerk all the time.

Punching the remote's buttons, he landed on the local public broadcast channel. What looked like a televised garage sale being hosted by a wiry dude in a Gilligan hat filled the screen. For a passing moment, Dallas wondered if he knew the guy. His gaunt face and squinty eyes looked familiar, but no recollection sparked in his alcohol soaked brain. A glance at the clock told him it was one fifty-seven a.m. Another minute and he could flip to some boobies.

Dallas watched the clock hit one fifty-eight. The guy on the T.V. was talking about a life-sized, silk-lined casket bookshelf, and if you called right away with a major credit card, he'd include a collection of horror novels. Suddenly, mid-sentence, the rambling hick looked up from caressing the casket to stare straight into the camera.

"If you have turned to channel two at two minutes to two a.m., you've cracked the first code. That means you're a very sharp cookie, which makes you even more important to us. World's got enough morons. We need special people. People like you. We'll be in touch, but you have to prove that you cracked the first code. I'm going to say something. Write it down, memorize it, and then burn the paper."

Dallas stared at the screen, trying to get the game. Why did Stanley want him to watch this crap? He figured it would be a rerun of *Jeopardy* or something, so Stan could prove he knew the answers. Instead, he was suffering through some kook's cable access show. Stan was going to catch hell for this.

"Things only get as bad as you're willing to let them," the man on the T.V. said, staring straight at the camera, at Dallas himself.

Suddenly, his eyes lost their laser-blaster intensity and dropped back to the creepy bookcase. "... yours for only sixty bucks. You gotta admit, this would make a great conversation piece in your living room, even if you had crappy books on it..."

Dallas hmph'd and flipped the channel, the stupid cable-access show already tossed into a mental dustbin.

When the phone rang a moment later, Dallas had just landed on *Porky's* on Cinemax. It was the shower scene, his favorite, and he was in no mood to miss the good stuff. However, he also knew that Stan would just call back again and again until he did.

"Stanley," he barked, picking up the phone. "That was some really interesting television, buddy. Pretty awesome. Thanks for the tip. Now if you don't mind, I'm gonna watch a little softcore and call it a night."

Dallas took another pull from the flask, reclining on the floor with his back resting against the foot of the bed. The whiskey and classic cinema boobage were starting to work their magic when something Stan said snagged his attention.

"Wait a sec. Back up. I was chosen? By who? For what? Well shit, Stan. If you don't know that, then why did you call? Uh huh. Yup. Yeah, I remember the weirdy guy at Stein's. Yeah. Yup. Wait…" Dallas leaned forward, suddenly tracking Stanley's rambling. Standing, he cast around the room until he found the previous day's clothes. As he fished through the jean pockets, he growled at Stanley.

"I don't know what was on the card, Stanley, and I can't find it. Oh, well, why didn't you *say* that you have it? Crap on a cracker, you're making this tough. Okay. 'Turn twenty-two at two-hundred-twenty-two.' A code, and you cracked it. Hooray. What? Oh, yeah. 'Turn to two at two to two.' Channel two, two minutes before two. Clever, and you're right. That's exactly when the garage sale weirdy guy made them comments about being contacted and being special." Dallas's brow furrowed in deep thought.

"Hell, I'm glad I caught that. Damn right that guy was trying to contact me. I'll bet… Hmmm. I'll bet he's C.I.A., or F.B.I., or Special Forces, maybe even NASA. Holy hell, Stanley," Dallas breathed, possibilities exploding through his mind.

"I'm a shadow recruit. Damn right, I am. I bet they got terrorists all over, and they need someone to take out the local cell. Like MacGyver. The A Team. That's gotta be it, and they need me." Dallas started to pace with excited energy. "They need me. The guy said that. 'You're needed.' That's what he said."

Dallas nodded between sips from the flask.

"Well, sure you helped, Stanley. They knew that when they saw me. I'm a good delegator. The important people can't be doing everything in a situation. Oh, by the way, that's what they call it when shit hits the fan. A situation. Now I just gotta connect with the main unit. Which would be. Um. Huh… I don't suppose you know where the main unit is?"

Dallas listened again, his face a mask of concentration. "No shit, Sherlock! Of course, they wouldn't just blurt that out over the T.V. Obviously, the guy gave the next piece of code. For when I get contacted again. By them. So I can. You know. Break the code."

Dallas nodded again. "That's what I said! Probably a question that I have to answer right. Exactly. Now," he continued in a no-nonsense tone. "Why don't you tell me what you got for the answer, and I'll let you know if that's right…"

As Dallas listened to Stanley and scribbled on a half-torn envelope, he smiled at the sense of purpose swelling in his chest and wondered when he'd be contacted again.

Chapter 5

THE MORNING SUN WAS in his eyes when he woke, and something much less adult than *Porky's* was playing on the T.V. Unfazed by spending another night on the bedroom floor, Dallas sat at the foot of the bed, giggling at *Ernest Scared Stupid* for a few minutes before rubbing his face and pulling himself to his feet. The bed was more of a recreational accessory to be used with company. If he just needed to get some shut-eye, it didn't matter if he landed on the bed, couch, floor, his pickup's back seat, front seat, the backyard, the front yard, whatever. One of the wonders of alcohol was how it made anywhere into a perfectly fine place to sleep. Only downside was waking up.

Fall was shaking leaves off the trees, a stern reminder to the Wisconsin Northwoods that winter wasn't far off, so folks in the area were getting their furnaces ready. After making his rounds, he headed back to Stein's for an early dinner and maybe a game of pool. As he walked across the parking lot, memories of hustling some out-of-towners with Herb came to mind. Dallas and Herb had squared off against a couple of mullet-heads in Vikings jerseys. Dallas had taken the lead, and they played the hustle like pros. After schooling those purple-clad posers for every bill in their Velcro wallets, Dallas, Herb, and Stanley had celebrated by emptying Stein's beer cooler. It was, Dallas recalled fondly, an awesome night.

He was halfway through the parking lot en route to Stein's front door when he stopped abruptly. He would not think about that monster. That demon. He was going to get a drink, shoot pool with whoever wanted to shoot pool, and *not* think about that night. With a deep breath to shore up his resolve, he made his way into Stein's and staked out a space at the bar. Soon, the whiskey shots and beer chasers had floated his unwanted thoughts back to his unexplored subconscious where they belonged. He was a goddamn hero, and if any other blood-sucking monsters showed up, he'd give 'em what for, just like he did with... with...

"... the vampire. That's good to hear," a voice close to his ear said.

Dallas didn't remember saying anything out loud. "Wasshat? Yoush talkin' t'me?" he asked.

As his eyes focused on the face in front of him, he thought he recognized the man. Widow's peak, scraggly goatee. Not a local, that was for sure.

"The vampire. You'd give them what for just like you did with the vampire. I know all about it, Dallas."

Dallas's face split into a grin. "GODDAMN HERO!" he roared, slapping the bar.

"Dallas, I need to ask you a question," the man said, voice dropping to a conspiratorial whisper. "Do you know how bad things can get?"

Dallas leaned back and squinted at the man. How did he know this guy?

Oh, I probably fixed his furnace, he reasoned.

"You bet I do," he answered. "You don't replace your filter, s'gonna cut your effin. Your effinsee," he tried again and then licked his lips and said carefully, "efficiency. By like, five pershent."

The man frowned, his mouth working for a moment. Apparently reaching some sort of internal decision, he asked again, "Do you know how bad things can get?"

Was the guy a little deaf or something? Dallas was still trying to place his face. Guy probably worked up at the paper mill and couldn't hear so good anymore.

"Yes. I. Do." Dallas spoke slowly and loudly. "Change. Your. Furnace. Filter. Every. Year."

A look of understanding crossed the man's face.

Thank Christ, Dallas thought. He couldn't stand idiots.

"Okay, buddy. Nice chatting. You have a g'night now," Dallas offered, returning to the rocks glass of whiskey requiring his more immediate attention.

"You're right. This ain't the best place. Too many people. I'll be in touch again." With an approving nod, the man stood, clapped Dallas on the shoulder, and headed out of the bar.

Hmph, Dallas thought as he took a drink, simultaneously waving to Stein for another. *Another happy customer.*

Some indeterminate amount of time later, Dallas staggered to his truck, Deloris. The raised up four-by-four Dodge was the love of his life. It had a custom electric blue paint job, chrome jaws on the grill, and matching chrome fenders, running boards, bed rails, and exhaust, and windows tinted black as night. He'd named the truck after the first girl he'd ever slept with. She was tough, sexy, and scary as hell, so it seemed like a natural fit. Giving Deloris an affectionate pat on the rear bumper, he belched and resumed his song.

"Packers! Go, you Packers, go and get 'em, Go, you fighting fools upset 'em,

Smash their line with all your might, A touchdown, Packers, Fight, Fight, Fight, Fight!

On, you Green and Gold, to glory. Win this game the same old story,

Fight, you Packers, Fight, and bring the bacon home to..."

"Do you know how bad things can get?"

Dallas acted on reflex. He grabbed a wrist and yanked, pulling the voice's owner off-balance and driving his face into the side of Deloris. A wet *thwump* preceded the appearance of a slobber mark on the truck's electric blue paint. Bouncing off the truck, the man recovered, crouched, and swept a leg out, catching Dallas behind the knees. Dallas went down with a curse, rolled, and pulled himself to his feet, the flurry of motion ending in a well-placed punch connecting with the man's jaw at the exact moment that fifty-thousand volts coursed through him.

Dallas stiffened and fell over again with a high-pitched scream-turned-gurgle. The volts charged through his veins like a swarm of ornery electric eels, standing his hair on end and leaving his toes numb. The stranger massaged his jaw, cursed, and looked around the lot before leaning over the still twitching Dallas.

"What the hell is your problem?" he whined, glaring down through squinty eyes. "Shit. It feels like you broke both sides of my face."

Dallas looked up in disbelief. "Me? You frickin' attacked me. What did you expect me to do? Send you flowers?" Wincing, he lifted his shirt and stared at the burned skin with growing indignation.

"And you tased me? What kind of pussy uses a taser? Well, you should'a kept the juice flowing. You should'a killed me," he advised, voice raising in volume. "But you didn't. You blew it, and now you're in a world of hurt." Dallas pushed himself to his feet, turned his profile to the stranger, and raised his fists.

"You got two options here. Try to do that again, and I beat you bloody, or run for your frickin' life. And just so you know, if you run, I'm taking my girl Deloris here and driving right over your punk ass, backing up, and spinning the tires."

The man dropped the taser, put his hands up, and took a slow step backward.

"Hey, calm down. I just wanted the password, that's all. Things were fine before. Why are you being such an asshole about the password? It's protocol."

Dallas lowered his fists and squinted.

Password? Protocol? he thought, then revelation sparked like the prongs of a taser.

"Wait a sec, you're him. The T.V. guy. That's you!"

The man glanced around the dark lot. "Shhh. Yes. Now just give me the password, and let's get outta here."

Dallas considered the man carefully, thinking back on his earlier conversation with Stanley. "You ain't looking to get your furnace fixed," he reasoned slowly. Pieces falling into place, Dallas realized he was talking to a bona fide member of the C.I.A. Or F.B.I. Or maybe NASA.

Why do they have so many letters, he grumbled to himself.

"No sir. Sharp guys like you don't worry about the furnace. Oh, wait. You like letters. You don't worry about the HVAC," Dallas conspired with a heavy wink. "And yeah, I got your password."

The guy never saw the punch coming. Dallas slugged him so hard in the gut it doubled him over, his breath coming out in a pained, "Uff!" before he slumped back against the side of the truck.

"That's for the taser. Now to answer your question, things only get as bad," he paused and patted his pockets. "Um, things only get as bad," he stalled, shoving his hands into first his front jean pockets, then his back pockets. Finding what he was searching for, he flourished a torn and much-folded envelope, pulled it open, and read out loud, "As you're willing to let them. Which, by the way, you totally shouldn't have let me gut-shot you like that. I expected more from you C.I.A. fellas."

Widow's peak looked up at Dallas, still catching his breath after getting floored by the cheap shot. Already squinty eyes narrowed even further as he replied, "C.I.A.? Oh no, Dallas. I'm part of something much more important. Something you can be a part of too, if you stop acting like such an asshole." Standing, the man brushed gravel from his jeans and straightened his shirt.

"You got the password. Hooray, you passed the second test. Can't say I'm too impressed, though. It was one of our easier ones." Reaching some sort of decision, the man grudgingly extended a hand. "Randall. Warrior of the Society."

Dallas shook the offered hand on reflex. "Dallas. Owner and Proprietor of That Blows HVAC and goddamn Hero of Trappersville."

Randall nodded. "We know who you are."

A testosterone-soaked silence descended between the two men.

"So. What now?" Dallas finally asked.

"Now you need to reflect on things, Dallas. Might help you get your bearings."

With that, Randall turned on his heel and walked to an orange and yellow moped parked in the shadows. It wasn't until after Randall had sputtered off into the night that Dallas noticed a familiar white rectangle lying in the dirt by Deloris.

"Find us. You're needed," he read aloud after picking it up. "Find you? Why bother? Every time I turn around, you pop up like a sneaky ninja with a taser."

Turning it over, he discovered that it was different from the first card. Instead of a cryptic message on the back, it had a cryptic map. At least, it seemed map-ish. Cartoon trees, drawings of triangles on boxes, a few squiggly lines, and a small "X" covered the card's back, but there were no names or anything else to indicate where the map was supposed to be.

Dallas ground his teeth in frustration.

"Frickin' C.I.A." he grumbled, shoving the card into his back pocket. "Lucky for me, I got a Stanley."

Chapter 6

Petro Patterson's wasn't really on the way to Stanley's, but it was a worthwhile detour. If Dallas was going to suss out mysteries and the like, he needed brain fuel. The waning moon and rising sun shone down on Patt's parking lot as Dallas pulled into an open spot out front. He put Deloris in park alongside a well-used pickup truck just as the owner ambled outside, plastic bag in one hand and keys in the other.

"Nice looking dog," Dallas offered as he stepped down to the pavement, referring to the old golden retriever standing ramrod-still in the bed of the truck. "Hey there, buddy! Who's a good dog?" he called. In response, the dog just stared, tail straight out, unmoving.

"Name's Bo. Had him since he was a pup," grinned the truck's driver as he leaned back to pat the dog's head. "He's famous, too. You heard about the vampire in these parts?" he asked with a chuckle and a sly wink.

The remnants of Dallas's morning buzz drained away, replaced with a sort of nothingness.

"Sure. Everyone 'round here's heard about that," he replied, the forced nonchalance making him momentarily dizzy.

"Bo here met him. In the flesh," the man said with a note of pride.

Dallas shrugged, feeling for all the world like someone else was moving his shoulders. "How'd you know it was him?"

"Paper. I come up this way a lot from Madison to fish. Nice to page through the local tabloids. Saw that red-headed guy's picture with the big headline, 'Wisconsin Vamp Ravages Town,' and I knew I'd seen that face before. Then it hit me. He was here pumping gas. Yessir. Bo's a regular celebrity now," he chuckled. "Vampires in Wisconsin. Too funny." Reaching back to scratch the dog's ears, he asked, "You a dog fella, too?"

Dallas's forced smile faded as the dog added a low-throated snarl to its unyielding stare. "Uh, not really. Although if I was gonna get a dog..."

I wouldn't get some over-bred mongrel that's only good for catching Milk Bones and Frisbees, he thought, staring right back at the dog while scratching a sudden itch on his thigh.

Bo's low snarl stopped, replaced suddenly with a plaintive whine. Tail wrapping between its legs, the dog licked the man's hand as it wriggled backward in the truck's bed.

"Huh. Guess Bo ain't feelin' too social, mister, no offense," the man said with a quizzical look at Dallas. "Well, we'll be on our way then. And don't forget to tell your pals you met an honest-to-God celebrity," he added with a good-natured laugh. "Vampires. What'll they think of next?"

Mood thoroughly ruined, Dallas watched the man back out of his spot and drive off.

"Well, at least Bo didn't have a taser." Putting it from his mind, Dallas entered Patt's and made for the beer cooler.

There's a certain sameness to roadside gas stations in rural America which Patterson's embraced. Tchotchkes clung to every inch of available space, encouraging shoppers to empty their wallets and walk away with nothing of value to show for it. Dallas remembered the way Herb used to go on and on about roadside gas stations. The guy loved them and had this crazy idea that if the rest of civilization fell and only roadside gas stations survived, everyone would pretty much be ok. The memory hurt like a bruise, the kind of hurt that you just had to deal with because nothing could make it go away. He continued past the aisles, drawn to the hum of the coolers while nineties pop music bounced and jarred the soggy space between his ears. A twelve-pack of beer and a few jerky sticks later, he was at the counter.

A young teenage girl leaned by the register, watching reruns of some teenie-bopper crap on a small television behind the counter. When the girl continued to favor the T.V. instead of him, Dallas cleared his throat.

"Today, please?" he asked politely.

"Whatev's," the girl replied. A bright yellow tipped finger pressed the register keys, each jab expressing complete indignation at the girl's lot in life.

Trying to stifle his impatience, Dallas's head turned and eyes roamed, a newly captured animal exploring the confines of its cage.

"Sorry. Screwed up," he heard the girl say without looking up. "Gotta re-ring you."

"Uh huh. Okay," Dallas responded, impatience coloring his tone. Still his eyes continued to rove, cigarette rack to jerky display to Slurpee machine to newspaper stand to magazine rack, only to start the circuit over again. The ding of each key on the register clanged against his eardrums, wearing on his already thin patience. Frustrated, he pressed his lips tightly shut and drew a deep breath in through his nose. When the smell of dried beef filled his nostrils, it eclipsed every other thought.

"You must really need this jerky," he heard the girl say. Perplexed, he cocked his head to one side as he looked at her.

"I can, like, hear your stomach growling. So I'm guessing no bag, right? You're just gonna scarf these down?" the girl asked, looking up at him with interest.

Dallas rested a hand on his gut and cocked his head to the other side. His tongue flicked out and around his lips, followed by a jaw-popping yawn as his eyes locked on the jerky stick she was holding toward him. Dropping into a squat, hands firmly on the floor between his boots, he looked up and watched the girl lean forward over the counter. Her eyebrows drew together in confusion while the jerky stick drooped forgotten in her hand. Focused solely on the jerky, he chuffed, licking his lips again and scooting a smidge closer to the counter.

"Um," the girl said, voice gone brittle. "So, no bag?"

Dallas blinked, looked down at his boots and back up at the girl. *What the hell?* he wondered, wiping a small tendril of drool from the corner of his mouth.

Making a show of tying his already-tied boot laces, he stood and passed a twenty over the counter.

"Oh, uh. No, thanks. I can carry it," he mumbled with uncharacteristic embarrassment.

Scooping up his change, he backtracked out of Patt's and hoofed it over to Deloris. Tossing everything in the passenger seat, he gobbled up a jerky stick in two bites, freed a can of beer, and drank deeply while excitement about the next clue and a fresh supply of brewskis conveniently erased the recent events from his mind.

41

Chapter 7

S TANLEY HAD EXAMINED THE small card from every possible angle before proclaiming, "I think it's a map," with the pride of a third grader showing off some handmade macaroni art.

To Dallas, it really did look like macaroni art. Stanley was pretty sure the mostly straight lines were roads and the squiggly ones were rivers or creeks, but it was still just a collection of strange doodles. Since there were more cartoony trees than cartoony buildings, they figured it was probably a map of somewhere in woods. Which woods in particular, bisected by which rivers or creeks in particular, and occupied by which buildings in particular though… Dallas had to keep drinking for fear of losing his gourd. What good was having a map if they had no clue where it was supposed to be?

"Okay, great. We've narrowed it down to, um, lemme think on this. Not the desert, and not the artic. That only leaves us almost all the planet to search. Geez, these guys are a real piece of work," he opined, frustration adding a sharp edge to his slightly slurred words.

"Hu-hold on, Big D," Stanley said, holding his hands palm-out toward Dallas. "We know a few things. They gotta be local, right? Don't m-make much sense to give you a map of someplace across the globe. No, sir."

Dallas shrugged, the gesture accompanying a non-committal huff.

"So it's a map of somewhere 'round here," Stanley concluded, radiating confidence like an EasyBake Oven.

Downing the last swig of the current Milwaukee's Best and slamming the can on the table, Dallas swore.

"We're still no closer to finding them. 'Around here' is a mighty big place to search."

Stanley nodded, mouth pursed in thought. "We could try the l-local library. They got all kinds of maps," he explained. "We could look at this little map next to the b-big ones and see what matches."

Dallas weighed the suggestion. It seemed like as good of a plan as any. If nothing else, the drive would make for a welcome distraction. He hadn't been to the library in years, as in all the years he'd been alive. Grabbing his jacket, he waved Stanley toward the door.

"C'mon, Stanwich. We've got a mystery to solve."

Trappersville could be described as a small town tossed haphazardly across a large area. As such, the drive would've normally taken about fifteen minutes. Dallas made it in seven. Rocketing into the library's small parking lot, he cranked hard on the wheel and sent Deloris into a power slide. Tires squealed on pavement, leaving skid marks across the neatly painted white lines of no less than three parking spots. The noise caused a face to appear in a ground-level window.

"This is a public library, not a friggin' motocross!" Glen Montal, the head librarian, yelled through the open window.

"Morning Glen!" Dallas hallooed. "Helluva day, right?"

"Dallas? Is that you? Geezus, man. You near gave me a heart attack." The bespectacled face disappeared from the window and reappeared a moment later when the library's front door opened from the inside. "And Stanley, eh? I should've known. What are you two hosers doing out and about, eh?"

"We got a m-m-mystery to solve!" Stanley crowed, only to grunt as Dallas slugged him in the shoulder.

With a withering look at Stanley, Dallas forced a laugh. "Not really, Glen. You know Stan. Figuring out which side of the toast to butter is a mystery for him, poor guy. No, we were just thinking it'd be, ah, educational to look at some maps of the area. You know. For..." he trailed off, at a loss for a good cover story.

"Looking for deer runs, eh? I should've known you weren't looking to read a book," Glen remarked with a lopsided grin. "However, I am impressed that you've realized the value of your local library. Get in here. I've got some maps that'll help. We'll find you a good spot for a deer stand. No trouble there," Glen said, nodding in approval.

Dallas liked Glen. He always had. When Dallas was in high school, the older man taught American History. Dallas thought that was hilarious since Glen grew up in Canada. At the end of the term, Dallas brought him French fries and gravy. In return, Glen let Dallas slide with a 'C.'

"Aerial maps would probably work best," Glen reasoned. Holding the door and beckoning the men forward, he shepherded Dallas and Stanley into the library.

Steering them toward the local geography section, Glen rummaged, muttering to himself in a distracted way. Soon Dallas was staring at a table full of aerial maps. According to Glen, the maps covered a six-county area and then some. Most of what they showed were large swaths of unbroken forest, parceled up between gray roads and curving, wiggly waterways. Dallas looked questioningly at Stanley, who beamed in response and bobbed his head.

Giving Glen a hearty thumbs up, Dallas said, "These are great. I, um. Should definitely be able to find a great spot for a, you know. Deer stand."

"No trouble at all," Glen replied easily. "You can just drop off some French fries and gravy later, eh?"

Back at Dallas's rambler, the dining room table had been cleared of empty bottles and cans. In their place were a variety of photocopied maps showing most of Marinette, Oconto, Menominee, Langlade, Forest, and even Florence counties. Stanley did the math and pronounced they were looking at a geographic region encompassing over five thousand square miles.

"Holy crapola, Stan. We've got a cartoon map on a business card, and we're trying to match it up with half of northern Wisconsin. I ain't drunk enough to think that's possible." he complained. "Gimme a sec."

Dallas fished around in the fridge and returned with a fresh Milwaukee's Best.

"All better," he announced. "Let's find 'em."

Stanley looked at Dallas with the eager eyes of a kid on Christmas Eve and set the business card on the upper left-hand corner of the first map. Gently resting his fingers Ouija-board style on the card, he slid it slowly down as both men's eyes flicked back and forth looking for similarities. Upon reaching the bottom of the map, Stanley moved the card to the right and started to slide it back up toward the top.

Three hours later, Dallas threw up his hands in disgust.

"Dammit, Stanley. This ain't getting us nowhere! We've been over and over these maps and haven't found a thing that looks like what's on the card." Snatching it from Stanley's fingers, Dallas flourished the business card while prancing around the room.

"La dee dah, I'm a C.I.A. douchebag. I'm so clever! Here's a worthless clue. Come find me."

Stopping mid-cavort, he held the card up close to his eye and squinted at the scribbly lines.

"Or maybe I'm just not looking close enough, huh? Maybe you have to glue it to your eyeball. Or maybe..."

Dallas's mouth stopped mid-sentence, and his nostrils flared once, then again. Turning his head to and fro, he snuffed, blew air from his nose, and snuffed again. Tiny map momentarily forgotten, he tilted and twisted his head, nose held high.

"Stanley! When did you run out to Cecil's? You can't just make a grub run and not say anything," Dallas admonished. "I've been working like a dog here while you went out for a Reuben and fries and," Dallas inhaled deeply again, nostrils stretching, "oh, you bastard. You got deep fried pickles, and you didn't share?"

Stanley's jaw hung for a moment before sputtering, "But D-Dallas, I've been here the whole time with you. I didn't go to Cecil's. We should, though. I'm starving."

"Well, someone went to Cecil's. Don't tell me you can't smell that," Dallas challenged, spearing Stanley with a questioning glare. "Smells thick as day old bacon grease." A couple of additional whuffs and Dallas's eyes widened to match his nostrils. He drew the small card in and held it beneath his nose. He sniffed once, twice, tentatively at first.

Becoming surer of himself, he pressed the card up against his nose and snuffed again.

"Geezus. This here card, it smells like Cecil's. Just like Cecil's. I kid you not, Stan. Here, try it." Dallas thrust the card toward Stanley.

Always accommodating, Stanley took the offered card and sniffed daintily. "Um, nothing Dal. I j-just smell, um. Card."

Snatching it back, Dallas breathed deep again. "That's why they're recruiting me, little buddy. Lighting reflexes, eagle eyes, and the nose of a bloodhound."

"M-maybe the guy who dropped it for you was there. So m-maybe Cecil's is close to the X," Stanley said, a glimmer of his previous enthusiasm returning.

The two men returned to the aerial maps, sorting and tossing sheets of paper until they found the one that covered the northern edge of the county. Tracing a finger up highway fifty-five, Dallas stopped in the vicinity of the little roadside restaurant. He tapped decisively on the spot and fished around the table for a pencil. Finding one, he scrawled a circle around the little rectangle-shaped building barely visible through the canopy of trees. Cecil's, photographed from above. Easy to look past, since the building and adjacent dirt lot were encroached upon from all sides by the ubiquitous Wisconsin forest.

His brain filled up with thoughts of the little restaurant while his nose was inundated with the smell of sour kraut and beer-battered pickles fried to hot, crispy perfection. A thin tendril of drool formed in the corner of his mouth.

"Must be hungrier than I thought," Dallas commented, wiping at his mouth with a sleeve and absently scratching his thigh. "But look, this can't be right. None of the stuff lines up."

Stanley pulled on his Columbo face. Squinting one eye, he rested an elbow on his wrist, stroked his chin, and scratched his head.

"What did that g-guy say to you?" he asked.

"Who? Glen? Um, let's see. To bring him some French fries and gravy."

"No," Stanley said. "N-not Glen. The taser guy. S-something about reflecting?"

Dallas scratched his own head Columbo-style to see if it helped him recall the details.

"He might've. Actually, yeah. 'Reflect on things,' or something like that." Dallas's face screwed up in thought. "He told me to reflect on things and get my bearings."

Looking down at the map and the little card Randall had dropped, he ran a hand through his hair. "But what the hell, Stan? How am I supposed to get my bearings when the damn little map ain't nowhere around nowhere?"

Stanley picked up the small card in one hand and the big map in the other. Looking around the room, he turned first one way, then the other, before moving with purpose down the hall. Stopping outside the main floor bathroom, he looked back at Dallas.

"Go for it," Dallas waved. "But light a match when you're done. Your dumps smell like roadkill chili."

"Dallas, come here," Stanley said.

"What? Need help finding it? Too bad. A friend in that kind of need ain't no friend I plan on helping," Dallas laughed.

"No, the m-mirror, Dallas. Reflect on things." Straightening his shoulders, Stanley stepped into the bathroom.

Curious, Dallas followed him down the hall. Stopping outside of the bathroom, he looked in and saw Stanley had one hand pressing the map up against the wall next to the medicine cabinet mirror while the other held the card in front of his chest, tiny map facing the glass. Dallas walked in behind him and looked first at the aerial map, eyes going straight to the little circle he'd drawn over Cecil's. Up the road a short ways was an auto body shop. A half mile or so west of the main road and across the river, the Skarsgard's farmhouse could be seen in a small clearing. Dallas knew it well. He'd dated old Skarsgard's daughter in high school and used to sneak up the trellis to her bedroom window. Not much else around since Cecil's was, like most of the establishments in Trappersville, tossed almost randomly in the woods.

Dallas's eyes shifted to the reflection of the card's hand-drawn map in the mirror. That line running at a slight curve from top to bottom, the one they thought might be a river or a creek, could have been the highway. Looking at the little rectangle-triangle things, two of them seemed to line up pretty well with Cecil's and the old Skarsgard house. If that was true, that other line could have been the Burnt Shanty Creek, a small tributary that fed into the Wolf River.

"Ho. Lee. Shit," Dallas whispered. Leaning over Stanley's shoulder, he pointed a finger at the mirror.

"Look here. The creek. Skarsgard's. Cecil's. That means the little "X" on their map is probably right around there." Dallas said. Mentally figuring distances in his head, he continued, "That can't be but a mile, maybe two, into the woods, but there ain't nothing out there. I think maybe an old, abandoned cabin. Otherwise, just empty woods. Why draw me a map to go there?"

Stanley's reflected eyes met Dallas's. "P-perfect spot for top secret stuff to happen, don't ya think?"

Dallas breathed deep. The scent of a Rueben with fries was still strong in his nose.

"I think it's time I paid those sneaky-deaky government boys a visit, Stan. No more popping in on old Dal. I'm gonna drop by their place unannounced and see how they like it," he announced, every pore oozing alcohol and resolution.

"But first, let's get some lunch. I'm starving."

Chapter 8

DALLAS COULDN'T REMEMBER HAVING been so hungry. The beer brat with a side of cheese curds went down faster than a third string quarterback behind a rookie center. The fried pickles had barely hit the paper tray before he'd swallowed them all in three bites, burning his tongue in the process. A second brat fared no better than the first, despite being loaded with all the fixings Cecil's had to offer. It wasn't until after he'd polished off a bacon cheeseburger with fries that Dallas felt satiated. After a long, belly stretching belch, he licked salt and grease from the fingers of one hand while scratching his thigh with the other.

Throughout the entire meal, Stanley sat entranced. Finally closing his gaping mouth, he leaned in with a serious look.

"H-holy smokes, Dal. You got a tapeworm? My uncle had one. Ate and ate, never gained weight. Finally ended up in the hospital. When they operated, it was big as a cucumber."

"Uh huh. Good story, Stan. So here's the plan. I'll go in on foot, take a peek at what their set-up is, and circle back here. Meanwhile, you're gonna hang back and cover my rear."

Stanley's face fell, reducing him to the kid who wasn't picked to play kickball.

"B-but Dallas. We tracked these guys together! You and me. We f-figured out their clues. Whadaya means I gotta hang back?"

Dallas rose up, rolling his shoulders and cracking his neck. "Besides you being worth less than a wet fart in a fight, what if someone's been tailing us?"

Leaning in for full effect, Dallas bridged his fingers on the table and spoke in an urgent voice.

"Look. We can't take any chances. You hang back, and if some little sneak has been tailing us, you take 'em out of the equation. You follow?"

Stanley's face went from overlooked-for-kickball to flat-out terrified. Leaning back from Dallas, he started to shake his head back and forth.

"Oh no. No way. I ain't getting n-n-nobody outta no equations. I got no gun. I got no criminal element. Not me. Even if I had a gu-gu... oh crappers..." Stanley looked ill. "Can't do it. Can't be killing no one. No, sir."

Dallas shook his head, palms out. "Oh, for Pete's... I wasn't... What the hell do you think is going on here, Stanley? I meant distract him. You know, stall tactics. So I don't gotta worry about no one sneaking up on me from behind."

Stanley lit up instantly. "Oh, I gotcha, big D." Winking conspiratorially, Stanley started to plan. "I'll f-fake a break-down. Maybe stab your truck tire with something, give it a flat. Some sneaky guy happens by, I'll make him ch-change the tire."

Dallas adopted Stanley's previous look of terror. "No no no! No one's stabbing Deloris nowhere. Christ on a stick, Stan. What's gotten into you?"

Chagrined, Stanley offered up a different thought. "Oh, right. Um, new plan. We'll t-talk about *Jeopardy*. I'll bet him five, no ten dollars that he don't know the answer to last week's Final Jeopardy question. That'll hold him for at least an hour. Maybe two," Stanley finished on an authoritative note. He immediately began trying to recall the previous week's question, and Dallas ceased to exist.

Shaking his head, Dallas strode through the door and out to the parking lot, turning his thoughts to the journey ahead.

A quick glance around confirmed that Dallas was alone. The few folks in Cecil's were thoroughly engrossed in hiking their cholesterol and stretching their waistbands. Despite having knocked off enough food to feed the Packers' entire defensive line, Dallas felt nimble. A fish sliding back into water, he slipped into the trees and moved at a gentle lope. At least a quarter mile or so had passed before he realized a couple of important things. One, he hadn't made any noise. Usually, even on his best days, he was bound to crack a twig or startle a squirrel. Today, though, he felt like smoke through the trees. Two, he had no idea where he was going. He and Stanley had done a pretty good job of approximating where the "X" was in relation to Cecil's. Even so, if he was looking for an old hunting cabin a mile or two into the trees east of Cecil's, that meant upwards of four to five square miles he might need to search to find the place. Disgruntled, he decided to stop running willy-nilly into the woods and think about a direction.

Squatting down on his haunches, Dallas screwed up his face in thought. Why had he run this direction in the first place? He was pretty sure he'd followed an east-northeast course from Cecil's, but it was hard to tell in the dense trees. A brief touch of wind rustled the surrounding leaves and his nostrils flared. Cecil's, directly behind him. Inhaling more deeply, he realized he could also smell the river, the grass, even the moss on the trees. There was something else as well. A smell that didn't belong with the others. Rising up from his crouch, Dallas cast around, sniffing and chuffing. For a moment it was there, then gone, then back. Each fickle shift of the wind made the scent dance mirage-like in and out of existence.

Even though it was faint, he recognized the smell. Taking a few tentative steps, he caught it again. Fixing it in his mind, he continued forward, pushing through the underbrush, stepping over fallen logs, and crouching under low-hanging branches. As he moved, the scent became incrementally more pronounced. He was passing by an old, crooked ash tree when his nose pulled him to an abrupt stop. Leaning in, he smelled a handful of leaves sprouting from a low branch. Beneath their leafiness, he smelled sweat, deodorant, maybe even cheap aftershave?

"Randall? It's Randall. Son of a bitch, that's gotta be him."

Dallas swung around in a slow circle as he searched for traces of the scent. It didn't take long to find it on another branch further into the trees. Soon, it was like a neon trail had been lit up just for Dallas. Every branch and leaf Randall had brushed against was emblazoned with his scent. Unquestioning, Dallas followed his nose.

Fixated on following the smelly trail, he almost forgot his original intent. Fortunately, a voice coming from just past the next rise brought him to his senses.

"... not much. I cast around for a bit, but I don't think we gotta worry about a wendigo. And that 'squatch scat was at least a week old. No fresh tracks, so it's probably up in the Michigan U.P., maybe even

Canada by now. Damn things got territories bigger than John Wayne's balls."

Dallas froze, dropped to his haunches again, and cocked his head to the side. The voice belonged to Randall, but he was clearly talking with someone else. Sure enough, a second voice rode in on the fickle breeze, clear one moment, faded the next.

"That's fine. We'll replenish our..." the second voice said before the wind snatched the conversation away. A moment later, it returned.

"... the next few days. Let's just hope that new... worth it so we can keep heading...," and then was gone again.

Gotcha now, you sneaky dogs. Looking around, Dallas tried to place the location.

"Crappers. Gotta mark something." Dallas rummaged around for a minute before fishing his ever-present pocketknife out of his jeans. Flipping the blade open, he was about to start scratching arrows into the bark of a few trees when a thought occurred to him. If he started marking trees, those guys would know someone had been through here and followed them to their spot.

Folding the knife up and returning it to his pocket, he pondered. Pondering, he realized he'd forgotten to pee before leaving Cecil's. After a quick glance around to make sure he was alone, he unzipped and let loose on the side of the closest tree.

Once finished, he moved quietly back in the direction he'd come from. After a half-mile or so, he suddenly had the urge to go again. Worried he might not make it back to Cecil's, he pulled over at another tree, unzipped, and soaked the bark with a warm stream.

With a satisfied sigh, he resumed his trek, only to find he still had to go. Grunting in frustration, he looked quickly around, unzipped, and peed yet again on a convenient tree. Convinced he was finally empty, he jogged the last half mile or so and crept carefully into Cecil's small, dirt lot. Reentering the restaurant, he found Stanley staring out the window. A glance at his watch told Dallas he'd been gone about forty-five minutes.

"Boo."

"Holy crap!" Stanley yelped. "D-didn't see you."

"You're a damn fine lookout," Dallas observed, rolling his eyes. "No matter. I found 'em. They're hunkered down deep in the woods, just like I thought." Grabbing Stanley, he dragged him from the restaurant.

"Where? Where are th-they hiding?" Stanley asked when they reached Dallas's truck.

The question brought Dallas up short, key halfway into the lock on Deloris's door. He hadn't paid much attention to his route through the forest. Come to think of it, he realized he'd just followed his nose. Didn't seem like a very reliable way to get through the woods, but Dallas wasn't wired for worry.

"Out there," he gestured irritably. "Dammit, Stan, I found 'em the first time. A natural tracker like me can find 'em again."

Dallas set a heavy boot on the truck's chrome running board and posed against the autumn sky.

"I'm a goddamn hero, remember? No problemo."

Chapter 9

T HE SUN WAS ABOUT to pull its daily disappearing act when Dallas arrived home and sent Stanley on his way. It had been a long couple of days, and Dallas realized he hadn't taken a shower since... well, it had been a while. Kicking off his boots, he headed for the master bathroom, shedding various articles of clothing along the way.

Dallas made his way up the stairs and down a short hallway, turned into his bedroom, and headed for the bathroom. Stepping into the tub-shower, he pulled the curtain closed and turned on the faucet. Soon, steaming water cut through the autumn chill, and Dallas felt an uncoiling deep in his chest. Shoulders that had been imperceptibly hunched relaxed, jaw muscles that tended more toward clenched gave way to a long yawn. For a moment, the briefest moment, Dallas closed his eyes, soaked in the shower, and didn't think.

Opening his eyes and seeing wispy clouds of steam rolling up from the cascading water, he couldn't help but think of how similar it looked to the tendrils of smoke rising from Herb's face, hands, and chest as he slowly burned away. With that thought, a thousand rubber bands throughout his body retracted. Face taking on a now-familiar tension, he set himself to wondering about other things, any other thing than that day. Grabbing a bar of soap and working up a lather with his hands, he mouthed words without really realizing he was speaking.

"That wasn't Herb. A damn monster, that's what it was. A blood-sucking monster."

Dallas crossed an arm across his chest and started to scrub the sweat off of his shoulder and arm. Switching hands, he scrubbed at his other side. Upper body scrubbed to satisfaction, he moved down to the left thigh, then the right, but stopped suddenly when his hand ran over a small, rough lump.

"The hell?" Dallas twisted into the flow of water to rinse away the soapy lather. Looking down at the side of his thigh, he yelped in surprise at the dark lump firmly attached to his skin.

The water stopped abruptly as he hit the faucet. He pulled back the curtain, climbed out of the tub, and headed back to the bedroom. The closet door was mirrored, allowing Dallas to get a closer look at the unwelcome hitchhiker. Eight legs and a teardrop shaped body that tapered to a tiny head buried firmly in his skin. Brown, a little splotchy, with telltale markings confirming his suspicion.

Dallas pinched the tick and twisted first one direction, then the other to no effect. Grabbing a book of matches off the dresser, he struck a match, blew it out, and held the still-hot sulfur to the tick's head. The little bloodsucker wriggled but still didn't release. A second match followed and then a third, but the damn thing didn't budge.

The naked man huffed in annoyance. Fixing this problem was going to take a more involved approach. Abandoning the matchbook, he returned to the bathroom. It took a bit of rummaging in the medicine cabinet, but eventually he found his nose hair tweezers. Carefully sliding one tweezer tong under the tick's body, he pinched down on the base of the head and slowly pried. Eight tiny legs gripped more tightly, and the tick stayed solidly in place.

"You're a tough little sucker, ain'tcha," he muttered in grudging admiration. Tweezers abandoned, he made a clothes-free trek into the attached garage, modesty being secondary to the immediate task at hand. Returning to the bedroom, he brandished a pair of needle-nose pliers.

"See these? Big D's got your number."

Once the pliers were in the same position as the tweezers, he clamped down and pried, leveraging the handle against his thigh. Muscles accustomed to prying rusty bolts loose for a living corded up while the pliers handle dug painfully into his quadriceps.

The tick didn't move.

"Un. Frickin. Real," Dallas cursed, flipping the pliers onto the bed. "The least you should've done is popped. Enough mister nice guy. I'm cutting you out."

His jeans were near the top of the stairs, along with his belt and one sock. Fishing into the jean's front pocket, he pulled out his pocketknife.

The knife was a gift from his dad for his sixteenth birthday. Maple burl wood handle, brass rivets, and a silver stamp on its side with his name engraved in bold, flowing script, it was one of his most cherished possessions. The blade was only five inches long, but Dallas kept it honed to a razor-sharp edge. Drying his hands on his bath towel and taking a quick nip from a nearby flask to calm his nerves, he sat on the bed and glared down at the bloodsucker on his leg.

"This here's a knife, ticky tick. Time for surgery."

He thwacked the tick with the knife handle, and it fell to the floor. Dallas blinked, surprised by the sudden twist in the epic struggle. The pest reoriented itself toward his bare foot and started to crawl purposefully forward. Grabbing the pliers, Dallas nimbly plucked the tick from the carpet and made his way to the kitchen. With a final glare at the little bloodsucker, he dropped it inside a Mason jar and screwed on the lid. If he remembered, he'd drop it by Stanley's later.

According to Stanley, there were at least sixteen known varieties of ticks plaguing the Wisconsin Northwoods. He collected the ones he found hoping to discover a seventeenth kind. Why someone would want to discover more ticks baffled Dallas, but everyone needed a hobby. He just hoped that if Stan did turn up a new kind of tick, it'd be one that didn't eat humans.

"Dallas not food," he admonished, shaking a finger at the scrabbling little pest. "Stanley is though. If he takes you out to play, I say chow down."

Tick secured, Dallas made his way back upstairs to finish his shower. As he passed the mirrored closet door again, he paused to inspect where the tick had been feeding. The bite mark had turned an angry red and oozed a thin tendril of blood.

"Frickin' wood ticks," he groused, continuing into the bathroom to finish his shower. Soon, all thoughts of the tick had washed down the drain, along with the blood from his thigh.

Chapter 10

DALLAS WOKE FEELING... GOOD. No, great. Gone was the perpetual hangover, and his mouth didn't taste like burnt roadkill. He couldn't remember the last time he'd felt this way. Sitting up, he was surprised to find he was fully in his bed. The sheets weren't a tangled mess, and both pillows were where they were supposed to be. Swinging his legs to the carpet, he stood, raising his arms above his head and stretching his tall frame. Shoulders and spine popped, the sensation bringing a wide smile to his face. Hungry, he pulled on a convenient pair of jeans and a clean flannel and made his way downstairs to whip up some honest-to-goodness breakfast.

The Hero of Trappersville rummaged through the fridge, pushing cans of beer and a half-empty carton of milk aside. Nothing fitting the traditional definition of breakfast surfaced, so he grabbed his keys and headed out to track down some actual food.

He was halfway to Ronnie's when he realized he was going to Ronnie's and only avoided stomping on the brakes by sheer force of will. He hadn't been to Ronnie's Grill since he'd confronted Herb and challenged him to make some garlic mashed potatoes. When Dallas had started to suspect Herb wasn't Herb anymore, he'd watched *The*

Lost Boys and learned a thing or two. Putting that newfound knowledge to the test had helped Dallas suss out the truth about his friend.

He squashed the unwanted recollections down deep, gritted his teeth, and pressed the accelerator. He wanted breakfast. Ronnie's made a damn good breakfast, and the odds of Lois working were probably slim.

Rolling into Ronnie's Famous Truck Stop, Grill, Bait Shop, and Gift Emporium, Dallas killed Deloris's engine and walked inside. Five or six truckers packing in some grub after a long night on the road were scattered among the various tables and booths. Ronnie, a retired trucker himself, had classed the place up a bit over the summer but still catered mainly to the masters of the eighteen wheels.

Mounting a stool and bellying up to the familiar counter, Dallas breathed deep and was rewarded with a cornucopia of smells. It was the olfactory equivalent of an IMAX movie after a lifetime of watching an old black and white T.V. For a moment, he was dizzy with trying to sort out more smells than there were stars in the northern sky. When a familiar voice spoke from behind him, it jarred him back to the present and shattered his euphoria.

"What are you doing here, Dallas?"

Swiveling on the fixed counter stool, Dallas turned and saw Lois, anger plain in every line of her posture. She looked different. Hair that used to be a brilliant blonde was dull and pulled back in a haphazard ponytail. Gone was the usual bright red lipstick and blue eyeliner. Instead, her eyes simmered over dark circles. She looked exhausted and pissed. Speechless, Dallas just stared, his thoughts a jumble.

"Too drunk to talk? Then get out. Ronnie doesn't allow drunks." Lois crossed her arms across her chest and lowered her chin, hard eyes staring out from beneath long lashes.

"Oh, hi Lois," Dallas managed. "No, not drunk. Surprising, I guess, but one hundred percent truth. I didn't have breakfast stuff, so I thought I'd get some breakfast stuff."

"Uh huh. Breakfast stuff. Well, my shift's done. Dee should be here soon, and I'm sure she'd be happy to serve the Hero of Trappersville. Enjoy the wait."

Lois turned on her heel and walked past the counter to the swinging door that led back to the kitchen.

"Lois! Wait! You don't have to, I mean. I didn't realize you were. Aww shit," Dallas trailed off, an uncharacteristic blush flushing his cheeks.

Lois hadn't had a single kind word for him since the night he'd killed Herb. The guilt he thought he'd ditched swung back around and blindsided him, followed by a spark of indignation that burned up to a familiar anger. Stubbornly, Dallas waited until Dee showed up and took his order. Lois made her way around the diner but didn't even spare him a glance. When his food arrived, Dallas mechanically pushed it into his mouth a surly forkful at a time, grumbling around each bite.

Finished but not full, he left too much cash on the counter and made it to the door when some sixth sense pricked its way through the fog of his thoughts. Turning, he saw Lois, a stolid mask of reproach fixed on her face as she stared at him from across the diner. Dallas held her unwavering gaze for as long as he could. Suddenly self-conscious, he was about to look away when he saw Lois raise her arm and hold out a doll. It was a boy doll with dark hair, a red flannel, and little blue jeans.

Dallas's brow furrowed in confusion. He had no idea why Lois was showing him a doll and tried to decide if he should be annoyed. Before he could ask what the deal was, Lois's other hand made an odd series of gestures. Her fingers wrapped and twisted around the doll's head. Her mouth moved, but she must've been speaking very softly, because Dallas didn't hear a sound. Actually, the more he thought about it, the more apparent it became that he couldn't hear anything except the rush of a distant ocean, waves rolling and receding. Each wave seemed to pull at his awareness, dragging his mind far away and leaving gobs of soggy cotton in its place. The button on his shirt cuff caught his attention. It was a button. A round button. But why did that matter? With a tremendous amount of effort, he refocused on Lois and offer a tentative wave goodbye, but she just turned and walked away.

Sound returned like a needle dropped on a record. With a huff, Dallas stomped out of Ronnie's Grill and climbed into Deloris. As he twisted the key in the ignition, he pushed thoughts of Lois and Herb forcibly down. No one ever said being a hero was easy, and Dallas had some C.I.A. douchenozzles to deal with.

The sun was spilling orange across the morning clouds when he pulled into Cecil's lot. More of a lunch and dinner spot, Cecil's was still a few hours from opening, and all was dark and quiet. Even so, Dallas decided not to take any chances. Pulling back onto the highway, he drove a quarter mile or so until only unbroken woods lined either side of the paved, two-lane road. A gap in the trees that looked big enough to accommodate Deloris appeared, so he drove off the road and killed the engine. Walking back to the shoulder, he looked at his impromptu hiding spot for the giant pickup. Only someone paying attention would notice the truck. Fortunately, most folks in these parts didn't pay much attention, especially when driving.

The morning air was crisp on his face as he jogged back toward Cecil's to get his bearings. Putting the small restaurant to his back, he started walking into the trees in what he hoped was the same direction he'd traveled the previous day. Buoyed by his conviction that he'd figure out where he was going soon enough, he strode confidently through the woods. It wasn't long, though, before he realized that he didn't have a clue where he was. Dallas slowed his gait and looked more closely at the surrounding pines and maples, hoping for a reminder of the path he'd followed just a day before. Finally coming to a stop, he ground his teeth in frustration.

"Dammit! C'mon Dal. You found 'em once, you can find 'em again. No big deal, right?"

A deep breath helped to bring his blood pressure down a point or two. Next, he exhaled, pushing all the air from his lungs. Closing his mouth, he drew a second deep breath through his nose. A hundred thousand smells that he'd been smelling the entire time suddenly registered in his conscious mind, a rush so intense he dropped to his knees. Letting the air whoosh out through his mouth, he drew another breath, more slowly this time. It was all there. Each tree, leaf, and blade of grass. Deer droppings, squirrel poop, and coyote scat. Bugs and birds and everything in between. And him.

Huh? he thought, coming back to the moment. He'd just showered the previous night, and the cool morning meant he wasn't in any danger of breaking a sweat. Even so, he could definitely smell something, and that something was definitely him.

Dallas lifted each arm and took a mighty whiff of each pit. Sweat, Old Spice, laundry detergent, no fabric softener. He'd be captain of the Vikings cheerleading squad before he used fabric softener. The shirt was mostly clean, no spilled beer or other such things on this one yet. Swiveling his head, he snuffed and whuffed, pulling the morning air in and out of his nose. He still smelled *him*, but it wasn't coming from him. Wholly confused, he paced a zigzag back and forth between bushes and trees. The zigs and zags became a lopsided loop, then a series of crisscrosses over the circle he'd just wandered. The more he concentrated, the more he could smell himself, always so close, always just out of reach.

He expanded the radius of his haphazard search. When he finally keyed in on the source of his scent, his head dropped down, and his long legs took him straight to a wide oak. Bending over at the waist, he placed his palms against the bark and brought his face so close it tickled the skin on the tip of his nose.

"That's it! That's me! I'm in the tree!" he crowed, any thought of stealth lost in his excitement. Wiggling and pacing back and forth, he sniffed again and again.

"Ha! Knew I'd find me. Ain't nobody can hide from old Dallas, especially not myself!"

The absurdity of the moment caught up with him. He sniffed more carefully and realized with a growing sense of surprise that he smelled his own pee. Expecting himself to be disgusted, he realized that it wasn't a bad smell, just a specific smell that stood out from all the others. Dallas stepped back and looked at the oak. Memories of having to pee on his trek back yesterday surfacing, he realized he had found one of the unlucky trees he'd repurposed as a commode. Dallas accepted the realization and gave up on trying to feel disgusted. His pee didn't really smell bad. It was just him. Nothing to get all weird about. Just a smell. His smell.

Standing straight, he raised his nose to the light breeze rustling the leaves. It took a moment, but he caught the scent again. Faint, but still unmistakably him.

"I'd make a damn strange tour guide, that's a sure thing," he chuckled.

It didn't take long to find the second tree he'd peed on the day before. A quick snuff confirmed it was his. With a satisfied nod, he cast about to catch the scent again and continued deeper into the woods.

Nearing the third tree, he pulled up short, a new scent pressing itself hard against his nostrils. Dallas's eyes narrowed, and a low growl passed his lips. The scent of urine was definitely not human. Other smells wended their way forward. Fur, musk. In a leap of intuition, Dallas recognized it as a wolf. The scent was fresh. Maybe an hour old, two at most. Eyes narrowing further, Dallas glowered in annoyance.

"Who the hell do you think you are? My tree. Mine!"

The sound of a zipper followed, and Dallas let a fresh stream go, taking care to completely obliterate the wolf's scent. Finished, he squared his shoulders and raised his chin in defiance.

"This tree's taken, wolfy!" Dallas declared. Business done, he turned to get his bearings and recognized the small rise he'd reached the previous day. Unlike before, when voices had reached him on the evening breeze, now there were just the sounds of the Wisconsin woods. Birds twittered, leaves rustled, squirrels chattered their domestic disputes. Ready for an end to the suspense, Dallas walked up the small rise and looked down upon something completely unexpected.

A clearing waited, maybe a quarter of the size of Lambeau Field, and bathed in the early morning sun. A small, decrepit cabin sat near the tree line, giving off an air of tired acceptance. Just past the cabin, an old pickup and a familiar moped sat at odd angles, as if the owners originally thought it'd be fun to collide demolition derby style but parked instead.

Dallas registered these details in an off-hand sort of way, but they didn't give him pause. It was what occupied the rest of the clearing that made him wonder about those C.I.A. guys. Tires, plywood cubbies, stacks of hay bales, and lengths of barbed wire were spaced along what looked to be an obstacle course. Between and around them, large plywood cut-outs decorated the rest of the course. Two-by-four frames held them upright, and most were facing the various obstacles. Squinting slightly into the rising sun, Dallas discerned that the cut-outs were painted to resemble...

People? Bears? Tigers? No. Nothing so common. Plus, those all had four limbs, and some of the cut-outs had decidedly more than four. Turning his head, he spied what looked like a man with tentacles instead of arms, and another that was quite clearly a buxom woman with a giraffe head holding a staff.

"C.I.A. my ass," he mumbled quietly. "Unless terrorists have gotten mighty strange."

With a cavalier shrug, Dallas straightened his flannel, pushed his hair back with his fingers, and started a brisk walk down to the clearing, singing his favorite song along the way.

"Packers! Go, you Packers, go and get 'em, Go, you fighting fools upset 'em,

Smash their line with all your might, A touchdown, Packers, Fight, Fight, Fight, Fight!

On, you Green and Gold, to glory, Win this game the same old story,

Fight, you Packers, Fight, and bring the bacon home to OLD GREEN BAY!"

He cut a diagonal path through the course toward the old cabin. About halfway in, Dallas watched an arrow fly past his shoulder and heard it thunk heavily as it struck the nearest plywood monster.

"You missed," he observed, looking with curiosity at the blunted tip of the arrow on the ground. It wouldn't puncture skin if it hit, but it would hurt like the dickens and leave a nasty bruise.

"I never miss," a voice Dallas recognized shot back. "If I'd meant to hit you, I'd a hit you."

"Uh huh. Whatever, Randall. Seems like the only time you can even come close to getting a piece of me is when you're a sneaky little shit about it," Dallas said with a mean grin.

The breeze stirred, and he lifted his head. A sniff confirmed what his ears suspected. His assailant was hiding out in a plywood structure twenty or so yards away. It was about the size and shape of a box truck, complete with painted wheels on the side. Turning toward Randall's hiding place, he moved confidently forward.

A glint of sunlight revealed the head of another arrow through a thin slit between two boards a split second before the arrow was loosed. Rather than dodging, Dallas calmly plucked it out of the air when the tip was mere inches from his chest.

Damn. I really am a badass, he thought with a self-assured shrug and proceeded to use the arrow's plastic fletching to scratch an itch on his back.

"If you're supposed to be a terrorist, this country's got nothing to worry about," he said.

A popping sound only slightly preceded the sensation of a fist-sized mass hitting him with the force of a freight train just above the kidney. The impact knocked him forward, and he grunted in pained surprise. Apparently, Randall wasn't the only one there. Turning as he stumbled, Dallas spied a blue bean bag on the ground right as another pop split the air.

This time, he was ready. Years of high school contact sports, a job doing physical labor, and a much higher than average bar-brawl to bar-outing ratio had honed Dallas's reflexes and made him the tough son of a bitch he prided himself on being. Turning his unintentional stumble into an intentional somersault, he tucked his shoulder and rolled off at an angle. The sound of a second beanbag whistling past was accompanied by a gruff, "Shit!" from somewhere behind him. Coming fluidly to his feet, he switched gears and charged the box truck structure where Randall was hiding. Last time Dallas checked, arrows tended to do a little more damage than bean bags.

Apparently, Randall wasn't expecting a head-on assault because he gave a high-pitched yelp and fired off a hasty shot from his bow. The arrow sailed wide as Dallas rounded the right side of the structure, flinging a hand out to catch the two-by-four frame's edge. As he suspected, the back was open, just like the back of a delivery truck would be. When he swung around, his momentum carried him straight at his assailant.

Randall wasn't a slug, but he didn't have time to both drop his bow and raise his arms to defend himself. Dallas's fist connected with the side of his face at the same moment the bow hit the ground with a twang.

"Ahhh!" the unfortunate man screamed in pain. "You broke my damn face again!"

Dallas didn't let up. He fired a few quick body shots into Randall's torso and followed with a sharp jab right between his eyes. The blow stunned Randall long enough for Dallas to slide his pocket knife free and wrap Randall up from behind, blade pressed firmly against his jugular.

"Whoa! Don't! Don't kill me! It's a test! It's just a test!" Randall screamed. His words devolved into gasping gibberish as Dallas torqued his shoulder and pressed the knife's tip until it broke skin, releasing a trickle of very bright blood down Randall's neck.

"Well, looky here!" he said in a clear, calm voice. Despite all the excitement, Dallas's heart rate was steady, and his breath came slow and easy. He felt completely relaxed, which he realized in a detached way might be considered odd given the circumstances.

With a shrug for life's perplexities, he continued. "When I got up today, I thought maybe I'd get some pussy. This wasn't quite what I had in mind, though."

Randall hissed through clenched teeth and momentarily tensed, but relaxed when he felt Dallas's iron grip on his wrist tighten.

"Easy boy. I think it's high time you introduced your friends and started to explain things." Dallas coaxed Randall into a sideways shuffle. When they reached the open side of the enclosure, he shoved Randall's head out.

After taking a deep breath through his nose, Dallas hollered out. "I know there's a punk with a bean bag gun and a lady who I really hope looks as good as she smells. C'mon out so we can get acquainted proper-like."

Silence hung for a few moments. Birds eventually resumed their incessant chattering, and a light breeze ruffled the leaves of trees circling the clearing. Otherwise, the only sounds were Dallas's calm and Randall's not-so-calm breathing until he heard a slow clapping.

"Well done! Excellent! Glad to see I was right," the voice said. "This vamp killer is every bit as tough as I'd hoped. Glad this little town has something to offer. Aletia, let's put down our toys and meet our new recruit."

"Qué demonios, Colton! I didn't get to use mine," a sultry and softly accented voice complained, words clearly coming from a pouting mouth.

"Tia, darling. Not on our company."

"You got to use your toy on our mala compañía."

"Manners, Aletia! Manners," the man named Colton chastised. "And I would've gotten my ass kicked six ways to Sunday right after our new friend finished up with Randall, isn't that right, Dallas? Now come out of there and say hello. No more arrows or bean bags, I promise."

Dallas gave Randall a shove and walked him out into the open. With a magnanimous smile, he removed the knife from Randall's neck and released the wrist he'd been holding behind the man's back. The knife's handle was making his palm itch, so he quickly folded it back up and returned it to his pocket.

"That sounds mighty fine," he agreed graciously. "I'm Dallas Emory Vinter, owner and proprietor of That Blows HVAC and Goddamn Hero of Trappersville, but you knew all that, I suppose." Placing a boot firmly on Randall's backside, he kicked and sent his former captive face first into the grass.

Turning his attention to the man that had greeted him with a beanbag to the kidney, Dallas continued.

"I imagine you're some type of commanding officer or whatnot, and you probably think I should be saluting. Well, I got news for you, buddy. One, I ain't enlisted in your little F.B.I, C.I.A., N.S.A.B.C .-whatever club you got goin' on here, and two, I don't salute little punks that ambush me, unless you call what happened to Randall's face a salute. So I guess you'd better get a beer to wash down your disappointment, but do it later. Right now, I expect you to start talking. You recruited me, right? Damn right, you did! So."

Dallas cracked the knuckles on first one meaty fist and then the other before crossing his arms across his chest. Staring straight at the man who still seemed to think he was in charge, he asked, "Who the hell are you, what the hell is all this, and when do I start hunting terrorists?"

Chapter 11

"A LONG TIME AGO," the man named Colton started, "humans weren't exactly top of the food chain, so to speak."

The air of potential violence had subsided a bit. Randall had settled onto a broad stump, alternately massaging the new, darkening bruise on his jaw and dabbing at the still bleeding cut on his neck. Despite having gotten the best of him again, Dallas knew Randall wasn't one to be trifled with. Never mind the sad goatee, unfortunate widow's peak and dorky moped. Wiry muscles wrapped his lean frame, and his eyes had the particular glint of one that fought dirty as a rule. Occasionally, he glanced up at Dallas with an expression that was less than congenial.

Well, can't blame the guy, Dallas thought without rancor. *I did bust his face a couple of times.*

The woman Aletia stood idly beside Randall, a mild look of disdain on her movie-star gorgeous face. One hand rested on a hip so perfectly curved scientists could've used it to calibrate their instruments. The other arm hung languidly at her side, an odd-looking corded thing dangling from her hand. Two strands of braided leather hung down almost to the ground. The end of each braid had a small metal sphere attached. From their scuffed appearance, and the weathered look of the leather braids, the strange whip appeared to be well-used, but Dallas couldn't quite discern its function. He didn't spend much time thinking about it, though. He much preferred to look at the dark, unblemished skin of her beautiful face framed in long strands of black hair. Eyeliner—so deep in color it was just a shade away from the skin beneath—was liberally applied, and emerald green eyes glinted dangerously beneath impossibly long lashes. The lips that at the moment were frowning in judgment of Randall gave the impression that, if they did smile, it was a smile that would guarantee you the best night of your life, followed by a trip to the emergency room.

Dallas sat transfixed, trying to figure out where she was from. Mexico? South America? Spain? Growing up in rural Wisconsin didn't give him much experience in such matters, but he realized he didn't much care where she came from. It was enough that she was here. Finally tearing his eyes away from the exotic Aletia, he looked at Colton. It was a little disconcerting, since Dallas felt like he could've been looking in the mirror. Colton was about his age, closer to thirty-five than thirty, and about his height, probably coming in around six-foot-one before pulling on the cowboy boots that could've come straight from Dallas's mud room. He had the same quarterback physique with wide shoulders, long arms, and the hands of a guy used to actual, honest-to-god, break-a-sweat work. His shoulder-length hair was a coarse, dark brown with hints of silver at the temples, giving his otherwise rough appearance a sophisticated edge. Here was a man that would never run home and cry to momma. Colton had the self-contained, hard-baked look of a man who solved his own problems.

Standing there in worn jeans and a faded flannel, with his thumbs looped in a wide leather belt fastened with a damn impressive brass buckle, Dallas figured they could've easily been cousins, maybe even brothers, and felt an immediate kinship to the man. That said, he was still annoyed that Colton was taking the long way around to answering his questions.

"Science would have you believe a thing or two about the evolution of our species and our relationship with the beasts of the earth," Colton continued, aware of but unconcerned by Dallas's scrutiny. "And those scientists would be right about most things. I'm not going to tell you science is a lie, because it isn't. History, that's the one who's a bald-face liar."

Colton rolled his shoulders and settled into his story, low voice rolling with a practiced cadence.

"You see, history was written mainly by churches and tyrants, and far too often, the latter held too much sway over the former. If you look far enough back in history, you'll learn that some churches knew the truth of things, but the tyrants didn't want all of those things being widely known. They didn't want the oppressed population getting spooked and unruly, if you follow. So when it came to writing the history books, most of what you get is a carefully redacted version of events."

Dallas held up his hand to interrupt.

"This sounds like the start of a nice story, but I think you'd better cut to the chase. I don't listen to history lectures until my third, no, my fourth beer."

Aletia gave Colton a look and twirled the two-corded whip in a lazy circle. Colton chuckled softly before saying, "Easy, now. He's right. We should probably clear up the basics before this good fellow loses his patience and takes it out on Randall's face again.

"Told you he's tough," Randall groused. "Not that I couldn't take you," he continued, pointing pointedly at Dallas. "You're just lucky Colton didn't want you hurt."

"Is that a fact?" Dallas asked innocently. "Well, that's awfully sporting of you, Colton. You're a right gentleman. Now, if you don't mind, answers, pronto, or I'm blowing this Popsicle stand. I swear, you government types take forever to do anything."

Colton shook his head. "Not government Dallas, and we're not hunting terrorists. I'm not really sure where you got that idea from. I believe Randall was quite clear when he said we're a part of something much more important. I mentioned that history has left us an incomplete version of what's gone before. More specifically, history would have you believe that there were humans, and there were animals, and that's all that there ever was."

"And fish. Bugs. Birds," Dallas interjected. "Wait, are birds animals? I guess not. So yeah, birds."

"Okay. Yes, animals and fish and bugs and birds," Colton agreed with a frown. "Now, if you don't mind?"

Dallas raised his hands. "Just want to make sure we're on the same page."

Moving forward until he was standing barely a foot from Dallas, Colton's gray eyes went hard as forged steel.

"I'll tell you what page we're on. We are on the human page. We are also the ones that know about those pages that history has conveniently left out. The pages that have been reduced to fairy tales, and bad movies, and T.V. shows staring too-pretty people. We're the ones that protect the human race from unmentionable things, the ones that keep you safe at night and solidly grounded in your quaint idea of the real world."

Spreading his arms to encompass the surrounding group, Colton said, "We, Dallas, are the Society."

The birds stopped their twittering, and the breeze no longer blew. A heavy silence descended, and even the morning sunlight seemed to dim as Randall, Aletia, and Colton all sat hushed, looking at Dallas expectantly.

"Okey dokey. Society. Check. Glad it's a word. I get kind of annoyed by all the letters them government types use. But don't you think 'society' is kind of, oh, I dunno, mamby pamby sounding?"

Aletia resumed her twirling, the sphere-tipped whip underscoring the moment with a quiet, malcontent whir. Even Colton's unshakeable confidence seemed to shake just a smidge.

"It's what we're called," he stated flatly. "It's what we've always been called. When we travelled with the Germanic tribes before Germany was called Germany, we were die Gesellschaft. In ancient Rome, we were the societatis. In every culture from every time, we've been the Society. It is not 'mamby pamby.' It is the name of a very old, very important brotherhood,"

"And sisterhood," Aletia corrected, the hollow whisper of her twirling whip twining with her words.

"Figure of speech, Tia. Figure of speech," Colton placated. "And please stop twirling that thing. It's like nails on a chalkboard after a while."

Returning his attention to Dallas, he continued. "I hope I'm making an impression here, Dallas. We aren't asking you to join a kickball league. You're being invited to join an ancient order of protectors with lines tracing back to the first time a Cro-Magnon used an antelope's thigh bone to club a manticore. You've been chosen to be a part of something truly important, something only someone of your unique experience and abilities could ever hope to be a part of."

Dallas rubbed his jaw. "Uh huh. We'll skip past the obvious question of, 'what the hell is a manticore?'" Pulling on his best haggling face, he matched Colton's unwavering gaze with his own. "What's it cost?"

Colton shot Randall a look.

"What? I didn't say nothing! Lucky guess, I guess," Randall shot back defensively.

"I knew it!" Dallas crowed. "Ancient order of special whatever, blah blah blah. Forget you guys. I ain't paying to hang out with a bunch of weirdos in the woods. I already do that for free. Crap on a cracker, have you met Stanley?"

Colton held his hands up. "Normally, yes, we ask for a reasonable donation from new members. Hunting monsters isn't cheap, and we can't exactly hold down nine-to-five jobs. New members typically give what they can. In return, we teach you, train you, and equip you to do battle with those very real monsters that most folks don't want to believe exist."

Dallas smiled his easy smile. "Lemme check the fine print here." Holding up a hand, he squinted at his palm and traced imaginary lines with a finger.

"Yup. Thought so. There's an exception for the Hero of Trappersville. Looks like he doesn't have to pay for shit and even gives ass-whoopings for free. And ass-whooping can be interpreted in a few interesting ways," he added, winking at Aletia.

"Seriously?" Aletia sneered. "Colton, I think we've misjudged here."

"Nonsense," he replied. "Forget the donation for now. The real question is this."

Standing to his full height, Colton extended a hand.

"We need you to hunt monsters. Are you with us?"

Dallas took a long look at the gathered group. Randall, despite his annoying voice and tendency to whine, probably wasn't all bad. Colton, he was solid as an oak. And Aletia...

"What the hell, right? I'm in. But seriously, you gotta change the name."

Chapter 12

"**L**EARN THE COURSE, RUN the course. It's that simple," Colton said with an expansive gesture. He figured that since Dallas had arrived, they might as well make use of the day. "Tia will show you the ropes while Randall and I check to make sure everything's secured."

Aletia hmph'd, and made a comment. Part of it was in a language Dallas didn't speak, but the English part about not signing up to baby-sit came through loud and clear. Certain that she was going to object to showing him anything, Dallas was pleasantly surprised when she took him by the arm and steered him toward the odd obstacle course.

"Demon dog," she pointed, indicating what looked like a rabid Rottweiler had taken a roll in the hay with an iguana and popped out a most unnatural critter. "Fast, mean, and smelly. Easiest to see with your peripheral vision, making them tough to take a clean shot at," she explained, tugging at a ragged tarp half-draping the monster. "Try to take a sideways shot on the run and hit the hound, not the tarp."

Taking Dallas by the elbow, she walked him to another monster. This was the buxom babe with a giraffe head.

"Werethekau. Well, one visage, anyway," she said. "Don't just look for a giraffe head. Could be a lion, rooster, or more frequently a hawk or eagle."

"Huh," Dallas responded. "So, do they all have fantastic racks?"

Aletia cracked a smile. "We did that for the idiotas like you. Reminds you to pay attention to all the details, not just the ones you want to focus on."

Dallas laughed. "And here I thought that's why they invented the light switch. What's with the staff?"

Her almost-smile left as quickly as it came. "Werethekau is a dios, a god. Well, one god of many. Most gods are rather caught-up in pageantry. They like props, so look for staffs, scepters, even gaudy jewelry. They can usually hide their true visage, but a careful observer can tell them by their accessories. Actually, incorporeal deities often rely on their talisman to anchor them to this reality. Which is to say that if you destroy their prop, the god has a fifty-fifty chance of disappearing. When you run the course, try to get the staff with your first shot. If you miss, go for the heart. In real life, hope there's only one heart to go for."

"Good to know. Good to know," Dallas nodded, shying away from the fact that he really had no clue what she was talking about. "What else you got?"

Aletia steered him back and forth, pointing out a werewolf, a collection of zombies, and even a Bigfoot. That one got his attention.

"For real? I mean, c'mon. You guys hunt 'squatches? What's next? The tooth fairy?"

Aletia leveled a cold stare at Dallas. "Pray to whatever gods you hold dear that you never run into a tooth fairy."

Dallas laughed, but Aletia didn't, so he stopped. When she continued to stare, he fidgeted. While fidgeting, the uncomfortable silence stretched until he cleared his throat.

"Um, how 'bout that one?" he asked, pointing to where Colton was standing. The plywood cut-out depicted a beautiful, dark-haired woman wearing a long robe, its deep red color matching her fingernails, lips, and strangely, her eyes. "That doesn't look so scary."

Colton walked over and made a sweeping gesture, encompassing the length of the woman depicted on the plywood. "Onryo. Vengeful spirits and actually quite scary. They're usually only found in Japan, but I killed one in Queens a few months back. It was a near thing too. I almost didn't make it out alive."

"Would've served you right, you horny gringo," Aletia quipped.

"Yep," Colton agreed easily. "We met at a sake bar," he offered by way of explanation.

"Sucky bar? That'll teach ya," Dallas said authoritatively. "That's why I stick to the classy places. You gotta have standards."

"Not sucky. Sake," he clarified, pronouncing it *sah-kay*. "It's a Japanese rice wine. Good stuff. Tia and I had just tangled with a particularly nasty Clurichaun,"

"Possessed Leprechaun," Aletia chimed in. "Real pain in the ass. Small, so you think they'd be a cinch to knock off, but they're surprisingly strong and have really sharp teeth."

"Temper like a wolverine with hemorrhoids, too," Randall added with a grimace.

Colton cleared his throat. "Anyway, as I was saying, Tia and I had just dropped one and were looking to unwind. She went whiskey-hunting, but I wanted a taste of something different. We had passed a little karaoke bar tucked into an alley. Sign in the window said, 'best sake this side of the Atlantic,' and it had been years since I was last in Japan." Colton shrugged as if no further explanation was necessary.

"She was an oiran, a royal courtesan. Well, she was when she was alive, which was in the late sixteenth century. With a few drinks in me, I thought she was just a beautiful woman with me in her crosshairs. After barely getting out with my pants and my life, I did a little research. She served in the court of Emperor Go-Yozei. Apparently, she fell from grace after embarrassing a local lordling. He tried to take credit for a song she composed that the Emperor adored. Rather than getting the recognition she deserved, the Emperor had the poor girl's tongue cut-out."

Colton paused in thought. "I imagine that's why she wasn't very talkative. I just thought she was the quiet type. Anyway, she kept pushing the karaoke book at me, pointing at songs, and making me sing. If I hadn't been so worn out from that tangle with the little Irish nasty and quickly filling up on what honestly was the best sake I'd had this side of the Atlantic, I might've noticed the more important details."

"She didn't have feet, and her eyes were glowing," Aletia said dryly, rolling her eyes.

"Tia said her hair was floating around her head, too," added Randall. "Not many ladies have floating hair."

"I said I missed some important details! Come off it, already," Colton said, starting to blush. Turning back to Dallas, he finished his story.

"Anyway, I'm a believer in consenting adults engaging in consensual adult recreational activities. However, if the adult in question happens to be around four hundred years your senior and a vengeful spirit, well... Let's just say it's a good thing I happened to have a twig of cherry blossom that had been blessed by a Shinto priest in my pocket."

While Colton and Randall shared a laugh and Aletia rolled her eyes, Dallas noticed a more familiar-looking cut-out. Well, familiar in a horror movie sort of way. The vampire didn't look anything like Herb. Dark hair slicked straight back showed a widow's peak that made Randall's own look amateurish at best. Beneath the widow's peak was a pale, drawn face with features pulled into a fearsome mask. Skillfully painted, its luminescent eyes practically glowed, and the too-wide mouth had blindingly white teeth with incisors that were easily three inches long. A silky black cape had been tied around the plywood neck, and its arms and clawed hands were up in a classic 'I'm gonna getcha' pose.

Dallas stared at the vampire cut-out, a sea of memories swelling to a tidal wave about to crest.

"I know that one. Damn right, I do," he said, voice trembling with emotions not easily defined. "But they don't always look like that, do they." It was a statement, not a question, but Aletia answered regardless.

"Vampiros can come in pretty much any shape or size, but they do tend to be attractive. They like fancy clothes and are usually dressed to the nines. Careful though. You can't just stake anyone you see in a designer suit or trendy sweater."

"More's the pity," quipped Randall, shaking his head at the injustices of life.

Ignoring him, Aletia continued. "See, the most common monsters we go after are the classics. Vampiros, werewolves, zombies. There are many others, but none are anywhere near as common as those three."

"Ghosts are," Randall chimed in. "But we tend to shy away from hunting ghosts."

"Too scary?" Dallas asked.

"No," Randall shot back while flipping Dallas the bird. "Just an over-saturated market. Any Joe Schmo can hunt a ghost, and even the bigger idiots in the bunch can find one or two. Ghosts are everywhere."

"Si, Randall's right," Aletia continued. "Pretty much anyone can find a ghost, so pretty much everyone does. Do you know how annoying it is to show up at a haunting site and have a bunch of pimply faced niños with EVP recorders stare at your chest?"

"You're putting me on," Dallas said. "I know vampires exist. I killed one at the bowling alley, remember? You can't get much more proof in your pudding, if you know what I mean. So I guess it stands to reason that if vamps exist, a few other things must exist, too. But ghosts? C'mon. I wasn't born stupid."

"I told you he took lessons," Aletia said to Randall, eliciting a snorting laugh from the other man.

"You don't have to believe in ghosts, goblins, and ghouls for them to exist," Colton chided. "They're real. We find them, we kill them. We just tend to ignore ghosts because, as Tia said, there are too many other people tracking them down and trying to grab headlines. We operate differently, more quiet like. We'd rather not make a scene. We find a real problem, get in, get out, and do our best not to leave a trail."

Gesturing around him, Colton invited Dallas to take in the small clearing, complete with the decrepit cabin and obstacle course.

"What you see here isn't our usual M.O. We got wind of a vampire in these parts, so we decided to pay a visit. Imagine our surprise when we learned you took care of the problem before we arrived. That piqued our interest. We used to have a Society Warrior in these parts, so we decided it would be a good time to replenish the local ranks, so to speak."

"What happened to the last guy?" Dallas asked.

"Dead," Colton stated matter of factly.

"We think," Aletia added.

"You think? You're either dead, or you ain't, right?" Dallas asked.

"Well, *most* of him is dead," Aletia explained. "There was a Mange-les-Morts celebration in Madison. In the Voodoo tradition, it's the day for feeding dead family ancestors in govis, these little clay pots. One dead ancestor didn't want to be dead anymore and possessed a Haitian witch. Tyrone thought he could handle it, que no había problema, but he'd been drinking Cremasse with a hundred and fifty proof rum. El muy estúpido was an organ donor, and now we're worried a few of his leftover pieces might be causing problems in Ohio. We have a girl in Ashtabula County looking into it."

"The point is," Colton interjected, "These woods seem to be a bit of a magnet for monsters, so we need someone on the ground to deal with it. We need you."

Dallas nodded slowly.

"You might just have a head on those shoulders after all, Colton. So, what do I gotta do?

"Well, for starters, you have to be trained," Aletia said with a smile.

Dallas liked that smile. He liked it very much. While he and Aletia exchanged a lingering look, Randall made his way to the cabin and returned with a big plastic tub.

"Weapons locker," he explained. Pulling off the top, he and Aletia unloaded an odd assortment of weapons. Nerf swords, ping pong paddles, hockey sticks, and even a large, wooden spoon.

Continuing her tutelage of the new recruit, Aletia went over the assorted arsenal with Dallas, explaining each item, what it represented, and what it was supposed to kill. The goal, Aletia explained, was to make it through the course and kill all the monsters using the 'monster-appropriate' weapon. If there was a Nerf sword by the manticore, you used the Nerf sword. If it was a wooden spoon... well, Dallas just hoped that if he ever did meet a Cyclops, scooping out its eye, represented by a squishy bean bag, with a wooden spoon was the best approach.

"Ignore how silly it seems," she said. "The point of this isn't just learning how to jump and roll. You have to learn how to think on your feet. When you encounter a supernatural, you won't have time to find the right ancient book with instructions for how to kill it. You have to *know* and you have to *act*."

"Oh, I think I know a thing or two about how to act and what toys to use," Dallas offered with a wink. Seeing her blush, he immediately cleared his mental calendar for the week and penciled her in.

"No seas tonto. Be serious and pay attention. You have to get through the whole course using the right weapons on the right monsters. To make it interesting, Randall and Colton will be hiding with paintball guns. They get an arm or leg, you can't use it for the rest of the course. They get a body or head shot, you're muerto."

"Uh huh, muerto," Dallas agreed, not really paying attention to her words. Not that he didn't want to. She just happened to have some spectacular cleavage that was occupying more of his brain than her words.

Rolling her eyes, Aletia stood and gathered up a collection of weapons. With Colton and Randall's help, she placed them around the course. Returning to Dallas, she finally managed to get him to look her in the eye.

"Up here, boy. That's right. Now watch. I'll run the course to show you how it's done, then it's your turn."

She turned to face the course, closed her eyes, and started counting. Reaching thirty, she launched forward, flowing like liquid mercury. Every move was infused with a panther's grace. Colton and Randall did their best to catch her off guard, but their paintballs all seemed aimed at the spot she had been a split-second before and splattered ineffectually against the various obstacles and monsters. Watching her was the most arousing thing Dallas had seen in recent memory, and he was damn close to pitching a tent right there in the clearing.

Ice baths, road construction, taxes. Dallas kept his face carefully blank while running his mind through a mantra of turnoffs. *Papercuts. Pat Sajak.*

Clearing the last obstacle, Aletia's run slowed to a trot, then a walk, then a confident saunter that ended back where he was standing.

"Like that," she said casually, while Colton and Randall clapped and whistled.

"Yeah, um. Looks like you've done this a few times," he managed, walking awkwardly up to the start of the course. "So now what? I just close my eyes, count, and then go for it?"

"Exactamente," she answered. "The boys will go easy on you this time. Focus on getting the right attacks in on the right monsters."

Dallas nodded, closed his eyes, and started to count.

"Twenty-eight, twenty-nine, thirty."

Opening his eyes, he was shocked to see Randall standing about ten feet in front of him, paintball gun already pointed at his chest. His surprise was rudely followed by three rapid pops coinciding with three sharp jabs to his chest.

"You little bastard!" Dallas roared, wrapping his arms across his burning chest.

Randall merely shrugged. "Now you know how it feels to get shot with a paintball. Didn't want you tensing up during the run-through. Fear of getting hit is always worse than getting hit," he explained in a patronizing tone. "Now count again. I promise I won't take any cheap shots."

Shaking off the stinging in his chest, Dallas glared at Randall, closed his eyes, and counted.

"Twenty-six, twenty-seven..."

Dallas heard the click of the trigger. Eyes still closed, he crouched and rocked to the right. A whistling split the air where his head had just been, but he was already moving to the first obstacle. Opening his eyes, he made it to the low wall, ducked into its offered protection, and picked up the first weapon.

"Oh, come on!" he complained, holding the ping-pong paddle. Rustling through his recent memories, he knew it was supposed to represent some type of religious talisman, but he had no idea what to do with it. After a short, annoyed sigh, he cocked his head and listened. The birds had gone silent again, hiding from the commotion.

He could hear the rustling leaves, but nothing else. Breathing deep to slow his racing heart, he listened harder and was rewarded with a myriad of tiny sounds. The slight scuff of a shoe shifting on dirt, the flapping of the tarp draped over the demon dog. Inhaling through his nose, the sounds intermingled with a million smells. Pollen swirling in the breeze, a small puddle of oil beneath the pickup, sawdust and wood glue, Aletia's sweet perfume, and Randall's sour breath. It was all there, each obstacle, each person, each bug, and blade of grass. All there, and he didn't even need to look to see it.

Dallas's mind went refreshingly blank. Gone were his attempts to remember all the monsters, all the weapons, all the rules of the game. He simply thought of nothing and opened himself up to the hunt. Ping-pong paddle in hand, he attacked.

He had no clue what the first plywood monster was supposed to be and didn't much care. A quick *thwap* to what he assumed was its head with the paddle was followed by a well-placed kick to its center, knocking it over and back a good five feet. A paintball gun popped, adding a strange percussion to the music of the clearing. Twisting, he moved with an apparent languidness that belied his true speed as paintballs sailed past.

After high-stepping through a series of tires and belly-crawling under a few strands of barbed wire, he reached the next obstacle. It was designed to resemble a picket fence separating him from three ornery-looking zombies. A hockey stick rested innocently within reach. Grabbing it, Dallas jabbed two of the zombies between the eyes with its blunt end before reversing it and swinging the blade at the third's neck. Caught up in the moment, he didn't realize his own strength and was mildly surprised by the explosion of splinters as the plywood cracked and the hockey stick shattered. Tossing it to the side, he loped off to the left and headed for a stack of hay bales.

Leaping, he cleared the bales, rolled, and came fluidly to his feet, growling with pleasure as he ran toward the Cyclops. Randall hastily jumped out from behind the plywood, giving Dallas a brief sensation of déjà vu before he had to shift left and right to avoid Randall's barrage of paintballs. Nearing the Cyclops, he snatched up the wooden spoon, scooped out the bean bag eye, spun in a quick circle, and launched the bag from the spoon straight at the retreating Randall. The bag hit with such force that Randall cursed, stumbled, and went down in a heap.

"Tag! You're dead!" Dallas whooped, running past the grumbling man.

Next up were the onryo, a manticore, the demon dog, and others he either couldn't recall or couldn't be bothered to recall. Either way, each monster was vanquished according to Dallas, and with each kill, Dallas felt himself swell with purpose. This is how it was supposed to be. He was a goddamn hero, and he would keep the town safe, his friends safe, Lois safe, no matter what it took. With another athletic jump, twist, and roll, he easily avoided a fresh hail of paintballs. Colton had finally decided to reveal himself and was doing his best to wing Dallas and slow down his mad assault on the remaining monsters.

"Goddamn it, sit still for a sec," he heard Colton grumble under his breath.

Dallas wasn't worried about Colton. The click of a trigger and quick blast of compressed air gave him plenty of time to shift and avoid the paint-filled projectiles. He didn't even have to think about it, which was good because all of his attention was on the monster up ahead.

The Hollywood vampire loomed large in his vision, glowing eyes, white fangs, jet-black hair, and matching cape. Dallas saw it and his imagination exploded, a rapid-fire panorama of visions retelling a story he'd told himself a thousand times before. Poor Herb, walking up to his house after working at Ronnie's or maybe bowling. A dark shape in his peripheral vision, then some blood-drinking fiend biting deep into his neck. He imagined Herb begging the demon to stop, pleading for his life, and then dying right there in his front yard, or maybe in his crummy kitchen. Then that demon, that fiend, that monster, doing whatever it was vampires do to make more vampires, and Herb rising up, no longer Herb but something *else,* something sinister, something dangerous. It all started with that beady-eyed vamp, that one right in front of him, the one he'd finally caught up to. Now, at long last, he could avenge his friend's death.

Dallas hit the plywood vampire cut out like a flannel-clad wreck-ing ball. One fist lashed out and shattered the widow-peaked head, sending glaring eyes and snarling fangs in opposite directions. The next fist punched straight through the cut-out's chest, wrapped up a fistful of billowing cape, and pulled it back through the fist-sized hole. Grabbing both shoulders, Dallas rammed a knee up and was rewarded with a satisfying crack as the plywood busted into two ragged chunks. Raising the torso up over his head, Dallas slammed it down to the ground and started to stomp. At some point, he noticed the wooden stake. Grabbing it, he dropped to his knees and slammed the stake down on the vampire's chest. Over and over again, he stabbed the painted wood while plywood splintered and the pointed stake in his hand blunted down to a rough stub.

"Dallas! Stop it! Hey, stop!"

Die, die, die, die, die! he raged, a maelstrom of hate and retribution driving each blow.

Something grabbed his wrist. Snarling, he sent Colton sailing ass over teakettle. Another figure stepped into his view. Dallas barely had time to register long legs, curved hips, and an arm rapidly twirling something before strong cords tipped with metal balls wrapped around him and pinned his arms to the sides of his chest. Something heavy hit him in the small of his back, knocking him forward. Landing awkwardly, he heard his shoulder pop and felt a lancing pain spider across his back. Like gas on a fire, the pain fueled his burning rage before it was doused by a bucketful of water being dumped on his head.

"Yerblaaaughhhh!" he sputtered, water streaming down his face.

"Are you done?" Colton yelled back. "What the hell was that? It's a practice course, not a *Full Metal Jacket* psycho field trip."

"I got to use my toy on the company, after all," Aletia commented with a grin.

Stunned and confused, Dallas lay in a pile, arms pinned and shoulder throbbing, and tried to slow his ragged breathing.

What did just happen? he wondered. *I was just running the course. Just doing what I was supposed to do, wasn't I?*

"Well, what good is practice if you don't take it seriously?" he asked, more than a little indignant. "Dammit, I think I dislocated my shoulder. Could someone get these damn ropes off of me? Hurts like a bitch at this angle."

Colton eyed him skeptically while Randall spit in the grass and shook his head.

"I gotta make a new vampire now," Randall complained. "That was a good one, too. Took me like three hours to paint it. Untie him or not, I don't care, but he owes me a new plywood vamp."

Colton walked over, rubbing his own shoulder from the impact of his fall. "Well, passion isn't a bad thing, I guess. I'm just not used to recruits being so enthusiastic. You're stronger than you look too. Also good, as long as you remember whose team you're on." Fiddling with the ropes, he freed Dallas from the constraints and handed the corded whip back to Aletia.

"What's that thing called, anyway?" Dallas asked her. "I figured you had a little S and M streak, but had no idea it could do that."

"Bolas. Es realmente grandioso, no?" she replied, giving them a quick twirl for effect. "Been around since forever. Inca used them, South America cowboys, Spaniards, you name it." Squatting down beside him, she held up one of the metal weights attached to a braided leather cord.

"These can be swapped out depending on what you're hunting. Limestone weights inscribed with the right Egyptian hieroglyphs can bind a mummy. Silver does a nice job of subduing werewolves. Wood weights have their uses, too. You just better make sure you've picked the right wood. Rowan, ash, oak, whatever. Right wood, no hay problemas. Wrong wood, es un problema."

"Nice to see you've got such a keen eye for good wood," Dallas quipped, his former humor returning. "Now, before the next lesson, I need a little help here." Standing awkwardly, he waved with his good hand while trying not to move his left arm.

"Randall, I'm sorry I smashed up your vampire. I guess it struck a nerve and old Dallas, he struck right back. Important thing is come-uppance. How'd you like to get even-Steven?"

Randall squinted suspiciously, eyes shifting from Dallas to Colton and back. "Boss?"

Colton merely shrugged. "I think I know where he's going with this, and yes, you have my permission to hurt him. What do you need, Dallas? Would a sturdy doorframe work for you?"

Dallas sighed in anticipation of the impending pain. "Yeah. I guess that'll do fine. Let's get it over with so I can run your little course again."

"Better idea," suggested Aletia. "Let's get it over with so we can have a drink."

Dallas looked at the small circle of his new companions and smiled back. Despite the silly name, he figured he was going to like this Society just fine.

Chapter 13

S *ETTING A DISLOCATED SHOULDER sure gives a man a powerful thirst*, Dallas observed while working on his third beer.

After reaching the decrepit cabin on the edge of the clearing, Dallas had braced his shoulder against the door frame and given Randall specific instructions: pull back on his arm and body check him into the stud at the same time. Dallas would never know if Randall just wasn't any good at that sort of thing, or if he intentionally took three attempts before Dallas's shoulder gave a satisfying *pop* and snapped back into the socket. He did know that each attempt induced enough pain to stun a rhino, and that Randall had giggled while Dallas screamed and writhed. Third time really did pay all though. Once his shoulder was put right, the wave of relief gave him gooseflesh all the way down his body followed by a definite need to drink.

Despite its sorry state, which included a half-collapsed roof and windows grinning broken chunks of glass like a geezer's leftover teeth, the cabin was surprisingly cozy. A circle of camping chairs, a few coolers, and some lanterns occupied the space beneath what was left of the roof. A small propane stove sat off to the side, surrounded by a small collection of pots and pans still containing the remnants of an earlier meal. Colton had opened one of the coolers and, to Dallas's great delight, displayed a healthy number of ice cold beers. Accepting one gratefully, he'd collapsed into a chair and set himself to drinking.

"Hot damn! What a day," he whooped. "I haven't had that much fun since I don't know when."

Aletia took the chair next to him and clinked her beer can against his. The hunter drained half the can and then said, "The obstacle course is a small part of the training we do for new recruits, but important, none the less. Monsters tend to be faster and stronger than humans. We need to make sure we can keep up."

"'Cept for zombies." Randall cracked his own beer and took a seat. "Zombies are slow. Even a Twinkie-chomping lardo can usually get away if they need to."

"Maybe for a bit," Aletia said. "But remember, zombies don't get tired. They'll keep coming. If your trasero isn't used to running farther than from the Barca Lounger to the fridge and back, you'll get tired, and then you're dead."

"Sure, sure," Randall agreed. "Obviously, if you're a fat ass and don't got a weapon, but who'd ever be without a weapon? Seriously, just bottleneck 'em in a doorway, get a long, pointy something-or-other, and take 'em out one by one. Even fatty-boombah-latties can do that."

"Ignore Randall," Aletia advised, returning her attention to Dallas. "He refuses to lose an argument, no matter how stupid. Point is, we put new recruits through this training to gauge what kind of shape you're in and how much training you need." She leaned in with a smile that was more than just friendly. "Seems like you could go all night and hardly break a sweat."

Dallas felt his face flush, which was weird. He didn't usually have enough self-awareness to worry about getting embarrassed. Wiping his suddenly sweaty palms on his pant legs, he gave what he hoped was a charming smile and not a goofy grin.

"Oh yeah, damn right I can! I'm like the night train." Tipping his head back, he started to sing.

"The thought of you is driving me insane. Come on baby, let's go listen to the night train!"

"That's good," Colton's voice spoiled the moment like a chaperone at a middle school dance, "because we'll be doing the course in the dark tomorrow night."

Chagrined, Dallas returned his attention to his current beer. "So Aletia here was saying that's just part of the training. What else do I need to do?"

Colton looked thoughtful for a moment before asking, "How would you kill a zombie?"

"Head shot or fire," Dallas replied quickly.

"Vampire?" Colton asked.

"Stake to the heart or fire."

"Werewolf?"

"Silver. Could be a bullet, could be a blade, and um... Maybe fire?"

"Chupacabra."

Dallas paused and scratched his head. There was one on the course. What was it they used again?

"Cyclops?"

Dallas brightened. "Oh! The wooden spoon!"

"Not just any wooden spoon. It has to be carved from the oldest branch of a Kermes oak from the island of Crete," Colton reminded him.

"Oh. Right. Old oak Crete spoon. Got it."

"Onryo?"

"A twig!" Dallas said authoritatively, followed a moment later by a less convinced, "Um, with cherries?"

"Sprig of cherry blossom blessed by a Shinto priest," Colton corrected, "but it can't be any old cherry blossom nor any old monk with plastic prayer beads and a postcard from Buddha. What I'm getting at here is that hunting monsters is a complex business. There's a boatload of book learning in your future."

Dallas grinned. "Nah. I'll let Stanley do that." Finishing his beer, he looked at his watch. "Speaking of, time flies when you're kicking ass. I gotta head back, or Stanley's gonna think I was the one abducted by one of his aliens."

"Stanley?" Aletia asked, eyebrow raised.

"Aliens?" Randall asked, deadpan.

"Uh, yeah. Stan's a buddy of mine. Thinks he got abducted by aliens back in high school."

"Did he?" Colton asked seriously, brow furrowed.

Dallas started to laugh and then realized that maybe it wasn't such a crazy notion after all. His definition of normal had stretched a bit recently.

"Well, I guess that's a question I can't right answer. He swears it's God's own truth, and who am I to rain on a buddy's alien parade?"

With a shrug that conveyed Dallas wasn't prepared to waste any more brain cells on the issue, he continued.

"Stanley's a weird guy, but he's a good one to have around when you need to lose at bowling or win at *Jeopardy*, and he just loves book learning. I'll bring him round at some point, but right now, I should get out of here. I'm starving, and a couple of cold ones ain't gonna do the trick."

"You need a ride back?" Aletia asked, looking up from under dark lashes.

Dallas considered all the connotations of the invitation. His libido started to hoot and holler, but it had been an eventful day, and he had a lot to process.

"Nah," he managed after a brief internal struggle. "A little walk through the woods will do me good. See y'all tomorrow."

And with that, Dallas rose and strode from the cabin, heading back into the trees. He wasn't concerned about getting lost in the dark. A neon trail still blazed whenever he snuffed the air. Following his scent from the previous day, he made his way back toward Cecil's, mind awhirl with more thoughts than he was accustomed to thinking at one time.

Chapter 14

THE NEXT WEEK WENT by in a blur. When he wasn't fixing furnaces for the folks around town, Dallas would drag Stanley to the little cabin in the woods for training and learning, learning and training.

It had taken a healthy dose of Dallas's not inconsiderable charm to smooth over the group's ruffled feathers when he dragged Stanley in the day after his first trip to the clearing. The Society, Colton had forcibly reminded him, was secret.

"But he knew Herb, that vampire I did in. Plus, Stanley's smart. You said there was book learning to be done. Stanley here loves books, don't you, Stan?"

"Oh, heck yeah!" Stanley's head bobbed in agreement. "T-tom Clancy books, Do-It-Yourself Potlucks for One books, um." Stanley wrung his hands, at a loss to properly explain just how expansive his taste in books was. "All s-sorts of books."

Randall shook his head, and Aletia rolled her eyes, but Dallas persisted.

"Look, we're a package deal. If I'm in, Stanley's in. He'll pull his weight, all hundred and thirty pounds of it. Scout's honor," Dallas pleaded, crossing his heart and holding up his other hand. "And he's seen some weird shit, too. Stanley, I told 'em about the aliens. Tell 'em about the aliens."

Stanley's eyes went wide as flying saucers. He related the story as requested: leaving school, walking through the soccer field, the bright flash of light, and waking up flat on his back with all of his clothes on backward, even his undies. The telling took longer than the story actually merited, but Stanley was so excited to have an attentive audience that he stuttered more than usual. He also pointed out to Dallas more than a few times that if he had known he'd be telling the story, he would've brought the umbrella to prove he wasn't just hit by lightning.

"I'll bet he's even got some weird alien powers now," Dallas added authoritatively, when Stanley's mouth finally wound down to a stop. "And there was that newbie fee you talked about. Stan here can pay, can't you, Stanley?"

While Stanley excitedly pulled a collection of singles and fives out of his wallet, Colton put it to a vote. Aletia shrugged her agreement on the condition that Stanley never, ever be allowed into a fight and stuck to research only. Randall said he'd be fine with Stanley hanging around because he thought his stuttering was hilarious. That left Colton.

"Well," the Society's leader started slowly. "I'm intrigued by the aliens, there's no doubt about that. It wouldn't be the first time the Society's work has tipped in that direction. Also, good hunters usually have a librarian of sorts, someone they can turn to for solutions to tough problems."

He paused, scratching at the few days' growth shadowing his jaw.

"Oh, why not? Two can do what one could never, so I guess it works out alright. Stanley, consider yourself part of the team. Just please—please—keep this to yourselves. Secret societies don't stay secret very long if you run your trap about 'em."

The rookie hunter trained while Stanley studied, and both were properly exhausted by the work. Evenings were spent drinking beers in the cabin, swapping stories and good-natured ribbing while genuine friendships blossomed. Dallas learned that Colton was originally from Minnesota but went to college in England. Dallas didn't hold either fact against him though. The two men were cut from the same sturdy denim and flannel, and they spent hours discussing everything from fixing sticky carburetors to the crappiest receivers in the NFL. Aletia was quickly climbing Dallas's list of the most awesome woman he had ever met. Even Randall didn't seem like such a bad guy once you got past his tendency to whine. More surprisingly, Randall and Stanley found they shared a passion for both *Jeopardy* and *Veronica Mars*.

Dallas had never lacked for friends and admirers, but now half the town thought he was crazy. Even the folks that saw him stake Herb would roll their eyes when they thought he wasn't looking. It made him realize that he had felt very, very alone over the past couple of months. Now, sitting around a small campfire, drinking beers, having a few laughs, he felt something he hadn't in quite a while. Belonging.

"Penny for your thoughts?" Aletia held out a beer to Dallas and slid her camping chair closer. They'd had a particularly grueling session on the course and decided to call it a day.

"Pretty little thing like you, I'll share them for free," Dallas winked. "I was just reminiscing. Been awhile since I've felt so relaxed. It's," he fished for the right word, "nice."

"Nice, huh? You never struck me as a 'nice' kind of guy. Your friend Stanley, he's a nice one. I don't think that boy has a bad thought in his head. But you?" She laughed, leaning back and languidly crossing her long legs. "I'd peg you squarely in the 'naughty' box. Muy travieso."

"You'd have me pretty well pegged, although I don't think you'll be getting any gold stars for sorting that out. I'm not a real complicated fella."

"Nice and simple, hmmm? Usted no tiene complicaciones? So that means you're single." It was a statement, not a question, but Aletia still raised an eyebrow.

"Me? Yep. Not that I haven't wanted to find a good woman and settle down someday. Just seems like I do pretty well at the first part, but kinda stink at the second part. How about you?" Dallas asked.

"How about me?" Aletia replied.

"So, you and Colton... you know."

"Know what?" she responded with a grin.

"Well, I just sorta figured, I mean. It's just. You know..."

"You keep telling me 'I know' something, but I still haven't figured out exactly what it is you think I know."

Dallas exhaled and tried to find his footing.

"Seems like you two must be an item, is all. I mean, I get Colton being a monster hunter. Even Randall. You, though... Well, it just seems like a nasty business for a pretty lady like yourself to be wrapped up in. I did the math. You plus Randall equals not frickin' likely, so that leaves you plus Colton."

Aletia looked shocked and then laughed. "Por Dios, how I love misogynistic men. Dallas, here's some free advice: never make assumptions. Now, where do I even start?"

She took a drink of her beer and drummed her fingers on her thigh.

"Let's clear up the basics. First, you suck at math. I'm not out here because I'm with Colton or anyone else. I'm out here for me. Second, have you bothered to think about why any of us joined the Society?"

Dallas reflected. The question had never really occurred to him. The group just seemed so natural, like they'd been tracking and killing supernatural creatures their whole lives. The idea of them doing something else, of having lives before this, hadn't crossed his mind.

"Guess I never gave it much thought," he conceded with a shrug. The conversation lapsed as the two drank their beers.

"So?" Aletia prompted.

"Okay, I'll bite. Why are they out here?" he asked.

"You'll have to ask them."

"Um, okay. But why are you? I mean, if you're not with Colton, what are you doing in the middle of the Northwoods in a busted up cabin, running around an obstacle course, and acting all badass?"

"Acting badass? Is that what you think? This is just an act? Increíble!"

Aletia's voice had lost its playful tone. She set down her beer, stood and reached up to pull at the collar of her shirt, exposing a snaking scar that ran the length of her collarbone.

"See this? Wendigo. Could've taken my head off."

Pulling her shirt back up over her shoulder, she pulled at the hem to expose the side of her stomach.

"Hydra. Well, one of the heads," she said, pointing at an oval of small, round scars.

Sitting down again, she rolled up her left pant leg to expose a jagged scar that wrapped around her ankle and halfway up her calf.

"Keelut. Inuit spirit that manifests as a hairless dog with really sharp teeth. And this one," she continued, pushing up her right sleeve to expose a scar that looked like another bite, "was an African rompo. Take the worst parts of a badger and a bear, and stick them on a skeleton body. Scary as hell. They eat corpses, but I was doing an out-of-body spirit walk. The shaman who was supposed to be watching my back until my spirit and body were reunited had just gotten cable and was watching *The Sopranos*. Lucky for me, he got up to take a piss outside and happened upon the rompo before it had done more than sampled my arm."

Aletia pulled her sleeve back down, leaned forward, and glowered at Dallas. "There are mucho mas, but we'd have to be in a more intimate setting for you to see them. Now, do you still think I'm just *acting* badass?"

Dallas started to sputter an apology when Colton sauntered over and saved him.

"She showing off her scars again? Pretty great, aren't they?" Dragging his camping chair into place, Colton settled in. "Usually, Tia only starts baring her scars when she's pissed. What'd you do?"

"I didn't do anything!" Dallas protested, looking at her for confirmation.

Aletia glared at him without speaking for a long moment before calmly turning her back and walking over to where Randall and Stanley sat playing Scrabble.

"Looks like you got on her good side," Colton observed. "Did you take the scenic route or just drive straight there?"

"Aww, hell. I didn't mean to get her all worked up. Not even sure what I did wrong."

"Don't worry yourself too much. Tia's taken a shine to you, which means she'll give you just enough rope to hang yourself with and then give it a sharp tug." Colton shook his head in admiration. "She's a gem, a beautiful, multifaceted diamond. Careful though. Diamonds also happen to be tougher than tough. So," he drawled, settling more comfortably into his chair, "what were you two talking about, anyway?"

"Well, honestly, we were talking about you. I mean, not just you, but all of you, and the Society, and how you all ended up here. And not just like 'Wisconsin' here, but, you know, 'all over the world hunting monsters' here."

"Ah, that," Colton said. Giving Dallas a sideways look, he asked, "Did she happen to tell you?"

"Nope. I might've implied that she was maybe just out here doing this monster hunter stuff because of the possibility that, um, you and her might be, uh, you know..." Dallas trailed off lamely.

"Me and Tia?" Colton exhaled and ran a hand through his hair. "Lord knows I've dreamt that dream more than a time or two. Fortunately, I'm also just the right amount of smart to know that if you juggle knives, you won't end up playing piano at Carnegie Hall. Nope, you've got nothing to worry about, partner. At least, not from me."

After a thoughtful sip of beer, Colton looked more closely at Dallas. "Did she tell you why she joined the Society?"

Shaking his head, he explained, "I started to ask, but then things kind of took a turn. Now I'm curious. Why did she join up?"

"That's for her to share, not me. Just be a little more careful the next time you ask her, so you don't end up with a cracked jaw or broken wrist."

After laughing at Dallas's disgruntled look, Colton slapped him heartily on the back.

"Don't pout. It doesn't suit you. Now drink up. We're celebrating, after all."

"What are we celebrating?" Dallas asked.

"The fact that you're on your way to becoming one helluva hunter. The Society really is lucky to have you."

Dallas felt his face flush as he smiled a broad smile.

"Damn right. So, can we change the name to the Monster Mavericks?" he asked.

"No."

"Demon Demolition Squad?"

"Nope."

"Frickin' A-Team. Not the A-Team, that's taken. But Frickin' A-Team. I bet we could use that. Or maybe A-Squad?"

A few beers and suggestions for names later, Dallas finally called it a night and headed home. It was still called the Society, but there was always tomorrow.

Chapter 15

T HE GET'N'GOBBLE WAS BUSIER than a confessional at the Second Coming. The Packers were playing the Patriots, so folks were hurriedly stocking up on cholesterol and corn syrup before the game, Dallas and Stanley included.

"M-maple bacon donuts, Dal?" Stanley asked, holding up the package for approval.

"Put 'em in the cart, and stop asking stupid questions," Dallas replied, heading for the chips.

"Okay den. You g-get us some chips, and I'll make for the bean dip." On a mission, Stanley raced down the aisle and rounded the corner. The crash of two carts colliding caused Dallas to turn his head just in time to see the bar of Stanley's cart ram him squarely in the gut.

"Stanley!" he heard Lois cry out.

"Oh, hey Lois," Stanley answered with a wide grin. "Shopping for the game, too? What'cha got? Wow. You g-got some funny ideas about game food. What's with all the green stuff?"

"It's for Herb. Herbs, I mean. Just, you know, getting some herbs. And I'm fine, thanks for asking."

Dallas could hear the smile in Lois's voice and realized with a pang that she wasn't upset with Stanley. It rankled. Stanley didn't save her life, he did. Even so, Dallas was the only person in town Lois had a beef with.

"Herbs, huh?" Stanley asked. "That's good, that's good. I always p-put the herbs in the hot dishes, or a nice goulash, or cereal. What'cha making?"

"Um, it's sort of a, well... I mean, I wasn't really cooking, exactly."

"Laundry. Got it," Stanley approved with a hearty thumbs up. "You got basil? Basil's great for getting the p-pit smells outta your shirts, yes, sir."

As Stanley moved back, Lois stepped into sight. Other than that morning at Ronnie's the previous week, Dallas hadn't seen her much around town and was struck again by how she'd changed.

The Lois that moved to Trappersville about a year earlier was a vibrant spitfire of a woman. Tanned and toned, trimmed in bright nail polish, eyeliner and lipstick, hair like liquid sunshine, a mouth that could tame a lion, and a laugh that swept all the shadows from a room. Looking at her now, standing behind her grocery cart and talking to Stanley about herbs and laundry and whatever else fell out of Stanley's head, she was as beautiful as ever. Even so, Dallas still noticed differences. Like a light on a dimmer, or a fire burning down to a bed of embers, something in Lois just wasn't as bright as it used to be. As Dallas looked, he tried to put his finger on what it was that he saw. Was it the slightly hunched set of her shoulders, the shadows under her eyes that the bright blue eyeliner couldn't quite hide, or the way her smile didn't go quite as deep as it should? Whatever it was, it made Dallas suddenly lonesome.

Lois turned her head. Their eyes met, causing Dallas to flinch involuntarily. The smile she'd had for Stanley dropped and shattered like an upended carton of eggs. Lois's lips moved, her hand gestured...

Dallas looked at the jar of olives. There were green olives inside the clear glass jar. Olives stacked haphazardly on top of one another in the yellowish liquid. Olives. Green ones. His eyes moved of their own accord to the next row of jars. Black olives. Like green ones, but black. Lots of them in a jar. Lots of black olives just filling up the glass jar, right up to the lid screwed on top.

He nodded to himself. Olives. Green ones and black ones. Check, check. Olives.

"Dallas?"

Stanley's voice sounded far away. He wasn't saying 'olives,' which was weird. There were obviously olives here, so what else was there to talk about?

"Hey Dal? B-big D? You okay?" Stanley asked.

A voice responded. It sounded familiar, but he couldn't quite place who was talking.

"Olives, Stanley. Green ones. Black ones. Olives in jars," the voice said. A pretty reasonable voice, too, seeing as how there were definitely olives in jars, right there on the shelf.

"I, uh, I thought you hated olives, Dallas," he heard Stanley say again.

Who is he talking to? someone wondered, someone that seemed a bit like Dallas. *More importantly, why is he talking about olives?*

"The hell you talking about, Stanley?" Dallas asked, turning to look at him. The second that his eyes stopped looking at the jars of olives, the air around his head seemed to pop. Sticking a finger in an ear and giving it a wiggle, he squinted first one eye and then the other as he focused on Stanley's face. "It's game day. No time for nonsense, and definitely no time for olives."

"You were just," Stanley started, before stopping, looking confused, and trying again. "I was t-talking to Lois and tr-tried to get you to come over. She's got a lot of herbs in that cart of hers, and a lot of them herbs are ones I've been talking to Randall about. Herbs do a lot of stuff, you know. Uff dah. You start looking at herbs, there j-just ain't no limit to what you can do. So I was telling Lois about the herbs I was learning about, and I was g-gonna have you tell her about the chupacabras and clurichauns and zombies and werewolves and d-devil dogs and Bigfoot and,"

Dallas cut in sharply. "Lois was here? When? What were you doing telling her about all that stuff? Secret Society, remember? Vince Lombardi on game day!" he cursed, shaking a finger at Stanley. "You gotta lock that shit down. Remember what I told you about the aliens?"

Stanley's face fell as he started to sputter. "B-b-but Dallas, you know I was abducted. I was! I got the umbrella. It wasn't no lightning storm. Them aliens, they took me, pretty as you please. T-took me up and shot me back and they was real and you *know* they was real!"

"Yeah, yeah, I know, Stanley. I know," Dallas soothed, trying to ignore the strange looks a few other shoppers were slipping their way. "But you gotta remember what I told you, right? Remember what we talked about?"

Stanley looked down at his feet and scuffed the linoleum tiles with a loafer. "Yeah, I know. 'Aliens don't like people talking about 'em. They're very private types, and if I talk about 'em too much, they'll come back and take my T.V.'"

"And you like your T.V., don't you?" Dallas coaxed.

"Yeah," Stanley admitted. "You're right, Dal. I won't t-talk about the aliens so much." Sudden concern drove the chagrin from his face. "Oh crappers, Dal. I told the Society all about 'em. You d-don't think they're coming b-b-back, do you?"

Dallas put an arm around his friend's shoulder. "No way, buddy. No way. But even if they do, your old pal Dallas is the Hero of Trappersville. I'll kick their alien asses straight back to Uranus." He barked a laugh at his own joke and pulled Stanley down the aisle, cart wobbling under the weight of their game time goodies.

"Now c'mon. Let's go watch some football."

Chapter 16

THE DREAM HAD CHANGED.

It had started the same. Dallas rode the crowd's upstretched hands, laughing and drinking as they sang their song.

Ding-dong, the vamp is dead. Mean old vamp, wicked vamp. Ding-dong, the wicked vamp is dead!

Like always, he felt the brittle edge of their laughter. Like always, he felt the slow-brewing terror, and like always, still closed his eyes. Opening them, he expected to be back in the bathroom from his high school days, Joey en route to sticking the red-headed kid's head in the toilet. This time, though, the recurring nightmare threw him a curveball. Stepping into the bathroom stall, he saw trees all around. Branches bent like gnarled fingers grasping at the sky were backlit by the full moon. The air was heavy and still with the promise of a deep snowfall. Odd, guttural sounds pushed their way through the tree trunks, lurching in lopsided circles around him and causing the hairs on his arms to stand on end. When he looked down, he was shocked to realize just how much hair there was.

Pulse racing, he snapped his head around and saw a flickering fire deep in the trees. Long, loping strides took him on a sideways path through the trunks and brush, circling closer to the orange glow. As he closed the final distance to the edge of the shadows, Dallas saw a solitary man crouched with his back to the flames, waving an old six-shot revolver at the darkness beyond his campfire's light. The noises around Dallas ripened and seemed to be very close, too close. Heart pounding, Dallas realized they were actually coming from him.

Must be allergic to the smoke, he reasoned.

"Hey buddy, maybe you could put that pistol down and help me out with a tissue."

Dallas spoke the words, but they didn't come out right. Either that, or someone's dog was barking and growling so loudly that he couldn't hear himself talk. Rather than doing the polite thing and helping out a stranger with a stuffy nose, the man trained the pistol on Dallas and fired three shots in rapid succession.

Dallas smelled flint and gunpowder, felt the air shift, and heard the soft whines of two bullets whizzing past. The third buried itself deep in his shoulder. Dallas had been shot before and remembered the pain clearly. He'd made the mistake of taking Stanley on a deer hunting trip. They'd barely made it twenty yards into the woods when Stanley dropped his rifle and sent a .22 bullet straight into Dallas's rear end. It had hurt like the dickens and really pissed him off, but was surprisingly not the terrible experience he'd always imagined getting shot must be. Hitting his thumb with a hammer hurt more. Banging his shin on the coffee table hurt more. That bullet, though, not so bad.

The dream bullet was nothing like what he'd experienced in real life. It felt like a rusty railroad spike had been soaked in salt and lemon juice right before being jabbed into his shoulder by an angry giant. His whole arm felt like it had been drenched in lamp oil and set aflame. His chest constricted, his jaw clenched. He tried to scream but heard only a loud, angry growl.

The dreamt pain pulled Dallas awake with a start. Frantic, he pulled at the covers of his bed. Grasping his shoulder, he looked for the blood he was sure must be there. When he found none and realized he wasn't actually in any pain, he collapsed back to the mattress with a shaky sigh.

"Geez, I hate nightmares," he muttered. A glance at the clock informed him there was still plenty of night left, but there was no way he was going back to sleep. Instead, he sat up and walked over to the bedroom window. Pulling up the venetian blinds, he looked out on the woods behind his house. While some leaves still clung stubbornly to the trees, most had dropped in concession to the coming winter. The resulting view of the night sky was sliced into a jigsaw puzzle by a myriad of dark, slender branches. A few clouds drifted across a field of stars and a half moon hanging so low it was only visible through the trees.

Dallas scratched at an itch on his thigh and gazed at the moon. Slowly, so slowly, it fell toward the earth below. He was still staring at where it had been when the sun's first rays washed across the horizon, painting the new day with ominous reds and golds.

Chapter 17

"GEAR UP, NEWBIE. IT'S hunting season." Randall turned from Dallas's front door and walked toward where his moped waited by Dallas's truck.

"You coming or what?" he called back over his shoulder. "Colton says we've gotta move quick."

"Shit yeah, I'm coming," Dallas hollered. "Gimme a sec to grab a few beers for the road."

Randall had called Dallas about twenty minutes prior. Apparently, a boo hag had turned up and was feeding on the late season campers near the Wolf River. Favoring speed over a detailed plan, the Society decided to meet near where it was supposedly holed up instead of at the regular camp. After calling, Randall had hauled ass to Dallas's place so he could lead him back to where the rest were waiting. He'd found Dallas dressed in black work boots, black jeans, a black turtleneck under a black, canvas windbreaker, and a black knit stocking cap which Dallas pulled down over his face, proudly displaying that it was actually a balaclava, not just a stupid hat.

"I got some of my old eye-black from my football days, too. Figured I'd black out my eyes so nobody sees me coming," he explained to a perplexed Randall.

He had also spray-painted an old tool belt black and strapped it around his waist. On it, he'd affixed a five-pound hammer, penlight, Maglite, Leatherman tool, his hunting knife, half a roll of silver duct tape, and a matt-black whiskey flask.

Randall had whistled through his teeth when Dallas answered the door.

"You look like Batman and Tim the Tool Guy's D.I.Y. lovechild," he chuckled. "What are you planning to do with all that stuff?"

The look Dallas gave Randall was sympathetic.

"I know you been doing this for a little while, but I can see why Colton's looking for new help. You gotta be prepared, right? Covert ops? Surgical strike? Get in, get out, get drunk, get laid, that's how Big D rolls. You think I'm diving into a nest of, a nest of, um. You know, a nest of... Say, what are we hunting, anyway?"

"Boo hag."

"Gesundheit."

"No, we're hunting a boo hag."

"Doo rag?"

"No, boo hag, you twit. Kinda like a vampire, but they eat life force from breath, not blood. Sometimes mistaken for skin walkers since they don't have skin of their own and are fond of taking someone else's to wear for a bit."

Dallas nodded authoritatively. "Well, that just proves my point. You think I'm diving into a nest of boo hags with nothing but my sunny disposition?"

"A boo hag. One. Not a nest," Randall explained slowly, rolling his eyes. "Aletia found a body, minus its skin. We checked with the local clinic and learned a couple of campers stopped in thinking they had

Lyme Disease. You know, fatigue, nausea, fever, sore joints. The thing is, none had tick bites. Ergo, boo hag," he sniffed, giving Dallas another long look.

"Good timing for you, anyway," Randall continued. "It's about time you stopped free-loading and went on an actual hunt. Also, you never know when we'll need some duct tape," he added with a sneer.

"Damn right, you don't," Dallas shot back. "And let me tell you, it is always—always—better to have duct tape and not need it than to need it and not have it."

Gesturing impatiently, Randall motioned for Dallas to get a move on and stomped over to his moped. Since the little scooter could only go about forty-five miles per hour, it was over twenty minutes before they turned off the main road.

"If it's so damn important, why the hell is he riding a mobility scooter?" Dallas complained, wrestling with the urge to drive over Randall and leave him in the dust.

When Randall did finally turn off the road, he headed down a narrow, rutted trail through the trees. Dallas navigated as carefully as possible behind the bouncing moped, wincing as branches scraped the sides of his baby. A few minutes later, they had apparently reached their destination. Randall dismounted and rolled the little moped back onto its kickstand. Draining his second beer, Dallas flipped the empty can into the back seat and belched loudly as he rolled to a stop.

"You know," Randall observed as Dallas stepped down from his truck, "some people might think you have a drinking problem."

"Is that so? Well, *some people* should remember that I have a roll of duct tape, and I know how to use it if *some people* don't shut their yaps."

"I don't want to end up dead or worse, because you're too drunk to do your damn job," Randall retorted, face going red.

"Where are you from, anyway?" Dallas asked. "Obviously not Wisconsin. There ain't no such thing as 'too drunk' here. Hell, they should just put beer in the bubblers. Now, where the hell is everyone else?"

Even as Dallas was asking, he knew they were close. The smells of the woods and the nearby river rushed through him. Mixed in with all those smells, he easily identified Colton's sweat and Aletia's perfume. Another snuff, and he realized there was something else. A bitter smell that puckered his mouth and made him pinch the bridge of his nose.

"Holy stink bombs, Randy. What'd you have for breakfast?"

"I didn't fart," Randall replied, indignant.

"Uh huh, and the Pope ain't naked under that robe. It's okay. Man's gotta do what a man's gotta do, and I suppose when you're riding that toy scooter you can just let 'em fly whenever you want. Common courtesy though, is that you don't rip one when someone's standing right in the flight path, okay?"

"I said I didn't fart," Randall stressed.

"Well, if that's so, what the hell is that stench?"

Colton's boots crunched over the fallen leaves on the forest's floor.

"What does it smell like, Dallas?" he asked.

"Oh, hiya Colton. Smells like Randall farted, which he totally did but won't own up to."

"Like a fart that someone who had a double-cheeseburger topped with Fritos and tabasco sauce might have?" Colton asked.

Dallas took a tentative sniff and nodded in awe. "Actually, yeah. I'd say that's just about right." He looked at Randall with disgust. "Fritos and tabasco on a cheeseburger? What's wrong with you, man?"

Colton held up a hand to stop Randall's retort. "It wasn't Randall. That's pretty impressive, Dallas. Not many people can smell a boo hag unless it's really close by, especially when it's in a borrowed skin suit. You've got a remarkably good nose. Now cut the chatter and move out."

Turning, Colton strode through the trees, with Dallas and Randall following close behind. The smell in Dallas's nose grew sharper and waned as the breeze shifted. Coming up on a large pine tree, Colton stooped and pulled aside an old, green Army blanket that had been camouflaging a small pile of supplies. Reaching down, he selected two wooden stakes, a saucepan, and a tin ladle. He handed one stake to Randall and slid the other into his belt. Stake secured, he extended the pan and ladle to Dallas.

"The hell is this?" Dallas asked, indignant. "Are boo hags allergic to SpaghettiOs? Am I supposed to just ladle out a batch of monster-killing oatmeal?"

"They don't like sharp noises," Aletia explained as she materialized from behind a nearby hedge. "You're going to flush it out so we can kill it."

"You want me to stand there hitting a pot with a spoon while you guys have all the fun? No way! No goddamn way!" Dallas crossed his arms across his barrel chest, flexing his biceps for emphasis.

Sauntering up to stand next to Dallas, Aletia slid an arm around his waist.

"I know it looks muy complicated. Don't worry though. You're a smart guy. Sometimes, it's easier if you count to four over and over and hit the pot every time you count. You can count to four, can't you?"

Dallas's eyes pleaded with Colton, but the other man just shook his head.

"This is your first hunt, Dallas. I know you took out that vampire, but that was part luck, and you know it. We don't barge in half-cocked. We're professionals."

Dallas held the saucepan and ladle where everyone could see them clearly.

"Professionals?"

"Look, I understand how you're feeling," Colton said, "but this isn't up for discussion. If you want to help, do as you're told. If you can't do that, go wait in your truck." Colton's eyes had gone hard, and his tone brooked no argument.

For a tense moment, the two men squared off, neither moving, neither blinking, but each throwing buckets of testosterone at one another. Randall's eyes flicked back and forth, seemingly eager for the fisticuffs that seemed inevitable. Finally, Aletia broke the tension by grabbing another stake from the pile and sliding it into Dallas's tool belt between his Maglite and the carabineer holding the duct tape.

"C'mon, Colton. You've seen him train. He can take care of himself. Here, Dallas. If it comes at you, stake it just like you did with el vampiro."

Colton didn't look happy, but he yielded.

"Just be ready, Dallas," he grudgingly sighed. "If there is no other option, you have permission to engage. Now," he turned to address the group. "The boo hag took a camper's skin and moved into their tent. The other folks haven't the foggiest that there's a monster in their midst, but they've been providing late-night snacks for the hag. Won't be long before it has to change skins, which means another innocent is on deck to be dead."

He let that sink in for a moment before continuing. "Tia scoped the campground. There aren't that many people camping this late in the season, and everyone's out fishing or hiking. Boo hags usually sleep during the day, so we should be able to get in, stake it, and be gone before anyone's the wiser. Dallas, you'll go around the back of the tent. Randall and I will be waiting out front. When it bolts, we'll take care of it."

Looking hard at Dallas, Colton continued. "If it does double-back and go for the pot-banger, Dallas will take care of it and Tia will watch his back. Agreed?"

Randall kicked at a clump of leaves. "Fine."

"Aletia?" Colton asked and was rewarded with an incredulous sneer.

"It was my idea, Colton. What you do you think?"

Colton nodded and extended his hand, palm toward the forest floor. Randall and Aletia followed suit, placing their open hands palm-down on top of Colton's. Realizing a game time huddle was about to happen, Dallas added his hand. As his palm came to rest on top of Aletia's, Colton spoke, his already deep voice taking on a resonance that held Dallas in thrall.

"Hear me. We are the light that keeps shadows at bay. When darkness gathers, we must not fade. Bright, we burn to light the way and never let our brethren stray. Warriors are we with shining blades. When darkness gathers, we will not fade." With a quick pump, they pulled their hands apart, and each clapped a fist to their breast. Dallas hastily mimicked the gesture, a wide grin splitting his face.

Like suiting up for the big game in high school, pulling on the jersey before the bowling finals, or grabbing a pack of condoms for a night on the town, the Society huddle made Dallas thrum with anticipation. As the group fell into line behind Colton and started their trek through the trees, Dallas bounced next to Aletia's shoulder.

"This is exciting," he whispered loudly.

"Shhh," she replied without turning.

"Like, really exciting. We're gonna bag a boo hag! I didn't even know what a boo hag was yesterday, and today I'm gonna bag one!"

"Shush, Dallas. Not now."

Dallas made it a few more steps without speaking.

"Are they ugly?" he asked. "They smell ugly. I've had some nasty farts in my day, but nothing that smelled like Fritos-tabasco burger farts."

"Callate! You really have to shut up now, Dallas. We don't want to spook it."

Finally taking the hint, he wrestled with his curiosity and managed to stifle it until Colton raised a hand and the group came to a stop. Turning, the hunter pulled out a sheet of folded paper and began to carefully unfold it while speaking in a low-pitched voice.

"Intel says the hag nabbed a solo camper on lot eleven and took over the site. Ditched the body about two miles downstream under a fallen tree, around here." His calloused finger poked the paper, which turned out to be a crude drawing of the campground. Colton's finger indicated a point near a squiggly line that Dallas correctly determined was the Wolf River. Stretching along the bank were a series of rectangles numbered one through fourteen. Camp site eleven was on the down-river side of the campground and fairly secluded.

"We're going to split up now. Aletia, you take Dallas in about halfway and find a place to sit tight. Dallas, you'll continue around the back side of the site. The camper's got a big, fancy tent facing the river. Sneak up from behind. Move soft as you can until you're about thirty feet or so out and then wait. You'll know we're in position when you hear a black throated blue warbler call, like this."

Colton tipped his head to Randall. In response, Randall pursed his lips and made a high-pitched buzzing.

"*Zee-zee-zeeee. Zee-zee-zeeee.*"

Randall smiled at Dallas, every inch of him oozing smug. "Just one of my many talents."

Dallas rolled his eyes in response. "Oh sure, you're very talented. I can see why they keep you around."

"Not now, you two," Colton snapped in a harsh whisper. "When you hear that, Dallas, you bang on that pot like nobody's businesses for a few seconds and then get back and stay out of sight, got it?"

Dallas nodded. "Yep. I sneak up, Randall does his mating call, I bang the pot, then get back under cover."

"Right. The boo hag should bolt from the tent. Randall and I will pounce and stake it. If it slips past us or doubles back toward the tent, I'd strongly encourage you to not engage and let Tia catch it. The girl's faster than a jackrabbit after a double espresso. If you've got the option, let her handle it. I'd rather it got away."

"Not going to happen," Aletia stated flatly.

"Understood, but if, by some unimaginable possibility, it does get past you, we'll track it and get it later. I don't want the newbie getting hurt."

Dallas snorted, but kept his mouth shut. With a final nod from Colton, the group split up. Colton and Randall made their way through the trees toward the riverbank while Aletia and Dallas continued toward the campsite. Dallas covertly watched her as she moved catlike through the brush, eyes glued to her shapely behind.

Too soon, they reached the point where she would hang back and Dallas would continue on his own. While disappointed that he wouldn't be enjoying the scenery nearly as much, he stepped past her with a reassuring nod. Moving as quietly as he could, which made him feel like an elephant in a room full of cymbals compared to her, he trekked toward site eleven.

It wasn't long before he saw the large, fancy tent. Typical of the type city folk liked to buy so they could be in nature without the inconvenience of really being in nature, it was an imposing collection of polyester and Gore-tex framed with carbon fiber poles. It looked innocent enough, but even if Colton hadn't told him where to go, Dallas would've known this was the place. The burger-Fritos-tabasco fart smell was close to overpowering. He had yet to hear Randall's bird call, but knew they'd be in position soon.

Dallas slipped his flask from its pouch on his tool belt and took a long swig. Replacing it carefully, he crouched behind a wide tree and reminded his jangling nerves that he was one hundred and ten percent bad ass.

"*Zee-zee-zeeee. Zee-zee-zeeee.*"

Dallas raised the pot and ladle and set to rapidly banging the two together. Before he could even count to four, a scream split the air. Something lurched inside the tent, causing the side to bulge, and the whole tent to lean precariously. Another scream was followed by a rending sound as polyester was torn asunder. The boo hag had apparently decided the front entrance was too easy and was tearing its way out of a window panel instead. Dallas watched two hands poke through a small hole and quickly rip a larger one. Arms pushed through, followed by a man's head. Terrified eyes looked left and right as part of his torso and a leg pushed through the growing rent in the tent's side. Stumbling on the fabric, the man fell forward and landed solidly on his belly.

The man lay face down for a moment, stunned by the fall, and Dallas knew they had made a mistake. This wasn't a monster. Just a middle-aged camper they'd obviously startled from a deep sleep. A tube sock-clad foot kicked ineffectually at the sleeping bag that the poor guy had dragged through the tent's torn wall. His faded Chicago Bears tee-shirt, plaid boxers, and rumpled, blond hair were the least monstery things Dallas had ever seen. At worst, the guy was a FIP. Those fucking Illinois people were always coming up to his woods and taking up space in his bars, but that didn't make them monsters.

When the startled camper looked up from the dirt, his eyes were confused and frightened. Dallas felt his face go bright red in response. If the guy had been a buddy of his, it would've made for a fine prank. In this case, though, Dallas just felt like a jerk. Dropping the pot and ladle, he walked forward, hand extended to help the poor guy up.

"Dallas! No!" Colton's voice cracked like a whip as he and Randall broke from the brush. They charged the tent, stakes drawn. The camper saw them, too. With a snarl, he turned and locked eyes with Dallas.

The next few moments moved in surreal slowness. Dallas saw the man's mouth stretch as if to scream, but what came out sounded more like a strong wind through a tunnel. The man's teeth were bared, and the lips were sliding further and further up the gums. Soon, they'd slid far enough up that the man's eyes disappeared beneath the skin of his cheeks. As he pushed himself up from the ground, a glistening skull wrapped in a lace-like web of red and blue veins crowned in the mouth. The head's abandoned skin slipped down and flopped back like a blonde-haired hoodie, lips ringing the neck like a gummy worm necklace. The man's arms seemed to deflate, and odd shapes rippled and distended his chest. First one, then two, then a whole collection of fingers and thumbs worked their way out and stretched the lips impossibly wide so shoulders and arms wrapped in twisting muscles and pulsing, blue veins could shrug free. With a final shake, the skin sagged down the hag's torso like a falling bathrobe, revealing a lean and completely skinless woman.

"Run!" Colton screamed. "Dammit Dallas, move your ass!"

Before Dallas's shocked brain could even begin to process the complex instructions someone was yelling at him, the boo hag closed the gap between them. Even without eyelids, Dallas was sure a look of recognition passed over the monster's staring eyes before it lurched in the opposite direction like a gory, overgrown fifth grader doing the shuttle run in gym class.

No skin. Dallas's brain skipped on the same thought, like a busted record. *It ain't got no skin.*

The boo hag screamed another rushing-wind scream and charged straight for Colton and Randall. At the last instant, Colton dove into a sideways roll while Randall thrust out with his stake. It was a well-practiced move, but the boo hag was impossibly fast. Ducking, it grabbed Randall below the armpits and lifted him into the air. Still running toward the river, the boo hag carried Randall aloft like an Olympic torch, immune to his kicks and screams.

"She's got me! She's got me!" he cried out in a high-pitched voice. "Holy crap, the bitch got me!"

Dallas's trance was broken by a sharp whistling past his ear. A split-second later, a knife handle appeared in the boo hag's back, causing it to stumble. Randall sailed like a discarded rag doll through the air for a few more feet before he slammed into a tree trunk. Dallas clearly heard the crack of Randall's skull as it connected with the tree and watched him fall like a sack of stones to the dirt.

By this time, Colton had regained his feet and was charging the boo hag from behind, stake raised high above his head. The hag's arm reached back impossibly far, a double-jointed nightmare, and red fingers wrapped around the handle of the knife embedded in its back. Pulling the blade free, it pivoted and lashed out as Colton's arm came down in a killing blow. Parrying the stake with the knife, the hag's free hand curled into a fist and caught Colton beneath the jaw. The blow sent the hunter reeling to the ground, and the stake skittered away from his hand. Seeing an opening, the hag swung the knife down, blade heading straight for Colton's chest.

Dallas was roughly knocked aside as Aletia crashed past. Another blade sped from her hand and impaled the boo hag's forearm, causing it to drop the knife. Instead of stabbing Colton straight through the heart, its empty hand thumped him hard on the sternum.

"Hands off, puta," Aletia growled while freeing her own stake from her belt. The two squared off, Aletia clad in black and moving like a panther, the boo hag's glistening muscles rippling like a collection of bloody garter snakes.

After ripping the new blade free from its forearm, the hag bent to pick up the fallen knife. Feinting with both blades, it danced around Aletia and knocked aside the woman's thrusts. The hag's own slashes and stabs came from every direction. Aletia moved like David Carradine's hot sister, but couldn't gain the upper hand. Dallas watched in horror, knowing that at any moment, one of the hag's blades would score a hit.

As that terrible thought rolled through his brain, a glint of light slashed across Tia's stomach. Her tight black shirt split open, exposing a bright line of red.

Whatever thread had been holding Dallas in thrall snapped when he saw Aletia crumple, drop her stake, and grab her lacerated stomach. With an infuriated roar, he charged toward the battle.

"Now you done it!" he yelled. "You done poked the bear and got it all riled up. You think you can jump out all freaky and skinless and start roughing up my friends? You got another thing coming."

Swinging a fist like a wrecking ball, Dallas connected with the hag's face. A second punch caught it solidly in the gut, lifted it off its feet, and sent it stumbling backward.

"Listen up, haggy thing. You done poked the bear. And this bear, he's like a bear that ain't had enough to eat. He's real ornery-like, and he's got these claws and these teeth and he's all sorts of pissed. You poke that bear, you're gonna end up nothing but a pile of shit in the woods, 'cause this bear, he's gonna rip you apart and eat you up and shit you out. You hear me? This bear's gonna shit you out right here in the woods. This bear's gonna shit in the woods!" Closing the distance, he started firing off more punches and swings at the hag, ignoring the unpleasant sensation of slimy mucus coating his fists.

"What are you doing?" the hag hissed at him, retreating from his furious attacks. "You'd seriously go after one of your own?"

"One of my own? You sure as hell ain't from Wisconsin," Dallas shot back. "Something as ugly as you has to be from Minnesota."

The hag shook its head, scattering droplets of mucus in a halo. "What's this world coming to? Serves me right, thinking a little time in the woods would make for a nice vacation. Hunters I can deal with, but now I have to worry about one of my own? It's enough to break a girl's..."

A wooden stake exploded through the hag's chest. Colton wrapped his arm around its neck and cut off its wind, so its scream was just a hoarse rattle that faded to a wheeze, then a sputtering cough. Dallas dropped his fists and watched a slow burn start around the stake and work its way outward.

Like Herb, his rapidly cooling mind thought. *Thing's gonna burn from the inside out, just like Herby.*

Colton released the boo hag and yanked the stake out, letting it drop to its knees and fall on its side. Lidless eyes stared up at Dallas, mouth wide in shock and pain.

"Why? You're one of..." it gasped. "One of..."

The rest of its intended words came out as puffs of ash. The fire that had started in its chest worked its way out along the arms and legs, blackening the exposed muscles, popping the tendons, and reducing bones to charred sticks, which collapsed into dust. The head was the last to smolder away, leaving two bright orbs staring straight at Dallas before they finally blackened to ash.

For a long moment, no one spoke. The only sounds were the various pained gasps and grunts from the injured group until Colton limped over, placed a hand on Dallas's shoulder, and said, "It's official. You're one of the Society, and that's a fact."

Chapter 18

DALLAS COULDN'T REMEMBER THE last time he'd been this drunk. Dallas was also having trouble remembering where he was, what he'd done with his favorite beer koozie, and if his name was actually Dallas, or if it was Donny, or maybe Deluco. Deluco sounded nice.

"I'm Deluco! Buffted up some boo rag! Whishastake. Stake and bake! Hooah!" he cried out in answer. At least, he thought he was answering. Didn't someone ask a question?

A hand tousled his hair. In response, his head swung loosely on the soft noodle someone had replaced his neck with. It lolled around and pointed his face at the person the hand was attached to. Squinting for good measure, Dallas took in a gorgeous, smiling face. Dark hair framed smooth cheeks, full lips, and two dangerous eyes that looked into his from beneath long lashes.

"Damn. You're hot," he observed.

"You're not so bad yourself, Dallas," Aletia replied. "You're also muy, muy drunk. Maybe you should slow down, so we can keep this party going back at your place."

His place. He had one of those. Damn straight, he did.

"I got one'a those!" he crowed. "A place," he clarified. With a conspiratorial wink, he whispered loudly, "I got one." Nodding, he tried to look into those endless eyes, but his head was too heavy. Much easier to stare at the gorgeous cleavage. Much, much easier.

"Boobs," he reasoned, quite proud of himself for making that connection.

They'd been at Weasel's for about two hours, and every minute had been occupied with drinking. After quickly cleaning up around the campsite, they'd hustled back to their waiting vehicles and made a hasty getaway. Despite the collection of cuts and bruises, the group was in high spirits. The new recruit was barely out of training and had already knocked off a boo hag. It was time to celebrate.

"You did well today, Dallas," Colton said, words accompanying another pour of whiskey into Dallas's well-used shot glass. "Most folks, they see something like what you saw, they just wet themselves and run, but not you. You were meant for this, Dallas."

"Gundamn herosh!" Dallas thumped his chest, forgetting his hand was holding the shot glass and soaking his shirt with a fresh layer of Wild Turkey.

"Monshters 'n doo gages 'n I shtake 'em with a shtake. Don't take no shift. Na' me! Not from no hoo dag or vampers. Not from no one. Not from Herby. Not from my besht friend Herby. I shtake 'em and they get all burned up and Loish hates me."

Dallas's head dropped for a moment. Suddenly, it shot up, and he gave voice to a wordless cry. Maybe he was wailing at the ceiling, maybe at the night sky beyond, maybe even at the very heavens where some cruel god turned bowling line cooks into blood sucking monsters so their best friends had to kill them.

"Gundamns herosh Trapperswill!" he yelled and slapped the bar hard. The force knocked him off his stool to the wooden floor, and everything went dark.

143

Chapter 19

WAKING WAS A SUDDEN thing. Dallas sat up, surprised to find himself in his bed and even more surprised to discover he wasn't the least bit hung over. He rummaged his brain for some clue as to how he got home. When no easy answers presented themselves, he shrugged and climbed out of bed. He had to pee something fierce, so he jogged down the stairs, through the house, and out the sliding door to his wooded back yard. Sniffing as he trotted back and forth, he settled on a nice maple, opened his boxer fly, and let loose a long stream.

"Aaaaaaahhhhhhh," he sighed with relief, savoring the dual sensations of the crisp autumn air and a rapidly emptying bladder. The sun was just starting to announce the impending debut of a new day, and the stars were taking their bows in anticipation of leaving the stage. All in all, it was a fine morning.

Finishing his business, he trotted back into the house and rummaged through his fridge.

"No, no, no," he muttered, pushing aside cans of beer, half-empty jars of mustard and mayo, and a squeeze bottle of ketchup. "Where's the meat? C'mon, there's gotta be some decent chow in here."

The fridge was decidedly lacking in anything worthy of eating. Dallas had just started to concoct a plan to head back outside and track down a rabbit, or maybe a deer, when his brain came skidding to a halt.

"Wait a sec, what the hell am I doing?" he asked out loud. The kitchen appliances didn't have a response and sat in quiet judgment.

Must still be a little drunk after all, he reasoned. *I can't chase deer through the woods in my undies.*

Climbing the stairs back to his bedroom, he pulled on a pair of socks, jeans, a tee-shirt, and heavy flannel. Strapping on a wide leather belt, he checked himself in the mirrored closet door.

Looking good, Dal, he thought. *Those deer will never know what hit 'em.*

Ready to hunt, a flushing toilet caused him to spin toward the bathroom and crouch down in surprise.

The door opened, and out stepped Aletia. For a moment, he forgot everything, including his hunger, how to breathe, and how to make sure his heart continued to beat. For a moment, he was simply overwhelmed by the vision standing casually in the bathroom doorway.

"Buenos días," she said.

A neuron fired somewhere in Dallas's brain. It made its way along a neural pathway, one that seemed like it could eventually lead to his mouth, but there must've been a lot of traffic. After a few long moments, the neuron finally arrived at its destination and bumped into a few other neurons that triggered a response in the web of nerves intertwined with the muscles of his face. Dallas felt his cheeks twitch, tongue shift, and throat work, resulting in a deep, "Whoa."

She was gorgeous. Absolutely, undeniably, without a doubt, one hundred percent gorgeous. And naked. Very, very naked.

"You weren't thinking of slipping out on me, were you?" she asked, a thin layer of ice frosting her otherwise playful tone.

Deer, he thought. *I was going to get a deer.* That didn't make a lick of sense though, so he decided to keep that tidbit to himself. Instead, he walked closer, drinking in every inch of her skin.

"Guess I was thinking of rustling up some grub, but suddenly I've got a different kind of hunger."

Unbuttoning his recently buttoned shirt and pulling his tee-shirt over his head, he wrapped up Aletia in his arms. "You okay with brunch instead of breakfast?"

Aletia's hands worked at his belt buckle.

"Absolutely."

Chapter 20

IT HAD BEEN A good day. After some morning recreational activities with Aletia, Dallas made a Get'n'Gobble run and returned to his place for brunch and a little after-brunch nooky. The sun was high in the sky when they finally deciding to find their clothes and hit up Bay City Bowlers for a beer and a couple of games. They rolled, drank, and made small talk about small things. All the while, Dallas watched each moment he spent with Aletia top the previous moment as the best moment of his entire life.

Sure, Aletia was beautiful. He also knew from recent experience that she was a pint-full of tough with a kick-ass chaser, but that was just the tip of the iceberg. She knew the engine displacement of damn near every Chevy, Ford and Dodge truck on the road, and gave him a very hands-on explanation of why she preferred a shaft-driven motorcycle over a chain drive. The girl was sharp too, with a wit that struck like the crack of a whip. Even more alluring was the fact that she was worldly. Most of the girls Dallas had been with were anything but. The edges of their maps barely extended past the best dive bars with mechanical bulls and two-for-one Jell-O shots.

He'd always known that Trappersville was small. Even so, he liked to think of himself as a man of some experience. Someone who'd done things, like tried Greek food or ate hotdogs with sweet peppers and mustard, but not ketchup. Aletia, however, made him realize how small his world really was.

The girl had been everywhere. She grew up in southern Mexico near the Guatemalan border and had moved to Oregon when she was thirteen. In the ensuing years, she'd been from San Fran to New York, from Duluth, Minnesota to Duluth, Georgia, from the northernmost icy plains of Canada to the southernmost tip of South America. Iceland to Australia, Spain to Japan... It was incredible.

"So Filipinos don't speak Filipino?" he asked, confused.

"Nope. Tagalog," she explained, pronouncing it *tah-GAH-log*.

"And 'Filipino' is spelled with an 'F,' but the Philippines is spelled with a 'P H?'"

"Yep."

"Whoa," he sighed, leaning back in the molded plastic chair and looking down the alley.

"What's on your mind, cowboy?" she asked playfully.

Dallas shrugged, succumbing to an unusual bout of shyness. "Just thinking that you're pretty great, is all."

"Awww, you're cute when you blush, like un niño pequeño."

"I ain't blushing. It's just, it's hot in here. Johnson's got the thermostat up too high," he said, pulling at the neck of his shirt.

"Uh huh. It is a little warm in here, but I don't think it's the furnace," Aletia said with a suggestive grin.

Dallas grinned back. "Well, I guess I'd better get a fresh round to help us cool off a bit. Same?"

Aletia gave a thumbs up in answer, and Dallas rose to head to the bar. As he made his way past the lanes, he passed a number of regulars. Each nodded or waved a greeting, even Fancy Dan.

"Hot damn, Dallas. That girl's a beaut! What's she doing with you?" Dan called out.

Adorned in his usual eye-searing conflagration of colors and patterns, Fancy Dan practically glowed in the neon and black lights of the bowling alley. Squinting his eyes, Dallas responded with a well-executed middle finger. The two men had never exactly considered each other to be friends. Year after year, their teams had squared off during league bowling. The end result of those regular encounters was that Dallas thought Dan was a whiny little bitch, and Dan thought Dallas was a testosterone-laden brute. When Dallas's team won the summer's bowling tourney, it drove an even bigger wedge between the two men. The fact that Dan was one of the few folks who genuinely believed Herb was a vampire had helped thaw things between them a little, but not much.

Passing the shoe rental counter, Dallas involuntarily looked up at the board displaying the Roll-Masters Hall of Fame. His name stared back, prominently displayed at the top along with Herb's and Stanley's. Seeing it hurt in ways that Dallas couldn't explain. Dropping his eyes, he pushed through the saloon-style doors into the bar.

Rhonda, the ever-present bartender, was working her magic. Her gray mullet passed by in a blur as she hurried from one end of the bar to the other, filling pints, rinsing out rocks glasses, shaking the martini shaker, and yelling at her son to stop fiddling with the karaoke machine and give her a hand.

Waiting for Rhonda to take his order, Dallas's mind wandered a short ways to Aletia. She really was amazing. He hadn't felt this way about a girl since...

"Lois!"

Herb's ex stood next to him at the bar. She must've walked in right behind him. Strange that he hadn't noticed her when walking from the alley, though.

"We need to talk, Dallas," she said in a serious voice, her face unreadable.

Lois? When did she get here? he wondered.

Dallas glanced over to see if Rhonda was ever going to stop by... And there was a napkin on the bar. A square napkin. White, square. Definitely a napkin. It had been folded. Looking at it, he realized it had been folded twice. A twice-folded napkin. If he were to unfold it, it would be four squares. As it was, though, it was just one square. One white, square napkin, folded. Check.

"Don't be a jerk, Dallas. We need to talk."

Someone was talking, but not about napkins. That was weird. There was a stack of napkins right there. His eyes moved down the folds, trying to count them. Twenty? Thirty? Yes, thirty white folded napkins. Check.

"Dammit, Dallas. What's your problem?"

The frustrated voice didn't make a lot of sense. Why get mad at Dallas? Houston, sure. Lots of problems with Houston. The Oilers hadn't been around since Bud Adams moved them to Tennessee and renamed them the Titans. Dallas, though. Dallas still had the Cowboys. The cheerleaders wore white cowboy hats. Like napkins, he realized. They wore white napkin cowboy hats. Check.

"Oh crap, the spell. Hang on a sec," a nearby voice said.

Nodding vaguely, he fixed his eyes on the white square on the bar. Napkin.

"*Septul dhanna rigosstro vale.* I am here, and you will see. Distracted, you'll no longer be."

A thunderclap sounded between Dallas's ears, and suddenly, Lois was standing right in front of him. Startled, he jumped back with a, "Holy shit!"

Pressing a hand to his chest, he continued in a calmer tone. "Jesus, Mary, and a paternity test, Lois! Why you sneaking up on me like that? You damn near gave me a heart attack."

"Everything okay here?" Rhonda asked, finally making her way over.

"Hi Rhonda, we're fine," Lois responded, still peering up at Dallas with an inscrutable look on her face.

"Lois? Well, I'll be," Rhonda said. "I didn't even recognize you without your, um. Is that dress new? It's very. Black." Rhonda laughed nervously. "And that's gotta be a new shade of eyeliner..." Rhonda leaned across the bar, flooding Dallas's nose with a mixed bag of smells. Nicotine, a cherry throat lozenge, sweat, and a heavy perfume that wanted to be daffodils but smelled more like dill pickle. "Oh you poor dear, that's not eyeliner. You look exhausted!"

Lois's eyes finally broke from Dallas's. "Hi, Rhonda. I'm alright. I just, I've been..." she trailed off, returning her sunken eyes to Dallas. "We just really need to talk, and this probably isn't the best place. Can we go back to my place?"

"And why would he do that?" Aletia asked, her accented words clipped off to sharp edges. "Friend of yours, Dallas? Maybe someone I should be properly introduced to?"

Dallas's head whipped around and saw Aletia standing just inside the bar's entrance. Every inch of her radiated anger.

Oh crap, he thought.

"Aletia! Hey babe, this is Lois. She is, um, was, ah. Well, she works at the diner at Ronnie's, and she was, um. Remember that vamp I staked? Before he was a demon thing, he was my buddy, you know? Herb. My buddy Herb. He and Lois. Um."

"Herb and I were on a date when Dallas killed him." Lois stated in a flat voice. For a moment, it seemed like the lights in the dim bar dimmed even further, and shadows seemed to pile up around her. "Who's the new tramp, Dallas? Doesn't look like your usual floozy. She seems even more," Lois tapped her chin, looking for the right word, "trashy."

"Said the goth wanna-be in Bumblefuck, Wisconsin," Aletia shot back. "Where did you get those clothes, puta? Rags 'R' Us or the Sack Barn?"

Rhonda barked at the two women. "No funny stuff in my bar, dammit! You two either simmer down or get the hell out. The last time a fight broke out in my bar, I had to replace the burned carpet."

Aletia's long legs moved her to Dallas's side, and a possessive arm slid around his waist. She glared at Lois with all the animosity of a cobra eyeballing a mongoose for a long moment, but then her expression changed. She looked confused, then surprised, then angry again, the reactions passing across her face in a flash. With a forceful shove, she pushed Dallas behind her and dropped into a crouch.

"Get back, Dallas!" Aletia commanded. Her hands made a series of quick gestures, finishing with her arms extended and fingers intertwined.

Lois stepped back hard, as if she'd been slapped in the face, and her already serious expression turned mean.

"I said you stop it right now! Knock it off, or I'm calling the cops!" Rhonda huffed, shaking a thick finger.

"Cops won't help," Aletia growled. "Fortunately, there just happens to be a bruja hunter in the room, and she has one of these!"

Aletia's hands broke from their strange intertwining, and one grabbed for a long necklace beneath her shirt. Pulling it out, she brandished a darkly shining pendant. Lois took another step back and then regained her footing.

"You're going to make cracks about my clothes when you're wearing jewelry from a gumball machine? Some nerve. *Holen dah, mik'spentu ran!* Warding broken, worthless token!"

The pendant that was dangling from the silver chain split with an audible *crack* and opened like a pistachio. Dark pieces of faceted gemstone fell away, leaving a bright red gumball firmly affixed to the chain.

While Aletia gaped at the gumball, Lois took a deep breath and let it out very slowly.

"When you're done with your flavor of the week, come to my place. We need to talk," she said to a stunned Dallas. "It's about Herb." With a parting glare at Aletia, Lois turned and shoved her way out of the saloon-style doors.

Dallas watched her storm off, noticing for the first time the black shift and matching loafers she was wearing. It was such a break from her usual brightly colored halter tops, slim-fit jeans, and trendy high heels that he wondered if it really was Lois walking from the bar. His brain chugged in place, trying to put the pieces from the last few moments together.

"Your dead vampire friend's ex-girlfriend is a bruja, a witch?" Aletia asked, astonished. "You really know how to pick 'em. We have to tell Colton. Vampires, boo hags, and now a bruja? This place is a total hell spawn hot zone."

Dallas shook his head emphatically. "No, not Lois. She's no witch. Look, I don't know what all that was just now, but that's Lois. She's not. I mean, she can't be. No way."

In response, Aletia held up her silver chain with the red gumball.

"That was a two hundred-year-old talisman, fashioned at the request of William Stoughton himself after he presided over the Salem Witch Trials. That puta cracked it like a Cadbury Egg and turned it into a gumball. A gumball!" Aletia shook it for emphasis. "And you are seriously telling me she's not a witch?"

Grabbing Dallas's arm, she dragged him toward the exit.

"Come on," she ordered. "We're going back to camp."

"But she said it was about Herb," he finally protested. "She wants to talk about Herb. Lois hasn't talked to me in weeks. Not a word, except for the, 'get the hell away from me,' kinda words. If she wants to talk, I have to go see her. I mean, maybe she's forgiven me. Maybe she finally understands what I had to do when I," he coughed, throat gone momentarily dry. "When I killed... it. Him. When I killed Herb."

Unbidden and unexpected tears welled up and streamed down Dallas's face.

"I killed him, Aletia. I know I had to, and I know I saved Lois and a lot of folks, but Lois doesn't understand. Look, you have to let me talk to her. I don't know if she's a witch or whatever, but if she is, it's a phase or something. It has to be." The idea made sense and dug stubborn roots as he talked it through.

"She was real broken up when Herb died. She probably just, you know, got kinda confused, and maybe *Charmed* was on. I don't know, but if she thinks she's a witch, she's not a bad witch. Not Lois."

Aletia looked ready to spit, like she'd bitten into a mealy apple and realized it a second too late. After a moment, though, her expression softened. With a sigh, she placed a palm on Dallas chest before reaching around him and pulling him into a hug.

"I never told you why I joined the Society," she started, voice heavy with emotion. "Now's probably not the best time for the whole story, but..."

Aletia looked up at Dallas, eyes gone moist beneath her long, dark lashes.

"I know what you're going through. Go talk to her, Dallas. When you're done, though, you come straight back to camp. You have to tell Colton about this. If you don't, you'll leave me no choice."

Stepping back from him, she stood up straight, arms still on Dallas's shoulders.

"We're the Society, Dallas. We're all that stands between the world of men and the monsters of the dark. Brujas might be humans, not monsters like vampiros or werewolves, but they choose a side the second they cast their first spell. They open themselves up to the dark, and that's it. They become the enemy. But if she's a new witch, well..." Aletia looked down for a moment before seeming to reach a decision.

"Maybe it's not too late for your friend."

Dallas nodded eagerly and turned to go, but stopped when Aletia spoke again.

"But Dallas, if it is too late, you have to be able to do what's needed."

Neither spoke again as they walked from the bowling alley, but Aletia's words rolled back and forth through Dallas's mind like heavy crates on a storm-tossed ship, threatening to break open and unleash the full import of their contents on a strange and confusing world.

Chapter 21

DALLAS PULLED HIS TRUCK into Lois's drive, killed the headlights, and rolled to a stop. Like most of the homes in Trappersville, Lois's little rambler was set back in the trees and fairly isolated from her neighbors. For a moment, the only sound was the rumble of Deloris's V8 engine. With a determined turn of the key, silence prevailed. This wasn't the regular silence that Northwoods dwellers were accustomed to, though. Usually, a silent night was still full of the small sounds of the woods. Stepping from his truck to the gravel drive, Dallas felt the hairs on the back of his neck prickle and stopped to consider the cause. His head cocked first one way, then the other as he listened. Nothing. Not a sound. No breeze through the stubborn leaves still on the trees, no motors from the nearby road, no bird calls or rustle of small, nocturnal woodland creatures going about their evening mischief. It was truly and completely silent.

As he crunched his way toward Lois's front door, Dallas felt distinctly out of place. Each step, each breath, seemed to crash and echo around him while the silence waited disapprovingly for his rude noises to dissipate.

Finally reaching the steps leading up to her door, he steeled himself and reached out to knock. A split-second before rapping his knuckles against the storm door, he heard voices and froze. Lois's voice was easy to identify. The other voice was much quieter and sounded... Dallas searched for the right word.

Tinny, he thought. *Maybe the radio?*

Hearing Lois's voice again, he decided that must be it. She was probably on the phone and had left the radio on. Knocking lightly on the door, his sharp ears heard Lois say, "Shhh! Quiet," before footsteps crescendoed as they approached the door.

"Who's there?" Lois asked.

"Dallas. I, uh. You said you wanted to talk and, well. I'm here," he finished, lamely.

"Are you alone?"

"What? Yeah, I'm alone. Just me. What's going on, Lois?"

A deadbolt *thocked,* a chain *clinked,* and the door opened a sliver. Lois peered out, looking first at and then past Dallas. Satisfied that he was alone, the door opened further, allowing Dallas to step inside.

The front door opened into a small living room. To the left, a galley kitchen peeked out through a narrow doorway. Across the room, a hallway led to where he assumed were the bedrooms and bathroom were. Taking in the space, Dallas again found his expectations at odds with reality. Her home didn't look at all like he thought it would.

It seemed like every flat surface held a candle, most of which were lit. The candles themselves were black, deep red, gray. Some were tall, slender tapers in elaborate candelabras. Others were round or square pillars, their sides marbled with the cooled tracks of once-molten wax.

Beside, between, in front, and behind the candles, was an extensive assortment of oddities. His head turning in a slow arc, Dallas took in the strange ornaments, gleaming baubles, glass vials, and what appeared to be a whole family of squirrel skulls neatly arranged in a row. Eyes widening and nose twitching, he wondered at the variety of vases holding clumps of drying weeds and dead flowers.

His head finishing its left-to-right circuit, it reversed course and swept the room again. Tables and shelves that still had space between the candles and curios held books. Dallas wasn't exactly an avid reader. Sports Illustrated and bar menus did a pretty good job of satisfying any urges he might get to read the written word. That said, he still knew what books were and what they were supposed to look like. Stanley, for example, had a lot of books. They were normal things. Normal sized packages of words with front covers, back covers, and stories or facts or pictures in between.

The books in Lois's house didn't feel like books. Sure, they had covers and bindings and pages, but their resemblance to what he considered books to be ended there. Lois's books made him nervous. They were all sorts of shapes and sizes, and they all seemed to radiate *something*. His molars vibrated like there was a diesel generator somewhere nearby, a tad too far away to be seen or heard but close enough to be felt. Flummoxed, he let out a slow whistle.

"Gee, Lois. I, ah, like what you've done with the place. It's really, um. Exotic like."

Lois stood in the center of the room. Her hair was pulled back, drawing the lines of her face into sharp angles that caught the flickering lights of the candles and gave her visage an otherworldly appearance. The effect was accentuated by the dark black shawl that was pulled tightly around her shoulders. It made her pale face appear to float detached from the rest of her body, and her hands gripping the shawl looked more like a strange, twisted broach than the usual collection of fingers and thumbs.

"Thanks for coming, Dallas, and thanks for not bringing that other chick. I don't think me and her are going to be BFF's, if you get what I mean."

"Oh, Aletia. Right. Um, I'm sorry about that. She's a, well, she's um." He thought for a moment. The Society was a secret organization, but Aletia's display at the bowling alley made him wonder if it was a secret that was supposed to be actually kept, or a secret that was something it was okay if people knew as long as they knew that they knew a secret. It was a little confusing.

"It's alright. We can talk about her and your other friends later." Lois moved to clear a space on the sofa, shifting a collection of books and what looked like scrolls to a still-empty space on the side table.

Scrolls? Who reads scrolls? Dallas wondered.

"Sit," she instructed. "You want anything? A beer?"

"Beer'd be great, I guess," Dallas responded, still feeling very unsettled. He'd only been a member of the Society for a couple of weeks but felt like he'd learned enough to know a thing or two about a thing or two, including how to add up black clothes, lots of candles, weird stuff, and old books, and get *witch*.

"I see you've got a head start on me," he observed, pointing at an empty Milwaukee's Best can sitting in the center of the coffee table.

Lois looked at the can, and her expression softened a smidge.

"Just be quiet for a little bit longer, okay?"

Dallas shrugged, his discomfort sawing at his patience like a rusty blade at an old rope.

"Sure. Whatever. You tell me to come over, say you want to talk, and then tell me to be quiet. Makes perfect sense. Guess I'll just sit here and not say a thing."

Crossing his arms and plopping heavily onto the couch, he hmph'd and pointedly looked at nothing, which also happened to be the beer can on the table.

"No, not you…" Lois replied. "Oh, never mind. I'll be right back." Lois disappeared into the rambler's small kitchen and returned a moment later with two beers, holding one out for Dallas.

Settling in next to him on the couch, she pulled the tab and took a long, slow drink. Dallas did the same and then sat quietly, waiting for some clue as to what this was all about. The silence stretched until he couldn't bear it any longer.

"Why the hell are you witch, Lois?" he blurted. "And don't deny it. You can't go around being all witchy, turning necklaces into gumballs, dressing in black, and having all this weird stuff all over the place, and tell me you're not a witch. Walks like a duck, talks like a duck, I always say, and it is pretty damn obvious that you're a duck. So whatever you got into, whatever phase you're going through, you just knock it off. You get your regular clothes and your tan back, fix your hair, and you just stop being a witch, alright? No one wants a witch around these parts, and if you keep being a witch, you're gonna get…" he snapped his mouth shut and stared at his beer can.

"You just can't be a witch," he finally managed. "End of story."

During his outburst, Lois hadn't said a word.

"Well, okay then," he said with a slow nod. It had actually been much easier than he'd expected, but Lois was a smart girl. She just needed someone to shake her up a bit and set her straight. She'd be okay now, he was certain. A huge weight he hadn't even really known was pressing down on his shoulders suddenly lifted. He'd go back to Colton, to Aletia, and he'd let them know Lois was going to be fine. He'd talked some sense into her. She was going to be fine, and they didn't need to worry about it.

Mood drastically improved, Dallas took another drink of his beer, let out a satisfied sigh, and smiled.

"Now that we've got that all squared away, you said you wanted to talk. What's up?"

Lois took a breath, held it for a moment, and let it out through her nose. Another breath, then she opened her mouth to speak. This time, the breath rushed out of her open mouth instead of her nose. Shaking her head, she looked at the coffee table.

"I don't even know how to start," she muttered. "It's like talking to a man-sized toddler."

"He's always been like that."

Dallas whipped his head around, startled by the voice.

"Who was that? Who else is here?" he asked.

"Shhh," Lois said. "I've got this."

Turning, she looked at Dallas. "We need to talk about this summer, about what happened. About Herb." Lois paused, looking down at her folded hands.

"After you... after Herb died, I was a mess. For the first time in my life, I had found someone that I really connected with. Someone I could be myself with, someone who actually liked me and wasn't a total ass."

"Hey!" Dallas protested. "I liked you. Hell, I liked you a lot. Still do."

Lois just looked at Dallas.

"Oh. Well, yeah. I guess I get your point," he said. "What can I say? I am what I am, and that's all that I am." Dallas grinned. "But c'mon. You know we had a little something."

Lois raised an eyebrow.

"A tiny little bit of something?"

Lois continued to skewer him with her stare.

"Okay," Dallas finally conceded, "but even so, I think we can both agree you were on the verge of being totally into me, even if you didn't quite realize yet, right?"

With an exasperated sigh, Lois ignored Dallas and continued.

"I won't say I've made the best choices when it comes to guys, but I will say this. Every bad boy that I've dated, I've *known* the guy was a jerk. My eyes were always wide open. I either ignored what I knew was true or convinced myself that they might change, but I never, *never* dated a jerk that I didn't know was a jerk. You knew Herb for a long time. He was a lot of things, but tell me honestly, do you think he was a jerk? An asshole? A bad guy?"

Dallas's faced screwed up in thought. She had a point. Herb was probably the nicest person Dallas had ever known. Hell, half of the trouble Dallas got him out of was usually the result of Herby getting into a jam because he was too damn nice.

"So? Herb was a nice guy. I'll give you that. But I don't see what that has to do with the price of beer at a Brewers game."

"I knew Herb before he was a vampire, too, remember?"

Dallas yelped in surprise. "You believe me? I told you so. I told you he was a goddamn bloodsucker, and you saw. You saw him burn right up when I staked him. He didn't skip town. No sir. Goddamn vamp, that's what he was, and I saved you, and you know it."

Lois's mouth compressed to a tight line, and her brow wrinkled above eyes gone dangerously dark. Visibly regaining her composure, she continued.

"I never said Herb wasn't a vampire. Other folks might be able to rationalize away what they saw that night, but not me. Yes, Herb was a vampire, but he wasn't a monster. I hate to burst your carefully constructed bubble, Dallas, but you didn't save me."

Lois looked at him imploringly. "Herb and I worked together four, five days a week, for over six months. He was always... sweet. Kind of a mess, definitely a dork, but sweet. When he became a vampire, he didn't turn into an asshole. If he had, I would've known. No, when Herb was changed, he didn't become a monster. Not even a jerk. Herb blossomed. He became someone amazing. If you hadn't been so busy being jealous, you would've seen it."

"I wasn't being jealous! Me? Jealous of Herb?" Dallas forced a laugh and tried not to grimace when he heard just how forced it sounded. "That's crazy talk. Me, jealous of Herb."

Suddenly very uncomfortable, Dallas rose to his feet and walked toward the kitchen.

"You got more beers in here?" he asked, leaning into the kitchen entrance.

"Fridge. Help yourself," Lois answered in a monotone, and then continued more quietly, "This is going to be harder than I thought."

"You're doing great."

"Who are you talking to?" Dallas demanded, walking back into the room with a fresh beer. "I keep hearing someone. Who's here?" he asked, loudly, looking around.

"You punched him, Dallas. When he beat you at bowling, you walked right up and socked him in the jaw. If that wasn't jealousy, what was it? A well-intentioned, but poorly executed high five?" she asked, ignoring his question.

"I know that was a shitty thing to do," Dallas admitted, still looking around the room for the third voice. "But I also apologized. Even bought the guy a drink after. Look, guys do that sometimes, especially during bowling. I wouldn't expect you to understand, but bowling is a highly competitive sport. Tempers can flare up, but it doesn't mean anything."

"He was on your team and had just helped your team win the championship tourney. Stanley was on his team and didn't punch him. Neither did the guys on the other team. Just you, Dallas. Admit it. You were jealous of Herb and his newfound gifts."

"Gifts! Yeah, that guy in the woods that they found, he got one of Herby's gifts. Or those college frat boys and the stripper they found in the dumpster at Nekked's. I'm sure they really appreciated Herb's gifts. And Helen, bless her perfectly heart-shaped behind and fantastic rack..." He paused, looking contrite. "Sorry, but it's true. The girl was a Penthouse Letter in the flesh, but what did Herb do? Turned her into a vamp and tossed her in a tanning booth."

Lois squeezed her hands into fists. "The guy in the woods was an accident! It was Herb's first time trying to feed, and he got scared. Helen was an accident too. He had just become a vampire and didn't have a clue how any of it worked. Helen might've been a wet dream for the guys in town, but she wasn't the brightest bulb in the tanning booth and didn't realize UV light would kill her. It wasn't Herb's fault. He barely knew what he was. How could he have warned her?"

Dallas looked at Lois like she'd just grown a second head. "What are you talking about? Look, you can be all heart broken and weird about your dead vampire boyfriend, but that's no excuse to start making up all kinds of stories."

"I'm not making up stories, Dallas. It's what happened."

"Really? And how would you know what happened? Were you there?" Dallas crossed his arms across his chest and stared down at Lois.

"No, she wasn't there, Dallas. I was."

Dallas's breath caught in his throat. The soft voice had a tinny, hollow sound. For some reason, he remembered playing telephone as a kid with two tin cans and a string. The voice kind of sounded like that. When he thought about it, the voice also sounded like,

"Herb?"

Dallas's head swiveled to and fro. Turning back to Lois, he voiced his sudden anger.

"What the hell, Lois? What kind of sick joke is this?"

Lois spread her arms. "No joke, Dallas. It's Herb."

"Where? Is this some witchy stuff? If that's really Herb, then where is he?"

"Well, for the time being, he's in there," she replied, pointing at the can of Milwaukee's Best on the coffee table.

"Howdy-do."

Dallas blinked. It sounded like the tinny voice came from the beer can. As in, from the beer can.

"What in the...," he started. "It can't be. It just," he groped for words. "Can't be."

Lois stood and faced Dallas. "You were right, Dallas. It is witchy stuff. I'm a witch, and I brought Herb back."

"Back? Like, back from the dead?" Dallas asked, incredulous.

"Worse. Turns out vampires aren't really heaven material, so I was in a pretty bad place. Lois saved me, Dallas."

"But why's he in a beer can?" Dallas asked in a scared whisper.

"I wanted to be in that Bela Lugosi bowling bag Slow Johnson was selling at the pro shop, but Lois said it wouldn't work since I didn't own it when I was alive." Herb explained in a reasonable, if still tinny, tone.

Dallas tried to process that and failed. When he looked to Lois for help, she shrugged.

"I told you. After Herb died, I was a wreck. I wanted him back, so I started looking for a way. It didn't take long. Trappersville's library is surprisingly well-stocked, and eBay is a great place for supplies."

"eBay?" Dallas repeated. "You got Herb-in-a-can on eBay?"

"Sit down, Dallas," Lois coaxed. "I'm trying to explain."

"You're going to explain how my best buddy-turned-vampire that I stabbed in the chest with a busted pool cue and then watched burn to a crisp ended up in a can of Milwaukee's Best because you went to the library and did some shopping online? Like, that can actually be explained?" Dallas asked, as a deep panic started to unfold.

"Pretty cool, right?"

Dallas chose that moment to collapse back onto the couch. Lois looked at him to make sure he wasn't going to throw up. Apparently satisfied that he was okay for the moment, she walked to the kitchen and returned with another beer.

"I never really told anyone this, but there was a reason I moved to Trappersville," she said quietly. "My mom's side of the family was originally from these parts. Well, I guess if you go back far enough, they were from Norway, but when my great-grandparents immigrated to America, they settled here. I grew up in Lincoln, Nebraska, but mom made me spend a few summers up here with her sister when I was little. I used to think mom was... eccentric until I met my aunt Helga. That woman was something else. The stuff she would do..." Lois shook her head and smiled sadly. "I didn't realize it at the time, but she was trying to teach me."

Lois paused, her eyes losing focus as she looked at her past.

"Anyway, my last boyfriend before I moved here was the worst of a string of bad mistakes I'd made, and I needed a fresh start. Aunt Helga had moved back to Norway, but I remembered how beautiful and serene northern Wisconsin was, and mom always talked about how great the people were. I figured it would be as good of a place as any, so I moved. Once I arrived, I started to look up mom's side of the family. Between the county's public records and the library's local history section, I found out quite a bit not only about mom and Aunt Helga, but about their mom and grandma, even their great-grandma. Turns out, 'eccentric' runs in the women of our family. So when Herb died, I had a good idea of what to do."

Dallas threw his hands up. "You've completely lost me. We were talking about Herb. In. A. Can."

"We are talking about Herb in a can," Lois replied, exasperated. "Sorry, Herb."

"No worries. I'm good." Herb replied amicably.

"Your… friend at the bowling alley was right, Dallas. I am a witch. I also happen to be descended from a long line of witches that trace their lineage back to the early 1500s in Iceland and northern Norway. We Norwegians were the earliest and most numerous Scandinavian settlers in Wisconsin. You can still find plenty of churches that have services in Norwegian all over the state."

For a moment, Lois's expression soured. "The church," she spat. "Witchcraft wasn't even called 'witchcraft' until the Holy Church decided it was evil in the 1600s. Before that, women with our abilities were honored members of the community. We provided protection, healthcare, education, farming advice, even marital counseling. Then suddenly, we were terrible creatures, in league with Satan, and a perfectly acceptable substitute for firewood if the town's ignorant schmucks felt like toasting marshmallows."

"But witches are evil," Dallas exclaimed, jumping to his feet and pacing restlessly. "Everyone knows that. I mean, casting spells and mixing potions and sneaking around, all warty and hag-like. Not that you're warty or haggish, but I'll bet if you keep this up, you're gonna be. I told you straight away to knock that witchy stuff off, and I can't think of a better reason. Lois, you're hot. Smokin' hot! Why would you want to get all warty and gross?"

"You must be blind," Lois responded.

"What? No! Look, I know you're in a funk, but you gotta believe me." Dallas sat back down on the couch and took Lois's hands in his own. "You really are a babe, Lois. You might not see it now, with your hair pulled back like that and no makeup and your kinda creepy clothes, but I'll tell you what. You hit that tanning booth, slap on a little eyeliner, and show off that tummy again, and you'll be back in hot-land. Guaranteed."

"But Dallas, I'm talking about you. Masturbation makes you go blind. Everyone knows that."

Dallas sputtered for a moment before Herb's tinny voice chimed in.

"Ooooh! You got burned, Big D. So burned!"

"Shut it, Herb, or I'll recycle your ass." Dallas dropped Lois's hands, annoyed at being laughed at by a talking beer can.

"All I'm saying is that you can't believe everything you hear," Lois explained. "Jerking off doesn't make you go blind. Witches aren't all ugly and covered in warts, and vampires aren't always evil monsters."

"Uh huh. So, you're a witch that comes from a long line of hot Norwegian witches, and Herb was actually a friendly vampire that just happened to kill people and drink their blood, and this is all just one big misunderstanding. Okey doke. Got it."

Dallas stood and made for the door. Turning back, he pointed a stern finger at Lois and shook it for good effect.

"Well, here's a little dose of wake-the-hell-up. You cast one more spell. Just one. You send Herb back to wherever dead vampires are supposed to be, and then you quit being a witch. Otherwise, you'll be picking the wrong side, Lois. You'll be on the side of monsters and ghosts and demons and all kinds of bad shit. I ain't gonna be on that side. I'm the goddamn Hero of Trappersville and a bona fide member of the Society, and we don't tolerate that. No, sir!"

"What are you saying, Dallas? That you'd attack me? Kill me?" Lois launched to her feet, returning Dallas's glare with her own.

"Hey, c'mon guys. Let's bring it down a notch, okay? Let's not do anything crazy," Herb pleaded.

"Shut up, Herb!" Dallas and Lois snapped, still staring at each other.

"Okey doke. Sorry."

Dallas heaved a heavy sigh. "Look, all I'm sayin' is that my Society pals aren't the types to let this slide. If I go back and tell them you're a witch and you brought back a vampire and stuck him in a beer can, they're gonna be pissed, and they're gonna come after you. Both of you. It's what they do, because humans belong here and monsters don't."

"You haven't heard a word that I've said, have you?" Lois asked, amazed. "Monsters don't belong here? Since when do you get to decide who does and doesn't belong here?" she sneered. Picking up a small book and throwing it at Dallas, she continued.

"Before you run back to your friends and grab the pitchforks, maybe you should read this."

Dallas caught the book like it was a bundle of scorpions.

"Good god, Dallas. It's just a book," Lois sighed, rolling her eyes. "My grandma wasn't the first witch in these parts, and Herb wasn't the first vampire. Supernatural creatures have found their way here for hundreds, even thousands, of years. They're a part of Wisconsin, Dallas. Just as much as you are, so you can't go around killing them all. If there are bad ones, sure, do what you have to do, but they aren't," she looked at the can containing Herb, "*we* aren't all bad."

Still eyeing the book suspiciously, he asked, "What's this, then?"

"Just look," Lois said, followed by a forced, "Please."

Dallas turned the small book over in his hands, fingers tracing its soft leather cover. It had decorative tooling along the edges and was tied shut with a leather thong wrapped around a small button sewn into the cover. Unwrapping the thong, he opened it and looked at the scrawling, handwritten script covering the yellowed pages in tight, flowing lines. The first page had a date written at the top, marking the beginning of what was apparently a very old journal.

"Seventeenth, July, 1896. This is like," Dallas crunched the numbers, failed, and crunched again. "Over a hundred years old. Whose is it?"

Herb answered, his soft and tinny voice still giving Dallas the willies.

"*Remember Jerry, my old neighbor? It's his great-granddad's diary. He was a travelling medicinal... am I saying that right?*"

"Yes," Lois affirmed.

"*Okay, good. So, turns out Jerry's great-granddad was a traveling medicinal salesman. The first few entries are pretty dull. Notes about the weather, how hard it is to get quality tapeworm weight loss tonics, some kind of mushy stuff about a girl named Mable. Skip ahead to the page Lois marked.*"

Curiosity piqued, Dallas sat back down and did as instructed. Clearing his throat, he began to read the entry aloud.

"Twenty-third, August, 1896. This journey has taken a most unusual turn."

Chapter 22

2 *3RD, AUGUST, 1896*

This journey has taken a most unusual turn.

My Ojibwa guide assured me there is rich trading to be done with French-Canadian trappers near the state's northernmost border. 'Many furs,' he promised, and so I traverse the wild expanse of this Wisconsin, braving its multitude of discomforts in hopes of future riches. While not pleasant, our travels had been uneventful until two nights prior.

We camped near a swiftly flowing stream in a small valley. As I reclined on a bed of fallen leaves and a heavy wool blanket, my mind began to drift. Perhaps, I thought, some industrious fellow could develop this valley. Spacious lodgings, fine dining, a variety of entertainers. A haven for weary travelers such as myself. Drifting on the edge of sleep, I even gave it a name. Wisconsin Dells. It was a pleasant fiction that was cut short by a most unnatural noise.

Imagine, if you will, a hog in passionate search of a carrot in a deep, mud-filled trough. That is the only image that can even remotely do justice to the sound. While I am not perhaps the most stalwart of adventurers, I am still a proud man and refused to cry out. Instead, I lay quietly, cracking my eyes to peer out upon the moonlit expanse of our modest campsite. Expecting a wild animal, I instead saw a child by the water's edge.

Rising from my makeshift bed, I moved toward the stream and called out softly, "Hello, are you lost?"

As I drew closer, I realized it was no ordinary child. What child wears beaver furs adorned with leaves and pinecones and walks by itself through the woods at night? What child has leathery skin and a full beard? If it was a child, I was suddenly quite sympathetic toward the parents' decision to abandon it in the woods. Such an ugly creature!

Seeing me, it spoke, but the words meant nothing. Just a collection of sounds like pebbles falling on still water, like rain on a canvas tarp. My confusion must have shown on my face, for the little creature grinned and spoke again in perfect English.

"Hello," it said. "Only children, simpletons, or medicine men are able to see me. Are you a child?"

It was such a strange question, I couldn't help but answer.

"I'm Reginald. Purveyor of wondrous curements for dreadful ailments and potent panaceas for persistent pains."

"Ah. A simple medicine man. So."

An awkward pause followed before finally I asked, "So, what?"

A twig snapped, and the ugly thing's bright eyes looked toward the sound.

"I must go, Reginald. Here. Take this."

It plucked a freshwater leech from its leg and held it out between two grubby fingers.

"It has feasted on my blood. It might help someone. Or not. Just like the rest of your 'potent panaceas.'"

A spark of indignation was quickly quashed by curiosity. Taking the leech in my shaking hand, I transferred it to a damp leaf, applied a dollop of mud, and wrapped the leech up securely.

"Thank you," I managed.

"Thank you," the thing replied before hopping into the water and vanishing beneath the surface. Soon, a few concentric ripples reflecting the moon's light were the only remaining evidence of its existence.

At that moment, my Ojibwa guide stepped through the brush.

"Who is here?" he asked.

Haltingly, I started to explain the ugly, bearded child. As I spoke, my guide's normally stern face folded into a terrified mask.

"Memegwesi?" he asked.

Not having the faintest idea what he'd said, I shrugged. My lack of understanding must have been plain, for he continued.

"You say," he groped for the word, "spirit. Dangerous. Tricks. It give you a...?" again, he struggled for the right word. "A gift?"

I'd never seen my guide so distraught, which suddenly and firmly convinced me that the leech I'd received could be immensely valuable.

I managed a smile and a shrug.

"No," I lied easily. "It made some strange noises and vanished into the stream."

In the ensuing two days, my guide has barely spoken to me. I suspect he knows I have a secret, but I honestly don't care.

• • • • • • • • • •

30ᵗʰ, August, 1896

Where to begin? Oh, Mable. Where to even begin?

We arrived at the trading camp on the Wolf River three days ago. I was well received by the French-Canadian trappers that call this small gathering of tents and semi-permanent sheds home. While modest, it was a remarkable improvement from my complete lack of accommodations thus far. There was even some discussion of it becoming a formal township. I suggested it be called Trapperstown, but my suggestion was met with laughter and shaking heads.

Overall, the trappers are a jovial lot and expressed an instant interest in my wares. By the end of my first day at camp, I had amassed a significant credit for fresh pelts. Settling into an actual tent (oh what bliss!), I opened a penny dreadful, sipped on rough Canadian whiskey, and eventually slept. A more auspicious start to my venture I could not have hoped for.

That is, a more auspicious start to my venture I could not have hoped for, until I was robbed.

I awoke the next morning to find my chest of medicinals vandalized. Someone had snuck in during the night, and no less than five of my vials were gone, including the one I had stored the small leech in. Short moments later, I heard screaming.

"Vous devez venir! Venez vite!"

I burst from my tent, looking for someone to translate the commotion.

"Come quickly," a burly trapper said, frowning and moving toward a ragged tent on the far side of camp. I hurried to match his long strides.

Arriving at the tent, the man who'd called for help stood back and held the flap open. The first thing I saw was one of my missing vials, empty and discarded on the dirt floor of the tent. I confess, I felt a tingle of glee. Of the missing vials, one was a potent diarrhetic. Bursting into the tent, I prepared to give the thief what-for and laugh at his misfortune. However, I quickly realized that what I saw was not a man writing with pained bowels. Instead, what I saw was man-sized and man-shaped, but was most decidedly not a man.

His skin had turned a glistening gray-brown, striped and patterned with black lines and closely spaced dots. His arms and legs bent and twisted like four snakes, all trying to flee the torso in different directions. No human appendages could ever move in such a fashion. Most alarming was the fellow's face. As I watched, his eyes sank into the gray-brown, mottled skin, nose following closely behind. His mouth stretched into a near perfect circle. Such a thing should not be possible, but after seeing his writhing limbs, my brain did not challenge the obvious reshaping of his jaw and cheeks. Some teeth had already fallen out and more were following. At the same time, row upon circular row of sharply pointed, glistening fangs pushed out in their place. Even the poor fellow's tongue was changing into a fleshy proboscis, round and hollow and lashing back and forth.

I swear, Mable. Each word I write is God's own truth. I stood transfixed by the horror, unable to move or make a sound. Despite all rational thought insisting the contrary, I was witnessing the transformation of a man into a man-sized leech. It bucked and twisted and flopped onto its belly. Moving like a collection of water snakes but with a speed that belied its size and assumed awkwardness, the monster slithered out of the tent. Men screamed and jumped out of its path as it pushed its way through the camp and toward the river. Reaching the banks, it plunged into the water and disappeared from sight.

Shaken to the core, I scanned the water, trying to find some indication of where the poor trapper-turned-monster had gone, but saw nothing. Nothing, that is, except a small, huddled shape on the far bank. There, blending almost perfectly with the rocks and mud, was the Memegwesi. It looked directly at me and waved in a manner that I can only describe as congenial before it, too, slipped into the water and was gone.

Chapter 23

"LEMME GET THIS STRAIGHT," Dallas said, closing the journal. "Jerry's great-granddaddy was a travelling salesman. He met a meme-whatsit, transported some magical leech across Wisconsin, and accidentally turned some poor guy into a monster? Come on, Lois. That's ridiculous. What are the odds of that happening?"

Lois just shrugged. "Think about it, Dallas. That journal is over one hundred years old, and it tells us that, even then, there were supernatural creatures interacting with people right here, right where we live today. Also, it wasn't just a fluke. Reginald's Native American guide knew about the Memegwesi, so their people must've had contact with them for generations."

"Right, which is why the Society exists. We kill 'em dead, no offense Herb."

"It's okay, Dallas. I mean, it wouldn't have been, but Lois brought me back, and we're gonna get me my body back too, so we're good," Herb replied, tinny voice chipper with anticipation.

Dallas looked hard at Lois. "What's he talking about, getting his body back?"

Lois hurried over to a bookshelf against the far wall and retrieved a large, black book with metal bindings, excitement plain in every step.

"It's all in here. It's where I learned the spell to reclaim the spirit of a lost one. If Herb still had a body, I could have put his spirit right back into it and brought him back to life. Pretty great, right?"

Lois started to flip through the pages.

"See? It's old English, so it reads a little funny, but it really is like a recipe. Take the flesh, usually the body of the deceased, and place it in the circle with an object precious to the deceased. Everything else is just ingredients in the right amounts at the right time, a few arcane symbols," she pointed at the strange geometric shapes drawn on the surface of the coffee table, "and the right incantations. In Herb's case, all I had was some ash from the karaoke bar, so I had to find a vessel for his spirit and something precious. As it turned out, Milwaukee's Best was precious to Herb, and the can was the perfect size to hold a soul."

"You know me, Dal. I've loved that beer since I was old enough to reach the top of the bar," Herb added.

"So," Lois continued. "I put his ashes in the can, stoppered it with wax, and anchored his spirit within. Not ideal, I know."

"Could be worse. At least now I don't have to worry about matching my socks."

Lois smiled. "But it would still be nice to get you back into a body."

Looking back at Dallas, she pleaded with her eyes.

"I know this is a lot to take in, but I really can bring Herb all the way back. I just need a body. According to the spell, it doesn't even really matter what body. The spirit will shape it when it is returned."

Dallas exhaled slowly. "For real? Like, for real, for real? You can make Herb Herb again?" He looked at the beer can on the table that held his best friend and fought back tears.

"Herby, does that mean it could be like it was? You, me, Stanley, drinking beers and bowling, and everything could be normal again?"

"Oh heck yeah," Herb replied. *"I mean, pretty much, yeah. Just like it was before, um. Mostly. I guess."*

Dallas frowned. "Whadaya mean 'mostly?' What's the catch?"

"Ah, well. Hmmm. Well, there's Lois, you know. I mean, me and her, we're a thing now, so there'd be that," Herb started, causing Dallas to laugh.

"You got nothing to worry about. I'm not going to try and steal your girl. Hell, you two have earned each other, that's a fact. I swear, Big D won't get in the way."

"How very generous of you," Lois remarked dryly.

"Well, that's good. Um, real good, Dallas. The other thing is... So, you and Stanley can definitely drink those beers up. As much as you want. Me, though... Well, here's the thing. When Lois brings me all the way back, I'm still gonna be a vampire, Dallas. Same rules. No sun, no church bake sales, and I'm gonna have to, you know, drink blood."

At the mention of blood, Dallas felt his face suffuse with it. As his face reddened, his quick temper flared.

"No, no, no! No way. Lois, what the hell? You said you could bring back Herb. Herb, not a vampire!"

"Dallas, that's who Herb is."

"No. Just shut up. Shut the hell up, both of you," Dallas snapped, running his hands through his hair.

"I can't believe this. Herb's a vampire, you're a witch, and now you're a witch that wants to bring back a vampire. What's next? You gonna bring some zombies over from the local cemetery and let 'em snack on our brains? Maybe get a werewolf from the local pound? Moses on a molehill, Lois! This is insane!"

Panic drove Dallas toward the door and away from Lois's pleas.

"I'm sorry, Lois, but that's it. You and Herb, you gotta get out of town. I can buy you a day, maybe two, but Colton's gonna find out about this. You pretty much guaranteed that when you started flinging spells at Tia."

"She started it," Lois protested, but Dallas wasn't hearing it.

"So pack your shit," he continued. "Toss Herb in your purse and leave. If you're still here in a few days, there's gonna be hell to pay, Lois. Hell. To. Pay."

Dallas slammed the door behind him and practically ran to his truck. Revving the engine, he whipped a tight U-turn and sped for the highway, for his house, for his waiting bottles and flasks. He'd killed Herb once and might have to do it again. Lois, too, if she didn't shape the hell up. It wasn't a thought he could face sober.

Pressing down on the accelerator, he tried to outrun his thoughts. Night had fallen while he was at Lois's. The dashed lines of the highway were caught in his headlights and sped past in a blur as he raced toward home. When he reached his house, he stormed inside, a thundercloud of confused rage. What was he supposed to do? Pushing his way into his kitchen, he rummaged through the detritus of bachelor life, looking for a beer or bottle of whiskey. The fridge was unacceptably empty, and the countertops only held a collection of empty bottles and cans.

"Figures," he griped aloud. "Of all the times a fella needed a drink, now's a helluva time to run dry."

Leaning back against the counter, he looked around the room in search of inspiration when his eyes landed on a mason jar. Picking it up, he looked at the small wood tick inside.

"I'd forgotten about you, ya little jackass." Holding it up for a better look, he contemplated the bug inside. "So what would you do, huh? Any advice for your old buddy, Dal?"

As if in response, the tick started to quiver and shake. Dallas peered at it, perplexed. The little bug seemed to be rippling, and its eight legs bent and twitched. As he watched, its torso bloated like a tiny balloon, and small, dark hairs began popping out across its back.

"What in the hell?" he managed to wonder aloud before a sledge-hammer slugged him in the gut.

For a moment, Dallas was sure someone had just shot him with a Colt .45. Dropping the jar, he clutched his stomach and cried out in surprise at the sudden and unexpected pain. Pulling up his shirt, he started to frantically look for the bullet hole he was sure must be there. Dragging his hands across his abdomen, he experienced a short moment of relief when no bloody hole was discovered. The relief was short-lived, though. As his fingernails raked across his flesh, they left deep, bloody gashes in their wake. Crying out again in response to this new and equally unexpected pain, he pulled his hands up. His fingernails were lengthening as he watched, growing into yellowed, pointed claws. The hair on his arms was darkening, thickening, and getting longer. Losing control of his hands, he watched them bend forward and back while his wrists made sickening popping sounds.

Groaning in agony, he doubled over and landed hard on his hands and knees on the kitchen floor. His back arched convulsively, and he felt each vertebrae snap. His eyes roved wildly, looking at everything and seeing nothing, until they landed on the Mason jar he'd dropped. Inside, the tiny wood tick arched and writhed, a tiny parody of his own torment.

"What the hell is happenaaaaaarrrrrrghhh?" he moaned as invisible hooks snagged his cheeks and pulled until his jaw snapped, sending lances of pain spidering across his face and down his neck.

"Wha wha wha wha," he chuffed in agony. Back arching again, he heard fabric rip and felt his shirt and jeans loosen. Still looking at the Mason jar, his vision warped and shifted. Colors were fading, but the myriad of shadows cast by the overhead light were sharpening. Swiveling his head in an unnatural way, he looked at his arms, at the strange, clawed paws that used to be his hands. The pain reached a blinding crescendo, and Dallas blacked out.

A smell roused him. As his mind pulled into focus, Dallas realized it wasn't just a single smell, but an entire spectrum of smells. Clarity followed the coalescing of his thoughts, and he realized he'd been aware of those infinite layers of scents for quite a while. Now, however, he knew that what he was able to smell was far beyond what he should be able to smell.

That small fact noted, he began to prowl. The objects of his environment were strange, unfamiliar things. Hard angles and clean lines delineated the smells into compartments that seemed contrary to nature. It was frustrating, so he moved toward where the smells were more familiar.

A thud on his snout brought him up short. Snuffling, he extended a paw and pressed. A flat surface that he couldn't see blocked him from the forest that was so close it threatened to overwhelm him with its nearness. Everything he wanted was right there. Why couldn't he move toward it?

Pressing his snout to the barrier, he inhaled a mix of odors that irritated his nostrils.

Windex, some small part of him noted. Grease and graphite. Plastic, metal.

Frustrated, he chuffed to clear his nose of the unwanted smells. He wanted to be in the forest. Why couldn't he be in the forest?

It's a door. A sliding glass door. I need to open it.

Claws raked across the unseen barrier, and Dallas cringed at the resulting noise. Turning in a tight circle, he raised his paw again and swiped at the unseen annoyance. Another screech rent his ears, and he answered with an angry howl.

I need to use the... handle. Door handle.

Curved claws started to scratch and scrabble. Wind and wood and earth and food were so close. Dropping down to all fours, he scratched with renewed fervor, trying to dig his way forward.

No. This isn't right. It's a door. A door! I just need to open the door.

Whining, Dallas abandoned trying to dig and simply rushed toward the woods he needed to be in. A cacophony of sounds and he was free! The force of his movement through the... the...

Door. Shit. I just smashed through a glass door. My door. Why would I do that? What's wrong with me?

Impulse and a fierce hunger drove him onward. The fresh grass beneath his paws turned to fallen twigs and drying leaves as he moved into the trees. A joyous howl sounded out. He was here. This was his territory. Rising up on his hind legs, he placed one, then a second forepaw against a tree and let loose a warm stream.

Mine. All mine.

Chapter 24

"DALLAS! HEY D-DALLAS! HOLY camoly. What happened?"

Flipping onto his back, Dallas grabbed impulsively for the covers, but his hand swiped air. The realization that there were no covers was the first of many sudden and embarrassing revelations. The next thing he realized was that he wasn't wearing clothes. That was followed by the sensation of cold brick on his backside and a chill wind on the rest of him.

"Yeeeaaaahhh!" he yelled, rolling and scrabbling to his feet. Once standing, he quickly covered himself with his hands. Eyes wide and roving, he tried to take in his unexpected circumstances.

"Where the hell are my clothes?" he demanded. "What'd ya do with my clothes, you pervert?"

"I d-didn't do nothing, Dal," Stanley answered, blushing furiously and averting his eyes. "I just got here. Saw your truck, knocked, you d-didn't answer, figured you was in back, and here you are, naked on the patio."

Dallas stepped carefully over broken glass and through his busted patio door, followed by Stanley.

"Don't be looking at my ass," Dallas growled. Once inside, he ran to his bedroom and dressed quickly. After running his fingers through his hair, he took a few deep breaths. Obviously, he'd been a little out of sorts last night. For a moment, something that was almost a memory tickled his brain. Looking for booze in his kitchen. Looking, but not finding any.

That can't be right, he reasoned, *because I was obviously very, very drunk.*

It wasn't the first time he'd busted something and passed out after a bender, and it certainly wouldn't be the last. The being naked outside part was a little harder to figure, but Dallas didn't have time to untangle that particular mystery. More pressing matters were at hand, specifically finding out why Stanley was at his house.

"Why're you at my house, Stanley? Phone too complicated?" he asked, rummaging around for a broom and dustpan.

"I d-did call, Dallas," Stanley said. "Three times. Something big happened last night, and Colton wants all hands on deck."

The broom and dustpan were still M.I.A., but he did find the previous day's clothes on the kitchen floor. Well, he found what was left of them. Picking up his shredded shirt and torn jeans, he shook his head in bemusement.

"One of my best shirts, too," he complained, tossing it in the garbage. "All hands on deck, got it. Thanks for the memo, Stan. Tell Colton I'll swing by camp in a bit. I gotta get some plywood and close up this door. Should probably call the hardware store too, and see if they have any glass panes in stock, or if they'll have to order them. Shit, you know what the weather's supposed to be the next few days?"

"Dallas," Stanley pleaded, "C-Colton said it was important."

"Then you'd better stop talking and lend a hand. This door ain't gonna fix itself."

The sun had trekked a good way up the morning sky when Dallas's truck finally rolled into camp.

"What part of, 'It's really important so get here ASAP,' didn't translate? I'm sure I was speaking English," Aletia demanded as he and Stanley walked into the broken-down cabin.

"Nice to see you, too. I had a few things to take care of. Someone busted up my sliding door last night." Dallas shrugged, grinning in his usual devil-may-care way. "Or it was me. Dunno. I think I was drunk."

"And naked. Outside." Stanley offered, helpfully.

Aletia raised an eyebrow at that, but didn't say anything else. Instead, she waved to Colton and Randall.

"All accounted for, Colton. Want to get the newbies up to speed?"

Colton waved the three over. "Huddle up. Things just keep getting better. First a vampire, then a boo hag. Now I'm pretty sure we've got a newly turned werewolf. Midwest is just full of monsters these days."

"Image if there was a bruja, too," Aletia commented dryly. "That would totally suck."

Dallas strapped on his best poker face, but his blood pressure jumped. Desperate to keep the conversation well away from any witch-talk, he raised a hand.

"So, how do you know there's a werewolf?"

"A few neighborhood dogs went missing last night. Not yappy little clumps of fur, either. Big dogs. A pair of huskies and a malamute. A Rottweiler. We talked with a few locals who said they heard howls, and there was a fair amount of blood at a couple of the sites, too."

When Dallas responded with a blank stare, Colton explained.

"A newly turned werewolf tends to act more on animal instinct than rational thought. Marking its territory and establishing itself as the local alpha is pretty common. It'll usually piss all over the place and then challenge and kill large dogs, coyotes, even other wolves if there are any nearby. More often than not, it eats them too. New werewolves tend to have ginormous appetites."

"Herb ate a pug," Dallas remembered. "Could it be another vampire?"

"Nope," Colton answered matter-of-factly. "Werewolves wouldn't bother with a pug unless they needed to wipe after a healthy bowel movement."

Stanley asked the obvious question. "Maybe it was j-just a regular wolf. They don't come into town often, but it's not unheard of. No, sir. So it could've j-just been a wolf, right?"

Before Colton could respond, Randall snorted and rolled his eyes. "We're the Society. You think we can't tell the difference between a regular wolf and a werewolf?"

"Prints," Aletia explained when Stanley started to stammer in his defense. "Werewolves are people turned into a half-man, half-wolf. They usually walk upright but have much bigger feet that a regular wolf. We found a couple of tracks at one of the missing dog sites. Definitely not a normal wolf."

Randall piped in again. "Probably made a racket going after those dogs. Where were you last night, Dallas? You hear anything weird?"

Dallas shook his head. "Sorry, nope. I went to see a... friend. Catching up, you know. Had a few beers and slept like a baby."

"Naked and outside," Aletia added.

"Well, sure," Dallas conceded, embarrassment showing. "Happens to the best of us."

"While someone busted your sliding glass door," she continued in a flat voice.

Colton's face collapsed into a frown as he looked from Dallas to Aletia and back.

Dallas scuffed the toe of his boot on the worn cabin floorboards. "I dunno, Colton. Probably me. I think I was drunk."

Shaking his head, Colton sighed. "Dallas, everyone needs a bender now and then, but I'm going to make a formal request that you rein it in a bit. For all we know, that could've been the werewolf. You have to stay sharp, stay frosty."

"Roger that. Say, about that monsters in the Midwest part. You don't think that, well, you know. I mean, maybe there are monsters that aren't really... bad. That could happen, couldn't it?"

Randall shook his head and clucked his tongue. The look on Colton's face could've soured all the milk in the Get'n'Gooble's dairy case. Aletia didn't say anything for a moment and searched Dallas's face with concern in her eyes.

"Entiendo, Dallas," she finally said in a quiet voice. "Your friend, your best friend, was taken from you. It's a horrible thing, something almost everyone in the Society has gone through." Placing a gentle hand on his shoulder, she continued, "But you have to understand. There are no good monsters. Así son las cosas. End of story. The only thing monsters want to do is kill us, eat us, or make more monsters, or some combination of those three. The ones that can pass as human might try to fool us, make us think they're just regular, everyday people,"

"Like, when they're bowling and stuff," Dallas suggested.

"Sí. Like when they're bowling, but when they aren't bowling, they're killing people. That's why the Society is so important. Why you are so important."

"Here's the rub, Dallas. We have to leave," Colton said, regret plain in his words. "There's been a Sasquatch sighting about halfway between here and Sault Ste. Marie. This one sounds legitimate, so we're going to check it out."

Dallas looked at Aletia, but she wouldn't meet his eyes. After a quiet moment, he nodded.

"And it'll just be me and Stanley tracking down this werewolf," Dallas said.

"Nothing to worry about," Colton said with a reassuring grin. "You've been trained by the best. Now, about that werewolf."

Chapter 25

D ALLAS FLIPPED THROUGH THE channels, restless and malcontent as program after program flipped by. Public access, news, *Andy Griffith Show* rerun, talk show, home shopping, weather, another news show, high school football, more news. Flip, flip, flip. Half-sentences formed a garbled commentary for the collage of images, but none of it registered. Despite staring straight at the tube and pressing the remote's buttons, Dallas's mind was far away.

Earlier in the day, before the Society had packed up and pressed on, Colton had told them what he knew about werewolves.

"First, it's not just a once-a-full-moon thing," he cautioned. "Werewolves turn the nights before and after the full moon, so you've got three nights to worry about. Next, do not kill it until after you've seen it turn. No matter how much evidence there is that someone's a werewolf, you won't know for sure until they turn. The last thing you want to do is make a mistake and kill an innocent human."

Colton held Dallas with serious eyes until Dallas nodded his understanding. Satisfied that his new recruit understood that important rule, he continued.

"They're fast, mean, and damn hard to kill when they've turned. Silver bullets work, but you can also cut off their head or burn them, provided you can keep them in the fire. If they got free, the burns would heal, and you'd be back to square one, with the addition of an exceptionally pissed off werewolf that you just tried to burn to death."

Next, he told them where the dogs had been snatched from, figuring that could help them suss out the werewolf's whereabouts. Once they had an idea of its territory, they could start to check up on the various folks inside of it.

"Don't just look for weirdos, though. It's never that simple. Instead, try to find a person who has some dog-like quirks."

Dallas felt an itch behind his ear and took to scratching furiously.

"Aaahhh," he groaned with pleasure. "Much better. Now, what were you saying?"

Colton shared a few remaining tidbits. Unfortunately, werewolves weren't as easy to track as other monsters. Unlike vampires, they had no trouble walking around during the day, and they weren't stumbling, groaning, smelly corpses like zombies. Until they turned, they were pretty much just human.

"There's always a tell though, even when they're in human form. Many don't like touching silver. They could be stronger than normal, have better reflexes, even better senses. They'll hear things no one else can hear, smell things no one else can smell. It's the wolf simmering just beneath the surface, waiting for that next full moon. But again, don't strike until you're one-hundred percent sure."

"Got it," Dallas had said while Stanley nodded along. "We look for an X-man that acts like a dog and doesn't like silver, wait until it wolfs out and then kill it. Piece of cake. Anything else?"

Colton had tapped his finger thoughtfully on his lips and looked at Randall and Aletia for suggestions.

"That should be enough to get them pointed in the right direction," Randall offered. "Hell, he's the Hero of Bumblefuck, Wisconsin. I'm sure he'll be fine. Or die. Whatev's."

"Damn right," Dallas agreed. "About the being fine part, not the dying part." Turning to look at Aletia, he asked, "So, how do we stay in touch? Like, to let you know we got the job done?"

Aletia opened her mouth, but words didn't follow. After a moment, she looked away with a shrug.

"We'll try to circle back this way in a few weeks," Colton said when Aletia didn't speak. "If there's still a problem, we'll lend a hand. If not, we'll drink. Now," he said, looking pointedly at Randall and Stanley. "I think I need some help loading up the truck."

While the three men gathered up weapons, books, and camping gear, Aletia pulled Dallas to the back corner of the cabin.

"I'm sorry, Dallas. It's been fun, but this is how it is. Lo entiendes, right?"

Dallas stuffed his hands in his jean pockets. "What? Me? Oh, sure. I understand. We had a good time. So."

Aletia searched his eyes for a moment. "You weren't getting attached, now were you? I thought you weren't the 'settle down' type."

"Hell no! Not Big D. Life is a highway, babe, and old Dal, he rides. I gotta admit, though. You were one helluva road side attraction."

"Wow," she said with a wry grin. "I'm going to decide that what you just said was intended to be sweet."

Her smile reached in and grabbed something deep inside his chest a moment before she pulled him into an embrace and pressed her lips against his. When she finally pulled back, Dallas thought her eyes looked just a tad moist. Of course, he might've been confusing them with his own.

Colton stuck his head back into the cabin.

"Time to roll out, Tia."

She waved him off and turned back to Dallas.

"Ten cuidado, Dallas. Be careful. Remember your training and go get that werewolf. If we head back this way, I'd really like it if you were still here."

Dallas placed a calloused palm on her cheek.

"Damn right, I'll be here."

Long after the sound of Colton's pickup and Randall's moped had faded, Dallas was still looking out the door of the cabin. Finally, Stanley's excited yips and questions had pulled him out of his reverie. They only had two more days around the full moon, and there was a werewolf to find.

Stanley had offered to follow-up on the missing dogs and do some research on the townsfolk. His thinking was that he'd put together a list of likely perps, and then he and Dallas could go interview the suspects. Since planning wasn't one of Dallas's strengths, he'd agreed, headed home, and flipped on the television. That had been over two hours ago, and restless didn't even start to capture what he was feeling.

Some sudden impulse drove him to his feet. Flipping the remote onto the couch, he started to pace. Front door, kitchen, fridge. Through the living room, stare out the sliding door at his backyard. Around the couch and back to the front door to look out the small pane of safety glass on his front drive. Back to the kitchen. Fridge, still empty.

After his fifth lap, or fifteenth, or fiftieth, he started to scratch. His left shoulder blade itched something fierce. No sooner had he finished satisfying that itch than his right shoulder cried out for his nails' ministrations. Switching hands, he scratched furiously, pressing deep into his flannel and scoring the skin beneath. Like a game of whack-a-mole, the itch moved to his scalp. Bringing both hands to the task, he scrubbed at his unruly hair, chasing the itch across the top of his head and down his cheeks to his chest.

Time must've passed, but Dallas wasn't getting the memos. His steps and hands settled into a strange cadence as his mind drifted. Pace, scratch. Pace, scratch.

Herb's back. But it's not really Herb. Can't be. He's in a can. Person can't be a person in a can.

Pace. Scratch. Rummage through the fridge.

Lois brought him back. How's that even possible? Witches ain't hot. Lois is hot, so Lois can't be a witch. Not frickin' possible.

Pace. Scratch. Stare at the backyard.

But she is a witch. She's got spooky books and candles and other crap, and there was that weird pattern on her table, and she said she's a witch.

Past the couch. Stare out at the front drive. Scratch.

She can't be a witch, and Herb can't be in a can. I drank too much, and Lois was messing with me. Forget it, Dal. Focus on the werewolf. Stan should be back soon. Dammit, I'm hungry!

The last thought yanked his feet to a stop, one hand reaching around his shoulder, the other mid-scratch on his thigh. His mind rolled the thought around as he considered the sudden urge to eat. While he didn't really have a list of things he wanted or needed to do, he knew with certainty that if he did put a list together, getting some food was definitely going to be on top. Underlined. Twice. With an exclamation point. His newly discovered hunger dragged him back from wherever his mind had been for the past...

"Two-thirty? Where the hell did the day go? No wonder I'm frickin' starving."

Saying the word flipped some kind of switch, turning his hunger into a physical thing. His stomach gave a long and gurgley gurgle, and his mouth started to water. Flipping through his mental Rolodex of grub spots around town, he considered his options, evaluated their menus, and discarded each one in turn. Ronnie's was definitely out. Weasel's, no. Stein's, no. Bay City? No. Cecil's? Been there, done that. Pizza? Nope. His hunger had a specific shape, a definite texture. He knew what he wanted, and no one was going to make it for him. This was a craving he had to satisfy himself.

Never one to sit idly by when things needed doing, Dallas grabbed up his jacket, swiped his keys off the table, and headed for Deloris, giving her a passing kick in the chrome testicles hanging from the trailer hitch. Thoughts of Stanley, werewolves, and all the rest fell conveniently aside, eclipsed by his new mission.

The Get'n'Gobble wasn't busy, which was good because Dallas was in no mood to queue. Bee-lining for the meat counter, he practically ran over the few unfortunate shoppers that had the rotten luck of being in his path. Upon reaching the case, he placed both palms against the glass and inhaled. When the smell of raw meat flooded his nose, his eyes rolled back, and a deep sigh escaped his lips.

"Hankerin', huh?" the woman behind the case observed. "I get 'em, too. What are ya feeling? Steak? Brats? Bacon? We got some nice pork cutlets wrapped up with cream cheese and asparagus, if that's your thing."

"Yes." Dallas's throaty reply might've surprised him if he were capable of any self-awareness. As it was, all he could think was, *Meat, meat, meat.*

"So, which will it be, then?"

"Yes," he replied again and clarified, "All of it."

The woman pushed at her hair net with a gloved hand. "Okey doke. One steak, one brat, one pork cutlet. How much bacon?"

"No, I mean all of it. Everything here. Unless you've got more in the back? That, too."

An eyebrow raised up as the woman considered his request. "A party, huh? How many people are you inviting? Heck, that much meat, I should grab the hubby and kids and make an appearance."

Dallas wondered at the strange suggestion. He wasn't having a party. He was just hungry. Really, really hungry.

"I'm really hungry," he explained, eyes still glued to the platters of dead flesh.

"Well, I can't sell you everything here. We're open until ten. What if other people want some?"

"Don't care," he growled, each syllable packed with malice and dipped in danger. "Pack it up. Shovel it into a bag, don't worry about wrapping it. Could you step on it though? Man's gotta eat."

The woman's eyes went wide before her face broke into a slow smile.

"Okay den, ha ha. I swear, you boys are always full of the pranks, aren't ya? Now seriously, what do you need?"

Dallas finally looked up from the meat. Rising up to his full height, he leaned forward, eyes boring into the woman's. Every muscle tensed, from his toes to his clenched jaw, as words ground out of his mouth like bloody sausage links.

"I want all of it. Now. I don't care how much it costs. I don't care if someone else whines. I don't care if you think I'm kidding around. I want all the meat, and I want it now. If that's going to be a problem for you, I'll smash the case and get it myself."

Huffing with indignation, the woman turned on her heel and walked through the swinging door to the back. She returned a moment later with a large, waxed box.

"I have to wrap it so I can weigh it," she said in a brittle voice. "Is that alright with you, or do you want to smash my scale, too?"

"Fine."

"Fine."

For the next few minutes, she grabbed handfuls of meat, slapped them on butcher's paper, wrapped, taped, and weighed them. Too slowly, she packed the box with meat and Midwestern passive-aggression. Dallas vibrated with barely suppressed anticipation and had to repeatedly wipe the drool from the corners of his mouth with his sleeve. Finally, the meat case platters were empty, and the box was full. The woman struggled mightily to lift it, but could only get it a few inches off the counter.

"Let me get another box," she complained.

Impatience driving his legs, Dallas rounded the meat case and shoved the woman aside.

"This'll do," he managed, lifting the box easily and heading back around, oblivious to the muttered curses the woman was throwing at his back.

When he reached the checkout, he upended the box onto the belt. The sound of a wet avalanche drew the pimply faced teen by the register out of his horror magazine and into the real world.

"Wow. Party?"

"No. Hungry."

"Wild. There's a sale on toilet paper. You'll probably be blocked up for a week, eating all this protein. When it comes, you're gonna need toilet paper."

A large and very annoyed animal growled, the sound coming from somewhere nearby. The teen's already pale face blanched, each pimple standing out like a bright red BB with an oily white cap. Dropping the magazine, he started to hastily scan the packages of meat and pack them back into the box. It was only after Dallas had passed a credit card across the belt, retrieved it, and carried the box to Deloris that he realized the growling noise he'd heard had been him. The realization brought a smile to his lips.

Chapter 26

"**I** C-CAN'T BELIEVE YOU ate without me," Stanley complained. "We're a t-team, right?"

"Oh, sure. A team. Which is why I was so annoyed. You were taking so long, I figured you'd gone to eat without me. Rotten thing to do to your teammate."

Stanley's face purpled with indignation. "B-but I didn't eat! I swear! I'm st-starving, but I was working hard, Dal. Really, I was!"

Dallas laughed, the action stretching his already distended stomach and pushing out a hearty belch. He'd packed away almost the entire box of juicy, raw meat in one sitting and was now feeling incredibly satiated and indescribably happy.

Sometimes all it takes is a good meal to put everything right, he thought.

"I know you were working, and I'm sorry I grabbed a bite without you. Won't happen again. I think there's still," he rummaged in the box and pulled out an asparagus wrapped pork cutlet, "one of these things. There's meat in there, somewhere, if you can get past the nasty green stuff."

Stanley's eyes went wide, and he bounced excitedly from foot to foot. "Oh, h-heck yeah, Dallas. I love the pork cutlets. And that's asparagus. Lots of iron, lots of vitamins. Make's your p-pee smell funny, but it's totally worth it."

While Stanley cooked up the cutlet, which Dallas thought was a bit weird, he reviewed the list Stanley had put together.

He unfolded it carefully and spread it out on the small dining room table. Dallas was impressed at the crisp, clean rows of hand-written text. Stanley was an odd one, to be sure, but he had amazing penmanship. It's why he was usually tasked with keeping track of important things like bowling scores and lists of possible werewolves in Trappersville.

Sliding a finger down the list of names, he wrinkled his brow and shook his head.

"Crappers. Kind of a long list. Are you sure you got some good suspects here?"

Stanley's head poked out of the kitchen, bobbing like a yo-yo on a short string.

"Oh, you betcha. I was watching *Murder, She Wrote*. S-season nine, episode seven. *Sugar and Spice, M-malice and Vice*," he said over the sound of a sizzling skillet. "It's a really good episode. One of my favorites."

Ducking back into the kitchen, he returned a few minutes later with his lunch and sat across the table from Dallas. Warming up to how he derived his list of suspects, he started explaining the episode for Dallas between forkfuls of pork and cheesy asparagus.

"See, Michael Haggerty's future son-in-law is mixed up with this Hong Kong b-bank run by drug dealers. Real nasty guys, those drug dealers. Guns, too. Bad news."

Dallas crossed his arms and cleared his throat.

"J-just listen," Stanley whined. "I'm getting there. See, turns out that gonna-be son-in-law, he ends up d-dead, you know. Everyone's looking at Michael, but not Jessica. No sir. She knows a thing or two about a thing or two, so she starts helping c-clear his name. It's tough though. That Michael, he was found with his dead son. Or almost son. In-law. I said that, right? He ain't a son-in-law yet, but he's g-gonna be. That's important."

Holding out a hand to stop the onslaught, Dallas shoved his words in edge-wise between Stanley's excited yammering.

"Okay! Good to know. Fine job, Stanley. You've convinced me. I can see you put a lot of thought into this, so where do we start? Who's our top suspect?"

"Fancy Dan," Stanley said, authoritatively. "I'd wager all the cheese c-curds in Kenosha he's a werewolf."

Dallas couldn't help but laugh. Seeing Stanley's crestfallen look only made it funnier. Fancy Dan, a werewolf?

"It's n-not funny!" Stanley sputtered. "I done my research. Fancy Dan's d-definitely a werewolf."

Dallas's laughter subsiding a bit, he obligingly listened while Stanley made his case. After mapping out where the missing dogs were taken from, Dan's trailer was pretty near to the center. Plus, the tracks Colton had found seemed to head in that direction. Dallas shrugged, pointing out that Dan's trailer wasn't too far from his house. While houses tended to be a little spread out in these parts, there were still probably twenty or thirty people that lived inside of the werewolf's assumed territory.

"Yeah, I know, I know," Stanley agreed, "but I checked 'em out. I know m-most of the folks in town, too, ya know. I crosschecked the folks on this side of town with some other stuff. There's more."

"Do tell," Dallas said, grabbing a fresh beer from the fridge and cracking it open.

"Well, we know it wasn't you, right?" Stanley started. "I mean, you didn't g-get those dogs, did you?"

Dallas snorted beer through his nose.

"Me? What the hell, Stan?"

"I know. I know. It wasn't you. So I started thinking, how does someone turn into a werewolf? They get b-bit. Sure they do. Another werewolf comes around, bites 'em. That's what Colton said. And g-guess what?" Stanley asked.

Dallas didn't say anything, still a bit insulted that Stanley would even imply that he'd done something to those dogs.

"Guess what?" Stanley asked again.

Thinking about it was really souring Dallas's mood. He'd been feeling just fine. He'd had a great lunch and was washing it down with a nice, cold beer. Everything was good, but then Stanley shows up suggesting that he, the Hero of frickin' Trappersville, might be a werewolf.

"Dallas, guess what?" Stanley repeated, knee bouncing and fingers drumming on the table with excitement.

"What, Stanley? What? Geez. You're like a four-year-old that just learned a magic trick. Get it out, for chrissake."

"Fancy Dan got b-bit. Last week. I saw him at the clinic. I had to g-get my flu shot. Always g-get the flu shot, you know. Flu's a nasty business. First, there's the fever, then you p-puke. Nasty business. You gotta g-get the flu shot. You got yours, right Dallas?"

"No. Now what's this about Dan getting bit?"

Stanley beamed. "He was at the clinic, coming out as I was going in. Had a b-bandage on his arm. Said it was a stray dog. Said it was hiding under his trailer and bit him when he was trying to get it out. Needed to g-get a rabies shot and everything. But Dallas," Stanley paused to let the drama of the moment build. "What if it wasn't no dog? What if it was a wolf?"

"Or what if it was a dog?" Dallas challenged. "I've had to run off more than my fair share of strays, especially if the garbage lid ain't on tight."

Stanley shook his head. "Nope. No, sir. When I was doing my research today, I saw Fancy Dan. He was coming out of the salon. You know the one where they do the t-tans and the highlights and what-not? That one. I saw Dan, and he was looking all suspicious like. Made for his c-car real quick and d-drove off in a hurry. So me, I went inside. I told the girl I th-thought maybe I'd left my glasses when I was there tanning."

"Your glasses? You don't wear glasses, and you sure as hell don't tan. Hell, scrawny thing like you, the sun couldn't even find you to make an attempt."

Stanley gave a sly wink, the gesture so unexpected that Dallas couldn't even start to think of a reaction.

"When the g-girl was in back looking for my glasses, I grabbed the appointment book! I had to look quick like, b-but you know what?"

Dallas waited, curiosity replacing his earlier annoyance.

"You know what, Dal?" Stanley asked again.

"Oh, for... what, Stanley? What?"

"Fancy D-dan had a wax. A wax, Dallas. To get all the hair off his body. So he gets bit by something, big d-dogs go missing near where he lives, and he had a *wax*."

A slow whistle slipped through Dallas's lips. It did make a certain kind of sense. Fancy Dan, the waxed werewolf of Trappersville. Looking out the window at the afternoon sky, Dallas decided now was one of those times when a decision needed to be made. It's what a Warrior of the Society was supposed to do. Make decisions and take care of business.

"Nice work," he commended Stanley. "I never much liked that douchebag, anyway. Thinks he can just run around being a werewolf in my town? No way. No goddamn way." Dallas flexed his biceps and pounded his palm with his fist. "We'll see how fancy he feels with my fist in his face."

Stanley shook his head. "Oh, no, Dallas. Oh, no. Can't be just p-punching him up. You heard Colton. We g-gotta be sure."

The urge to hit things he didn't like warred with his common sense, but eventually Dallas gave in.

"Fine. Let's go have a chat with that prancy little twit, but ten bucks says he's our wolf. C'mon, Stan. We've got a town to save."

About twenty minutes later, Dallas had his bowling shoes on and had settled in at the lane next to Fancy Dan. Even though the fall league hadn't kicked off yet, Dallas was pretty sure he'd find Dan at Bay City Bowlers, the town's premiere venue for the highly competitive sport. After checking in with Slow Johnson at the counter, his intuition was rewarded when he looked across the lanes and saw the usual cornea-melting collection of colors that defined Fancy Dan's wardrobe.

"Fancy Dan! You're a sight, that's a sure thing."

If ever someone tired of looking at jeans, flannels and sweatshirts, all they had to do was pull up a chair, flip on some sunglasses, and take a gander at good old Fancy Dan. At the moment, Dan was sporting a white silk neckerchief, a wide-collared, button-down shirt that pulled a daunting array of primary colors into haphazard but somehow still geometric patterns, purple velour bell-bottoms, and his usual powder-blue, patent leather bowling shoes.

Dan smirked and gave a theatrical bow. "Clothes make the man," he patronized. "You never know when the right person might walk through the door. I saw the Stones last summer in Chicago. After the show, I was in the bathroom when Mick walked in. That's right. *The* Mick Jagger. He saw me and gave me the sign." Dan held up his index finger and pinky and pumped his arm. "'Rock on, dude!' That's what he was saying. 'Rock on!' Nobody in no high waisted jeans and flannel, or even a lips tee-shirt, got that. I did, because I," he paused for emphasis, "have *style*."

Point made, Dan took up his ball, disco'd down the lane, rolled a seven-ten split, and cussed loudly.

"Dammit. Slow Johnson needs to oil these lanes."

"You're probably right," Dallas placated, earning a suspicious look from Dan. "I gotta say that hook had quite a bit of oomph behind it. You been hitting the gym, Dan? Pumping the old iron?"

"Gyms are for girls," Dan answered. "I've just got a naturally strong arm. Part of the package."

Dallas noticed Stanley's eyes go a tad wider. Sensing he was on the right track, he offered another question.

"Naturally strong. Uh huh. Hey, you smell that, Dan? What is that?"

Dan shrugged, rolled, picked up the seven, huffed at the injustice of being a top-tier athlete forced to bowl in mediocre conditions, and walked back over to tick his score sheet.

"You noticed, too? Rhonda must have broken out a new tub of cheap perfume. Smells like a whorehouse in late July."

Stanley gasped. "I c-can't smell nothing," he whispered, his awe laced with a hint of fear.

"You can't?" Dan exclaimed. "Ugh. I'm half-inclined to shove bar napkins up my nose."

Dallas gave Stanley a surreptitious thumbs up. Rising, he picked up his own ball and rolled an easy strike.

"Crazy days lately, don't you think?" he asked in a conversational tone. "You heard about those dogs going missing last night?"

Fancy Dan took a moment to answer. He was still staring at the pin deck on Dallas's lane where ten pins used to be standing.

"Lucky roll. Yeah, I heard about the dogs. So?"

"Well, seems kind of strange, a bunch of dogs getting snatched up like that," Dallas drawled. "What would someone have against the neighborhood mutts?"

"Dog fighting. Police busted up a ring in Milwaukee a few years back. Probably some unsavory types came through town, grabbed those five dogs, and bolted. Sheriff can look all he wants, but I doubt he'll find much."

"Five d-dogs, you say?" Stanley asked in his best Columbo voice. "I heard it was four. Two huskies, a malamute, and a rottweiler. F-four, not five."

Dan sniffed. "Four, five, whatever. Now be quiet. I'm trying to bowl."

While Fancy Dan rolled a seven, cursed again, and picked up the spare, Stanley leaned in and whispered.

"Ask him about the b-bite," Stanley encouraged. "You just ask him."

Dallas casually stood and picked up his ball again. With a quick approach, he released the ball and tweaked his thumb at the last moment. The ball spun wildly and curved into the gutter about halfway down the lane.

"Crappers," he groused. "You must be right, Dan. These lanes do feel a bit dry. Of course, it could be my arm. Got bit the other day, and it hurts like the dickens."

Dan snorted. "Figures. Always looking for excuses, aren't you? Man up, Dallas. Maybe you just aren't the bowler you think you are."

Something in Dallas's gut turned, and a snarl leapt to his lips, but he forced a smile instead.

"Yeah, you're right, I guess. Just a shitty roll. You gotta admit, though, a bite on the rolling arm could sure mess with a guy's game."

"Maybe with your game," Dan sneered. "Professionals like me don't let something like that interfere. Professionals know how to play through the pain."

Pushing back a loudly patterned sleeve, Dan brandished a large gauze square held in place with athletic tape.

"I got bit by a dog, but you don't hear me making excuses. You know, for such a manly man, you sure do act like a little baby."

"At least I know how to make a baby!" Dallas shot back. "The last time you tried, you bruised the poor girl's belly button."

"Whoa, whoa, now," Stanley jumped in. "Let's n-not get mean."

"Shut up, Stanley," the two men snapped in unison.

Dan crossed his arms across his chest, which was a bit disconcerting. The crazy patterned fabric made it look like his arms just disappeared.

"Are you two done?" he said with a sneer. "I need to roll."

Dallas grabbed his ball in one hand and Stanley's arm in the other.

"Yeah, you do that, Dan. Keep on rollin'," Dallas said, dragging Stanley away from the lane. Once they were safely away, he added under his breath, "I hope you enjoy it, *werewolf* Dan, 'cause your bowling days are done."

Two hours later, Dallas and Stanley watched Fancy Dan exit Bay City Bowlers, stroll across the lot, and climb into a Pontiac Fiero with a custom burnt orange and lime green paint job.

"Man, I hate that car," Dallas groused before asking if Stanley had the silver rope.

"Yes sir!" Stanley answered, holding up a long, slender chain about the width of a finger. Each link was solid silver, making the length worth thousands. Colton had informed them that it was forged by a jeweler in Poughkeepsie whose brother-in-law was turned into a werewolf during the blackout of '03. He'd also informed them that he expected to have it returned when they came back through town, or there'd be some serious hell to pay.

"Nice. We'll tail him, jump him, tie him up in silver, and toss him in the back of Deloris. Once we get him out to the cabin, we'll wait for the moon to rise. When he goes all wolfy, we'll put him down. Can't leave a trace, though. It has to look like Dan just up and disappeared. Got it?"

"Yep. I mean, y-yes sir. But, um. Maybe you don't really n-need me for the down-puttin' part." Stanley's eyes pleaded with Dallas. "Maybe I can just, you know, n-not be there for that."

Dallas considered his friend. Stanley was as gentle as a stuttering kitten. If he was going to be a monster hunter, he'd have to toughen up at some point. Dallas was about to say just that when he saw Stanley's lower lip quiver.

"Sure, Stan. That's no problem at all. From what Colton said, the silver should hold him good. You help me get him into the truck, and I'll take it from there."

Relief washed across Stanley's face. "Th-thanks, Big D. I just... it's just..."

"I know. Don't worry about it, buddy."

"Hey Dallas?" Stanley started.

"Forget about it, Stanley. I said it was okay. Let's not make it a thing."

"No, not that. It's Fancy D-dan. He's gone."

Dallas looked up and quickly scanned the parking lot. The orange and green Fiero was nowhere to be seen.

"Oh, that's just frickin' great. Let's get over to his house and hope he's on his way home."

Deloris's giant tires spit gravel as Dallas dropped her into gear and roared from the lot. Dan's trailer home wasn't far by rural Wisconsin standards, and they made good time thanks to Dallas's blatant disregard for the speed limit and stop signs. Unfortunately, they only had another hour or so until moonrise. If Dan wasn't at home, they'd have to find him quick.

"If he's not in there, maybe we should break in and ch-check out his place," Stanley suggested. "I mean, we think he's a werewolf, but maybe we should, you know, d-double check."

Dallas had pulled his truck over and was getting ready to go the rest of the way in on foot so they wouldn't be as easy to spot. Killing the ignition, he looked at Stanley with a dark frown.

"What happened to, 'All the cheese curds in Kenosha?' You said you were sure he was our wolf. He's got a bite, and he passed the tests."

"I know, I know," Stanley backpedaled, "but j-just in case. I mean, maybe we'll find them d-dogs, or like, I dunno, something."

Dallas drummed his fingers on the steering wheel. As much as he hated to admit it, Stanley had a point. He didn't much like Fancy Dan, but that wasn't quite reason enough to string him up, drag him to a cabin in the woods, and cut his head off.

"Well, let's go see what we see," he decided.

The two men moved as quietly as they could through the trees, approaching Dan's place from the rear. When they got close, Dallas jogged a short lap around the trailer, looking for the Fiero.

"Shit. Not home," he complained, returning to where Stanley fidgeted behind a broad oak. "Guess it's Plan B."

After tip-toeing to the backside of the trailer, Dallas boosted Stanley up so he could peek in a window.

"Any sign?"

"N-nope. All clear," Stanley reported.

The trailer only had one door. Luckily, Dan didn't invest as much in home security as he did in his outlandish wardrobe. A well-placed kick busted the jam and sprung the door open. It made a bit of a racket, but that didn't matter much this far outside of town. Like most of the houses scattered in the woods, Dan didn't have the inconvenience of nearby neighbors.

Dallas and Stanley stepped inside and stood for a moment in shock. Despite the plain exterior, the inside what about what someone might have expected Fancy Dan's home to look like, assuming that someone expected to see the worst parts of the 1970s packed into one small trailer.

"Ho. Lee. Crap," Dallas exclaimed, poking a low-hanging disco ball and picking up a Bee Gees album. "Disco ain't dead. Fancy Dan's got it on life support."

While Stanley rummaged through the kitchen, Dallas worked his way around the living room. After a couple of moments, he stopped and gave a slow whistle.

"Take a look at this..." Dallas whispered, waving Stanley over.

"You got p-proof? Werewolf proof?" Stanley asked excitedly, hurrying to Dallas's side from where he'd been checking the cupboards for kibble or flea powder.

"Psycho douchenozzle proof, more like it." Dallas stood looking at a cluster of framed photographs on the paneled wall. Each shot was of a bowling tournament winner from previous years. Doing a quick count, Dan had pictures of the various winners from the past seven tourneys. In each photo, he had taped his own picture over the bowler's actual face.

Trying to control a tremor of emotion, Dallas plucked one from its nail. Not bothering to pull the back from the frame, he instead whacked it against the wall and shattered the glass. Freeing the snapshot from the broken shards, he looked at the picture from the past summer's tournament. It was taken near the end of the after-tourney party. Hands shaking with rage, Dallas peeled off the Scotch-taped picture of Dan's face to reveal his own grinning, drunken mug.

"I don't care if he's a werewolf or not. I'll drag him into the woods and beat him bloody anyway."

At that moment, Dan stepped in through his busted door, a pistol held unsteadily in front of him.

"Dallas? Stanley? What the hell are you guys doing here? Why'd you bust my door?" He fired off the questions while his finger trembled on the gun's trigger.

"You get away from those. You just get away from those pictures right now," he demanded, voice warbling with emotion. "This is a home invasion, and I'm going to shoot. I'm going to shoot you both right now if you don't step away from my pictures." Dan's voice cracked and tears started to well up in his eyes.

"Stanley, now!" Dallas yelled in response. Lurching to the side, he heard the gun pop and the wall paneling crack. Rushing Dan, he tackled him to the floor, knocking the gun away in the process.

To his credit, Stanley didn't panic. Grabbing up the length of silver chain they'd carried from the truck, he ran toward the struggling men. As Dallas pulled Dan up from the carpet and held him in a tight bear hug, Stanley tried to wind the chain around him.

"S-stop kicking! Just s-stop k-kicking me!" he screamed, trying to pull the chain tight.

"Stop trying to chain me up!" Fancy Dan yelled back, faux alligator loafers jabbing out at Stanley's knees, gut, and groin. A wild kick finally connected, and Stanley crumpled with a noise part grunt and part squeal. Whipping his head back in the same motion, the back of Dan's head connected with the bridge of Dallas's nose. Stars burst and fizzled in Dallas's eyes, and then Dan was on the move.

Roaring in pain, Dallas lurched after the fleeing man. Panic-fueled adrenalin drove Dan out of the trailer to the grass outside, but his smooth soled loafers didn't offer much for traction. Trying to cut a zigzag path, he instead went down in a tumble. Dallas jumped from the front stoop and body slammed the smaller man, pressing him down into the mud and leaves.

"Oh god, not my shirt!" Dan squealed. "What are you doing? This is an authentic Domenico Dolce reproduction. I'll never get this clean. You're going to pay for this!"

"Shove it, Dan," Dallas grunted. "I got him, Stanley. Bring the chain and hurry your alien-probed ass up. He's harder to hold than a greased up garter snake."

A few cursing, crying, questioning, and more cursing-packed moments later, Dan was gagged with a shiny polyester necktie and bound with the silver chain, a padlock holding it tight around his arms and chest.

"Help me carry him back to Deloris," Dallas instructed. Stanley was still whimpering in pain, and tears poured freely from his eyes, but he did as he was told. Once they had Dan securely stashed in the bed of Dallas's truck, he drove Stan home and dropped him off with instructions to stay put.

"I'll let you know when it's done," Dallas said. "Until then, you just sit tight. Don't answer the phone, don't go out for a Diet Mr. Pibb. Nothing. Got it?"

"Okay, D-Dallas. Okay. I'll just, I'll stay here. But Dallas," he managed.

"Yeah, Stan?"

"B-be c-c-careful."

Dallas nodded, but like most advice that found its way into his ears, he was pretty sure he'd ignore it.

Chapter 27

DALLAS'S WATCH READ 7:43 p.m.. According to Stanley, moonrise should be right around eight o'clock. After dragging a still kicking Fancy Dan into the decrepit, old cabin the Society had used as their home base, Dallas had trussed him up with some heavy rope and tied him to an exposed stud in a partially open wall.

Looking up through the collapsed ceiling, he considered the autumn sky above. The sun had finally set, leaving the cloudless sky a progressively darkening shade of rich blue. Stars were whispering Morse code to one another, getting more and more vocal with the fading of the light. It was, Dallas realized, a beautiful October evening. For a moment, he wondered if he was doing the right thing. Maybe he shouldn't be out in the woods with a guy tied to a two by four and wrapped in silver. Maybe he should just walk away from all of this. Put Trappersville and all the stuff from the past few months in his rearview and just head deeper and deeper into the trees.

"Mmrrhph furph foo fooogh wuffmee?"

"Hmmm?" Dallas asked, distracted. "Shut up, will ya? I'm thinking about stuff."

A few quiet moments passed before Dallas heard panting breath and licking lips. Turning, he saw that Dan had managed to work the tie out of his mouth.

"Look. Whatever this is about, I'm really sorry. I didn't mean to do it, or if I did, I didn't know it was going to piss you off, and I sure as hell didn't know you were the crazy type. So I'm really sorry, and I won't do it again, whatever it was. Just please, please let me go."

Dan's pleas fell from his mouth in rapid succession, eyes wide with confused fear. Dallas felt a tug at what might have been his conscience, but something Dan said flipped a switch in Dallas, shutting off the remorse he'd been on the verge of feeling a moment before.

"Me the crazy one?" he repeated in indignation. "What was with all those pictures from the bowling tourneys? Those don't exactly put you in the 'sane' category."

"Aww, c'mon," Dan whined. "It's not my fault I've been robbed year after year. I should've been the winner at least three times, and you know it."

Dallas stomped over to where Dan sat, bound, mud-splattered, and half-gagged on the worn wooden floorboards of the old cabin. He'd never seen such a pathetic sack of sniveling snot in his entire life. Just looking at Dan made him unreasonably angry. Squatting so his face was level with Dan's, he leaned in so close their noses almost touched.

"Winners are winners because they won," he growled, the menace in his voice making Dan blanch. "You can try to rewrite history all you want, but at the end of the day, you're still a loser."

Standing, his frustration pushed him into a pace. Back and forth across the small cabin, Dallas's work boots thunked heavily on the floor.

"I swear, I've about had it with all you monsters trying to make it sound like you're special, like you deserve something. Herby, the boo hag, and now a goddamn werewolf! Real champions don't need no supernatural whatever. We just kick ass because that's who we are. It's what we worked hard to become. Oh sure. Vampire Herb was such a celebrity. Such a lady's man, such a good cook, such a goddamn good bowler. But what was he before he was a vampire, huh? I'll tell you what. A loser. A nobody."

Dallas stopped his relentless pacing and spun to confront Dan.

"And that goes for you, too. Nothing but a loser that thinks it's okay to try and take what isn't yours. Like those dogs. Jesus, man. What's wrong with you? Those dogs belonged to someone. I'll bet that someone loved each and every one of those mutts, but you didn't care. You just up and took 'em. Like Lois. I cared about her. I would've been good to her. I know what I'm like, but I would've changed. Didn't get the chance, though. Oh no. Mr. 'I'm really a nice vampire' Herb had to cut in. He would've killed her. I saved her."

The anger was working its way deeper, its dark and barbed tendrils pushing and ripping into every fiber of his being. His breath was coming faster, and every inch of his skin was starting to itch. His bones ached, and his teeth felt two sizes too large for their sockets.

"Well, too bad for Herby and too bad for you. See, there just happens to be a bona fide Warrior of the Society here. I know it's a stupid name, but let me tell you, stupid name or not, there's a whole lotta comeuppance waiting for your punk ass when the moon rises. Just a little bit longer, fancy werewolf, and you'll get what's coming."

During Dallas's tirade, Dan shrank further and further into himself. Wide, frightened eyes stared, and his mouth worked like a trout pulled from the river.

"I- Holy crap, Dallas. I have no idea what you're talking about. Werewolf? Dogs? What about Lois?" Voice shaking with unfettered terror, Dan's mouth kept running. "I know you staked that vampire, and I'm really glad about that, you know? I mean, hell. I totally agree that Herb shouldn't have been the bowling champ. We're on the same page there, aren't we?"

"You? On the same page as me? Maybe you and I could've been on the same page back when we were both human. But now?" Dallas let out a harsh laugh.

"Now, you're on the page with vampires and zombies and chupa.. rabras or whatever they're called and other nasty stuff. Me, though. I am solidly on the humans who kill monsters page, which is pretty great for me, but honestly, kinda sucky for you."

"You're gonna kill me?" Dan gasped. "Because I, because of the bowling pictures? That's crazy! You can't kill me for that. You just can't!"

Dallas squatted down again, elbows resting on his knees. He sat that way for a moment, contemplating the man he used to know as Fancy Dan. Now he was something else. Something dangerous. Wicked. Evil.

"No, Dan. I ain't gonna kill you because you taped yourself into some pictures. That would've gotten you a beat down at best, but not a killing. I'm gonna kill you because that moon's gonna rise, and you're gonna turn into a werewolf, and if I don't kill you, you're gonna hurt a lot of innocent people."

Dallas's stomach growled. "Man, I just hope the moon rises soon. I'm starving. Maybe I'll celebrate with a fancy meal after I'm done saving the town again."

Dan opened his mouth to protest. At that moment, the slowly rising moon cracked the horizon, painting the woods around the cabin with a cold, silvery light. Dallas tried to make out Dan's words, not because he really cared what the monster in disguise had to say, but because he suddenly couldn't hear the other man's voice very well. A different sound rose up to fill his ears, like the roar of an ocean pounding a rocky shore, like a thousand buffalo pounding the hard earth, like a mountain splitting open.

The sound was followed hard by a sharp spasm in his gut. A harpooned whale might've been able to relate to the sudden and explosive pain that wracked Dallas and sent him sprawling to the floor, but then again, Dallas guessed that getting harpooned wouldn't feel even half this bad.

Rolling onto his side, Dallas's arms and legs pulled in tight. Curled up like a pill bug, he rolled from side to side, a collection of incoherent grunts and gasps escaping his mouth. They might have been words, but his mouth felt too large, his tongue too long, to make any sort of normal collection of vowels and consonants. Another spasm straightened his spine, and vertebrae split like wood beneath the woodsman's axe.

A new sound cut through the heavy fog of his pain. A scream, high and loud and very close. Writhing and grunting, Dallas flipped himself back onto his stomach. Fingers tipped with thick, yellowed claws scratched and found purchase on the wooden floor. Pushing himself up, he felt his wrists, elbows, and shoulders crack in sequence and watched thick, dark hair sprout from his skin and start working its way up under his flannel sleeves. A primal growl rolled and roiled through him as the excruciating pain peaked and evaporated, leaving only two lingering sensations: a simmering anger and a deep hunger.

Rising up on his hind legs, Dallas looked down at the kicking, struggling, crying little human. Meat was right there. Within his reach. Sniffing, he shied away from the smell of cold silver. The scent seared his nostrils and fueled to his anger. Grasping with a clawed hand, he grabbed the chain and pulled, only to howl in agony and lurch away as it burned his skin.

Stupid. I know better. Can't take the chain off the meat. Need to get the meat out of the chain.

Eyeing the evil silver and ignoring the meat's incoherent screams of terror, Dallas grabbed two ankles. With a tendon-popping pull, he ripped the legs and waist free from the rest of the body and dragged them far across the floor.

Safely away from the silver, Dallas settled into satiate his deep hunger. Ripping away the purple velour with his sharp teeth, he exposed more and more flesh. Clamping down with strong jaws, he tore chunk after chunk of flesh free, chewed, and swallowed. Warm blood steamed in the cool evening air as it coated his chin and ran down his chest.

One leg finished, he picked up the second and continued to feed. Soon, he was happily chewing on a spongy loafer and licking blood from his fur.

Yum. Meat is good, Dallas thought as he looked around dispassionately.

He'd quickly grown accustomed to his altered view and found that he could actually see quite a bit more. The shadows had a depth he'd never imagined, and his heightened sense of smell gave new dimensions to everything he saw. It was, he realized, pretty damn awesome. Looking at where the remaining half of Dan slouched against the cabin wall, he chuckled to himself; the sound coming out as a series of heavy chuffs.

Guess I got something fancy to eat after all. Still hungry, though.

Tossing a half-chewed loafer aside, he lumbered over to the very dead torso sitting in a wide puddle of blood and gore. Carefully avoiding the silver chain, he gripped the shoulders and lifted what was left of Dan free of the chain and ropes. With a satisfied sigh, he rummaged around inside of Dan until his claws hooked the kidney. Pulling it free, Dallas settled back on his haunches and resumed his dinner.

Chapter 28

HIS WORLD WAS SHAKING. Everything around him shuddered, each tremor growing more and more violent. Flailing to keep his balance, Dallas tried to run, to find stable ground. For a moment, all was calm, and he breathed a huge sigh of relief. Just when he thought the world had finally decided to settle the hell down, another tremor shook him to the core. At the same time, he heard a voice calling out his name.

Dallas. Dallas! Are you okay? Dallas, are you alright?

I would be if the world would stop shaking.

"Dallas! W-wake up! C'mon, Big D. You gotta wake up!"

"Churphlegurr shoobey. Wazzahell. Why you shaking me?" Dallas slurred, finally rousing from his slumber with a cough turned curse.

Opening an eye, his entire field of vision was filled with a twitchy, angular face.

"Damnation, Stanley! What do you want? Why are you in my house again?"

Finally opening both eyes, Dallas saw a very confused-looking Stanley and a very shocked-looking Lois standing directly behind him.

"Both of you? What happened?" Dallas paused, a worried look crossing his face. "Did I get drunk and bust up my door again? Colton's gonna be pissed..."

As the dense fog he'd been wallowing in finally dispersed, Dallas began to notice details. One, he wasn't in his bed. Two, he wasn't in his bedroom. Three, there was an absolutely overpowering smell all around him, and four, he really needed to take a crap.

"Where am I, and where's the bathroom? I've gotta drop the kids off at the pool."

Dallas braced his arms behind him and tried to stand, but his legs weren't quite up to the task. Stanley reached out a hand to steady him and wrapped an arm around Dallas's waist when he realized Dallas wasn't able to stand on his own.

"Oh, thank g-god, thank god you're okay, Dallas. You was c-covered in so much blood, I thought that werewolf did you in, too." Releasing Dallas so he could stand on his own, Stanley stepped back and gave him an appraising look and approving nod. "Yep. I should've known. Nobody, not nobody, werewolf or nothing can t-take down Big D. You're tough as they come, Dallas, and that's a fact."

Lois stepped forward, her face still wearing a mask of terrified worry. "What happened here, Dallas?"

Frowning, Dallas tried to put his thoughts into some semblance of order. He thought he was doing a decent job until he turned and looked around the run-down cabin, the resulting view sending his almost-ordered thoughts back into a whirl. It looked like someone had taken buckets of red, gloppy paint and splashed it liberally over every surface. The floor, walls, and even the remnants of the cabin's ceiling were splattered with tacky, smelly red. Strange, asymmetrical shapes stood out, scattered haphazardly across the floor. Puzzling over what they were, he realized they were parts of what used to be a body. Bones, parts of limbs, a stocking-clad foot, a hand curled into a half-fist.

Worse, he realized that beneath the red, he could make out bits of purple and geometric patterns in what used to be a riot of colors. Fancy Dan's pants. Fancy Dan's shirt. Fancy Dan's body parts.

Fancy Dan's head.

It had been ripped off its neck and tossed into a far corner. By cruel coincidence, it had landed right-side up and was facing where Dallas now stood, sightless eyes rolled back, and mouth open in what had to have been a scream.

"Nahnahnahnahnah," Dallas mumbled incoherently, stumbling back and falling in a heap against the wall opposite Dan's head.

Finally getting his mouth and brain in synch, Dallas looked to Stanley and Lois. "What happened to Dan?"

"Dan was the werewolf, he t-turned when the moon rose, and you beat the crap outta him," Stanley pronounced. "That's what happened, right Dallas? I mean, that's how it was... Right?"

Stanley's eyes looked from Dallas to Lois and back, wide as a startled puppy. When neither one jumped on his theory, he tried again.

"Wait, no. Don't make sense. N-not enough of Dan left."

Looking down, Stanley chewed on a thumbnail in deep thought before popping his head back up.

"I got it! Dan wasn't the werewolf. My bad, my bad. S-sorry about that. But the real werewolf g-got in here and ate Dan, and then you beat the crappers outta that werewolf. And then you, um. D-drank a whole bunch and, um. Rolled in the b-blood and, ah... p-passed out. Right, Dal? That's what happened, right?"

Dallas finally tore his eyes away from Dan's face. Unsure of what to say, he turned to Lois. As he watched, the shock left her face, replaced with a surprising calm.

"No, Stanley. Dallas didn't fight off the werewolf. Dallas is the werewolf."

All the air in the room disappeared as Dallas sat, stunned. His brain chugged while trying to pull some semblance of meaning from the string of words Lois had just uttered. Dallas, the werewolf? Him? A werewolf? Like cinderblocks dropped from a skyscraper, heavy, crushing realizations slammed down around Dallas's head, each one shattering more of his paltry delusions.

"Well, duh," Stanley said, turning an exasperated look on Lois. "Obviously, Dallas is a w-werewolf. Everyone knows that."

"What?" Lois and Dallas gasped in unison, causing Stanley to backpedal in surprise.

"S-sure he is," Stanley sputtered. "I mean, not like forever, but when Colton was talking about the s-signs, you know. The being really strong and fast, the hearing things and smelling things, and the, you know, the d-doggy stuff. Dallas, you've been doing that for a few w-weeks now."

"Crap on a cracker, Stanley!" Dallas exploded. "You mean to tell me you knew I was a werewolf, and you didn't say nothing?"

Stanley's brief glimmer of confidence faltered. "But I th-thought you knew."

Indignation-soaked anger drove the weakness from Dallas's legs, and he launched back to his feet.

"Dammit Stanley, we were hunting the werewolf! Looking all over town, tracking down Fancy Dan, dragging him out here, and the whole time," Dallas seethed, "the entire time, you knew that I was a werewolf?"

Stanley's eyes shifted from Dallas to Lois and back. Nervously, he muttered, "But I d-didn't think you was the werewolf."

"Gosh, this is awkward."

The tinny voice was a fresh bucket of surprise dumped on the already gigantic pile of what-the-hell Dallas was struggling under.

"Herb? You brought Herb?"

In answer, Lois reached into her purse and lifted out the dented Milwaukee's Best can.

"Yes, I brought Herb, but now isn't the time to talk about that, or you, or what you've done. We need to clean this up and get out of here."

"I'll keep an eye out."

"Thanks, Herb," Lois said, carefully setting the can on a windowsill.

The absurdity of the moment burst through Dallas's stupor.

"Herby, keep an eye out? He doesn't have any eyes." A high-pitched giggle found its way past his lips.

"I can see. Well, I'm not sure if I'd call it 'seeing.' Like, I can see you right now, Dallas, but I can also see Stanley picking his nose, and Lois, and Fancy Dan's head over in the corner. All at the same time. That's not all though. I can see outside the cabin and even a good part of the woods around here. Weird, right?"

Another deranged giggle slipped past Dallas's lips.

"Oh, that's great. Stan got snatched up by aliens and she's a witch and I'm a werewolf and the dead vampire can see the whole wide world from a beer can. This just gets better and better."

A hard slap to his cheek brought his building rant to an abrupt end.

"I don't think you appreciate the significance of this situation," Lois snapped. "I know you're in shock, and this is a lot to take in, but I repeat–now isn't the time and this isn't the place to talk about it. Now get up, scoop up the leftover bits of Fancy Dan, and bury them in the woods. I'll start cleaning up the blood."

Still reeling with the discovery that he was a monster, a goddamn monster, and more specifically, a monster that had just killed and gobbled up an innocent man, he couldn't come up with a better course of action, so Dallas walked over to the closest piece of Dan.

Innocent, maybe, but he was still a douchenozzle, Dallas reasoned, trying to make himself feel just a tiny bit better about the whole ordeal.

"Stanley. Go to my truck. I've got a couple of five-gallon buckets in the bed. Empty them out and bring them here while I start gathering up Dan." A winding pain pulled at his innards. "Actually, scratch that. I gotta crap. I'll grab the buckets on the way back. You get my shovel and start digging a hole past the tree line."

Face gone an unfortunate shade of green and lips pursed to hold in his breakfast, Stanley nodded and ran for the cabin door. Dallas followed, holding his stomach and shuffling in a half-crouch toward the small outhouse around the back of the cabin.

Business attended to, Dallas walked back inside, the emptiness in his bowels a hollow shadow compared to the emptiness in his chest. Walking over to the first Dan-bit he could see, he bent down and picked up a severed hand and gave it a perfunctory shake.

"Hi there, nice to meet'cha. I'm the Hero of Trappersville, member of the Society, oh, and a werewolf. A goddamn bloodthirsty, murdering werewolf." Voice cracking at the end, Dallas used the hand to wipe at an unexpected tear.

"Dallas!" Lois snapped. "We don't have all day, so man up and start scooping dead guy."

For the next half an hour or so, Dallas hauled bucketfuls of body bits out of the cabin while Stanley dug a hole a few yards into the tree line. After emptying bucket after bucket into the hole, he finished by resting Dan's head carefully on top, eyes looking up at a crisp, clear October sky. Taking the shovel from Stanley, he moved the pile of dirt on top of the improvised grave. The truth of his nature finally hidden beneath the ground, Dallas levelled the dirt off, patted it down, and covered it with fallen leaves and an armful of small branches. The grave blended in with the surrounding ground, and Dallas gave a satisfied nod. He turned to go back inside, but Stanley grabbed his sleeve.

"What, Stanley? Christ, I just want this nightmare to be done, alright?"

"B-but Dallas. We g-gotta say something, don't we? For Dan."

Dallas considered it for a moment. He wasn't the religious type and would've been surprised if Dan was. What good would a few pretty words do for a dead guy? A guy Dallas had murdered?

His mind drifted to Herb. Herb had died, come back undead, got staked and burned to a crisp, and yet somehow was back again. In a really weird sort of way, sure, but still. So what did it really mean to be dead? Was there a heaven? A hell? And if such places existed, which one would a glammed-up ass hat like Fancy Dan go to? Dallas realized how little he actually knew about the man he'd been bowling against for years, which made saying something over his grave even more ridiculous.

"Sorry, Stan. I got nothing. You want to say something, go for it. Just make it quick."

"Okay, Dallas. Okay. I'll m-make it quick." Clearing his throat loudly, Stanley lowered his head and folded his hands.

"So, um. Dear lord or whoever. I mean, maybe God, or B-buddha, or Zoroaster, or Shiva, or," Stanley frowned and looked up at Dallas. "Who else is there?"

Dallas shrugged, so Stanley plowed ahead. "And whoever else might be up there. Um, we're gathered here today because Fancy Dan got k-killed, and we hope he's someplace better. I mean, I know he's in a hole. Well, some of him. The parts of him that Dallas didn't eat. But the other part, the part that you can't eat, we hope that part's someplace real nice. With, um. D-disco balls and a really big c-closet with lots of real nice clothes. And bowling. Please make sure Dan's the b-best bowler. Even if maybe, you know, the other folks there could kind of agree to let him win. I th-think he'd like that."

A lump the size of Dan's kidney formed in Dallas's throat. He'd never known Stanley had such a way with words.

Seems like there's a lot of stuff I never knew, he thought. Believing they'd reached the end of Stanley's improvised eulogy, Dallas again turned to go when Stanley suddenly spoke again.

"And, um, God-Buddha-Shiva-person, please d-don't think this was Dallas's fault. He thought he was keeping people safe. He really is a hero, even if he, um, well, kind of keeps killing the wrong p-people. But he's trying to do right. Me and Lois and Herb, we're gonna help 'cause he's our friend, and th-that's what friends do. Amen and Namaste and, ah. Sorry, I don't know anything other p-prayer words. The end."

Raising his head, Stanley looked at Dallas. When their eyes met, the tears Dallas had been trying to control broke free. As they streamed down his face, a little bit of the blood, a little bit of the horror, was washed clean.

Chapter 29

WITH NO REAL IDEA where else to go, the trio had returned to Dallas's house. Lois had practically gagged when she walked in and was slapped in the face with the ripe smells of bachelor pad and raw meat.

"Good god, Dallas. Guess I just get to keep on cleaning. Best day ever. Go take a shower and bag up those clothes," she instructed, referring to the rags that still hung on his large frame. "They're ruined anyway, so we'll burn them later."

Dallas had obliged. After a long, steaming shower, he returned downstairs wearing a fresh pair of jeans, tee-shirt, and a cleanish flannel. He found Lois wiping the last bits of dust from his entertainment center and stood in amazement at the transformation of his home. Gone were the empty pizza boxes, beer cans, and random piles of junk mail. He no longer felt the menacing stares of over-sized dust bunnies, and a lemony scent flooded his sensitive nose. Without the detritus of his bad habits cluttering up the kitchen and living room, the space looked twice as big.

"Wow. You did a helluva job, Lois. I mean, this is really, really," he sniffed again, "lemony. You didn't need to do all this, though. I would've done it..."

Lois crossed her arms across her chest and glared at Dallas. "I didn't do it for you. I did it for me. If I'm going to be stuck here for the next twenty-four hours, I'd rather not be sitting in month-old pizza grease."

"Twenty-four hours? What do you mean?" Dallas asked, puzzled.

"The full moon. Tonight's the third night, which means you're going to turn again. To make sure you don't run out and eat anyone else, Stanley and I are going to tie you up, lock you in the basement, and make sure you stay put until it's over."

For a moment, the old Dallas popped up through the confused self-loathing he'd been wrapped in since waking up at the cabin covered in blood and full of Dan.

"Sure, you can tie old Dallas up, but only if he gets to return the favor."

"Keep your paws off my girl, you dirty dog," Herb snipped, causing Dallas to whip his head around.

"Herb's here again? Where'd you put him?"

In response, Lois pointed at the coffee table in front of the couch.

"Oh, right. Hiya, Herby." Dallas waved at the beer can. "Don't you worry, buddy. I won't be making any moves on your girl. Actually, I got somebody kinda special..."

Dallas's brief ray of humor was bowled over by a dark realization.

"Oh crappers. My girlfriend's gonna kill me. Like, for real, kill me."

Lois levelled a dark stare at Dallas, every bit of her glare wrapped in cold judgment.

"So tell me, Hero of Trappersville. How does that feel, knowing someone wants to kill you for no reason other than they don't like what you've become? What you are?"

"Dammit, Lois, don't you get it? I killed a guy! I'm a murderer. Me! It doesn't matter that I don't know how I turned into a werewolf. I am one, and now Aletia and the Society have to put me down."

Dallas stopped talking, a new realization shoving its way forward. It was absolutely true. The Society had to put him down, and he was a member of the Society. Filled with sudden purpose, he lurched toward the closet. Pulling it open, he retrieved his hunting rifle.

"Dallas, what are you doing?" Lois asked.

"Yeah, what the heck, Dallas?" Herb echoed.

Dallas checked the clip and found it loaded. Grunting in satisfaction, he turned and headed for the front door.

Time to end this once and for all, he promised.

"Dallas! Stop. Don't be stupid," Lois yelled, but he ignored her completely. Grasping the handle, he yanked open the front door and almost collided with Stanley. The other man was carrying two loaded grocery bags and struggled mightily to keep from dropping them as he pulled up short to avoid colliding with Dallas.

"Oh, s-sorry, Dallas," Stanley offered. "What'cha doing? I g-got you some food."

"Out of the way, Stanley. Thanks for always being a good buddy and sorry things worked out this way." Shouldering his way past his confused friend, Dallas walked down his front drive, shifting the rifle in his grip as he walked.

Shit. Bullets ain't silver, he realized suddenly. Stopping, he hollered back at the house.

"Stanley! Will regular bullets kill a werewolf when it's not a werewolf, or do they have to be silver?"

Always helpful, Stanley hollered back from where he still stood in the doorway.

"Oh, um. I th-think regular bullets do alright when the werewolf's a p-person. You need silver when they're a wolf, though. I know that for sure."

"Shut up and get out of the way," Lois screamed, pushing her way past Stanley and running after Dallas. "He's going to kill himself!"

Knowing he didn't have much time, Dallas turned to make sure the blast would go away from the house.

No sense hurting anyone else, he thought, bringing the barrel up under his chin and stretching his arm, thumb on the trigger.

"*Noseph ruthera, bruckallow zizith!* Limbs of stone, can't move alone!" Lois screamed.

Dallas thought it was a funny thing to be the last thing he heard on earth, then he squeezed the trigger.

For a moment, he thought he had pulled the trigger, blown his head off, and now was stuck in some lame afterlife that was suspiciously similar to the life he'd just left. That didn't make a whole lot of sense, though, so Dallas concluded he hadn't yet shot himself and made a fresh attempt.

Bang! he hoped, but again, nothing happened.

Bang, bang, double-blammy! Pull the goddamn trigger. C'mon, thumb. What are you waiting for?

Again, no luck. The barrel was under his chin, and his thumb was on the trigger, but Dallas couldn't seem to finish the act.

I ain't no coward! I'm not scared, he screamed, belatedly realizing that he didn't actually scream since he couldn't move his mouth. Or head. Or anything, really. He was just,

Stuck! I can't move. What the hell is going on here?

"I'm taking the gun, Dallas. Then I'll reverse the spell. When I do, you're going to go back in the house, sit on the couch, and not, I repeat, not do anything stupid. Okay?"

It was rather impressive how Lois's voice managed to sound at once very calm, very reasonable, and also very, very pissed off. Dallas felt a tug remove his thumb from the trigger. He felt the weight leave his outstretched arm as the gun was lifted away, and the peculiar cold spot on his neck where the barrel had pressed into skin started to warm.

"That's awesome!" he heard Herb exclaim. *"Can you do anything to him right now?"*

"Pretty much, yeah," Lois responded. "The spell holds the person in a sort of stasis. Automatic things still work, like his heart and lungs. He just can't voluntarily move any muscles."

"So we could maybe pose him or something? Dress him up?"

"Oh, h-heck yeah!" Stanley chimed in. "Make him a ballerina. I want to see a Dallas ballerina."

Lois walked in front of Dallas, still holding the rifle. "What do you think, Dallas? You up for a little humiliation at the hands of your friends? I know! We could take pictures, too. Dress you up like a schoolgirl or put you in a Vikings jersey and post those pictures all over town." She leaned in, a wicked smile curling her lips but not reaching her eyes.

"Would you like that, Dallas? No? Then remember, I can do this to you whenever I want. When I reverse the spell, you behave. No suicide attempts. No trying to fly the coop. If you do, we'll be relentless in our pursuit of humiliation. Comprende?"

Stepping back, Lois handed the rifle to Stanley, taking Herb in trade. "Put that away, would you, Stan? Oh, and empty the clip. Only a bona fide idiot keeps a loaded gun in his coat closet."

Closing her eyes, Lois took a deep breath.

"I love it when she gets all witchy." Herb whispered.

"Shhh. I need to concentrate. I wouldn't want to accidentally turn his insides to Jell-O or swap his ears with his kidneys."

What? Whadaya mean, 'swap my ears with my kidneys?' You know what you're doing, right? Please say you know what you're doing. Dallas's thoughts turned into panicked critters that scurried around his skull in mad circles.

"Just kidding. I know what I'm doing. Now."

A gentle hush descended as Lois spread her arms and waggled her fingers at Dallas.

"Perchun modund. Ento dally. No more fun, spell undone."

Dallas's thumb twitched, and his eyes flinched shut, but of course nothing happened. He sucked in a large breath and started crafting it into a royal ass-chewing, but a single glance from Lois put the kibosh on that.

"Okay, fine. Relax, will ya? I'm over it," he muttered, running a shaking hand through his hair. "Although I'm sorely tempted for a quick game of kick the can, you read me Herb?"

"Loud and clear, Dallas." Herb said, his tinny voice full of smiles. *"I'm just glad you're back."*

Chapter 30

Dallas and Lois sat on the couch while Stanley perched on a chair and Herb rested among a large collection of empty beer cans. Dallas was glad Stanley's trip to the Get'n'Gobble had included grabbing a case of beer. After the day he was having, he certainly needed one, or as it happened, six, going on seven.

"You seriously have no idea how it happened?" Lois asked again.

Dallas shook his head tiredly. "None whatsoever. I mean, does anybody know what they were doing a month ago? I know I was probably drinking a lot, and there was this girl from Chicago I hooked up with a while back, and, um." Dallas scratched his head, face screwed up in thought. "Oh, wait. I fixed Jerry's thermostat around that time, too. No werewolves, though. Not even a dog bite."

Stanley's eyes lit up. "Oh, the d-dogs! I forgot to tell you. They're in the backwoods."

"What?" Dallas yelped.

"Yup. I got to thinking, well, if you was the werewolf we've been looking for after all, then it was p-probably you that got those dogs. You know, the ones that went missing. I found 'em back behind your house. Well, what's left, I mean."

Dallas's shoulders slumped. Some small part of him had still hoped this was all a terrible mistake, but now Stanley had just taken a big, fat crap on that possibility.

"Well, this is just great. Just frickin' great," he griped. "Not to mention totally unfair. I was supposed to be the monster hunter, not the frickin' monster."

"You're preaching to the choir," Herb said. *"Near as I can figure, a mosquito that drank from an old and really powerful vampire did me in."*

"There's over a hundred seventy k-kinds of skeeters," Stanley offered helpfully. "That's why you got to get the DEET. Maybe a skeeter that bit a werewolf got you, Dallas."

"Maybe," Lois conceded. "But it doesn't quite work, does it? I mean, mosquitos drink blood, vampires drink blood. Makes a weird kind of sense. But a werewolf?"

Dallas stood and walked into the kitchen, a dark certainty settling in. Suddenly, he had a very good idea of just what had made him into a damn monster. Since Lois had taken the liberty of putting stuff away, it took a bit to find the glass Mason jar. Luckily, she hadn't tossed it.

"Mosquito biting a werewolf don't make much sense, but what about a dog tick?" he asked, holding up the jar for the rest to see.

While Lois, Stanley, and Herb *oohed* and *aahed* over the wriggling little parasite, Dallas threw up his hands in disgust.

"Forget about the stupid tick. What am I going to do? Lois, you brought back Herb. Can you do something witchy and make me not a werewolf?"

Lois shook her head sadly. "I honestly don't think so, Dallas. I told you there was a way to bring Herb all the way back and get him a body again. When I was researching that, I tried to find a way to make him human and not a vampire."

"Forget it. Being a vamp is way better. Did you see me bowl?"

Lois patted Herb's can affectionately. "The point is, it seems like magic can move someone between *living* and *dead*, but only as themselves, whatever their 'self' is. Herb was a vampire. You, a werewolf."

"So what's the plan? I mean, there is a plan, right?"

Lois looked at Stanley, and Stanley shrugged.

"For now," he said apologetically, "we t-tie you up and lock you in the b-basement."

Dallas's rambler had an unfinished basement that was about as hospitable as a cave with a roughed in bathroom. Stanley carried down a sturdy wooden chair, and Lois brought down long coils of heavy rope. Dallas grumbled a bit about being trussed up like a pig but didn't resist. Only a handful of hours ago, he'd been scooping up and burying the remnants of the last person he'd been around in werewolf form. It was just one night. If this is what it would take to keep everyone safe, he'd tough it out.

"These, too," Lois said, dangling a pair of familiar fuzzy handcuffs. "Can't be too careful, right?"

Dallas eyed the cuffs skeptically. "I know they look legit, but those are more recreational than practical. I'll bet even Stanley could bust 'em."

"Humor me," Lois replied, dropping them in Dallas's lap.

He settled into the chair. "What should I cuff myself to?" he asked.

"Nothing. Just put them on with your hands in your lap. I'll take care of the rest."

For the next fifteen minutes or so, Lois and Stanley worked diligently to restrain Dallas. First, his ankles were bound to the legs of the chair. Next, coils of heavy rope were wound around his legs and behind his calves. Soon, his legs were so securely anchored that all he could do was flex his ankles a bit and wriggle his toes. Legs secured, they wound length after length of rope around his torso, pinning his arms to his sides and securing him to the back of the chair.

"T-too tight?" Stanley asked, tugging on the rope.

Dallas shook his head. The experience was definitely getting uncomfortable, but it had nothing to do with the ropes. He could feel the moon drawing closer, a sensation that was at once foreign and familiar.

"Just hurry up and get out of here, would ya? Clock's ticking."

Once Dallas was firmly attached to the chair, Lois looped two lengths of rope around a couple of stout four-by-fours supporting the joists, pulled them taut, and tied them off. Like guy-wires securing a tower, he wouldn't be able to topple the chair over.

"I think that's the best we can do. Shouldn't be much longer. Are you okay?" Lois asked, concerned.

"Oh sure," Dallas replied. "Peachy. Couldn't be better." Sighing heavily, he tried to stretch his shoulders, only to find that he truly couldn't move.

"Couldn't you just use that spell that makes me freeze?" he asked. "The ropes and all ain't exactly comfy."

Lois shook her head. "I can't risk it. After you change, I don't know if that spell will hold. I know this sucks, but it's the better option."

Resigned, Dallas relaxed his muscles as best he could and tried to ignore the queasy claustrophobia that kept swimming in dangerous circles just below the threshold of his control.

"Hey Lois? Dallas? Um, you guys down there?" Stanley's voice called down the stairs.

"Kinda hard for me to go anyplace else, Stan. What's up?" Dallas replied.

"Um, t-the moon."

Chapter 31

PAIN. PAIN SO RAW it blistered his insides, scraped the blisters off with a rusty wire brush, painted the remaining sores with gasoline, and lit them on fire. As the change gripped Dallas, his spine, ribcage, arms, legs, wrists, and ankles all cracked, split, and reformed, but the binding ropes left no room for his body to expand. Like tree roots pushing up from under the sidewalk's concrete, Dallas's altering body pushed against his restraints and found them unyielding. It was like being squeezed by a vice or run through a sausage grinder. Considering the two, he decided it was actually quite a bit like both.

"Help!" he moaned, the word drooping and warping as his jaw stretched and lowered. It didn't matter, though. There was no one to hear him. He was completely and utterly alone in his agony.

As suddenly as it started, the fierce pain of the change finally passed, leaving only the more natural pain of ropes cutting deep into his flesh. Dallas gasped, his breath coming in shallow pants. He was so tightly bound that even breathing was a chore. Angry at being trapped and desperate to see the moon, he flexed his muscular limbs and heard the ropes creak in response. A low growl burbling up from deep in his gut, he flexed again, straining every muscle in his transformed body. This time, his keen ears heard the ropes groan from stress and the popping of tiny threads as they split and tore. Panting with exertion, he braced himself for one more attempt.

The ropes burst, the wooden chair shattered, and Dallas was free. Only the flimsy, furry handcuffs held him. Rising up to his full height, head grazing the joists above, he rolled his shoulders and readied his arms to snap the links that bound his wrists.

"*Hestra numto boll tar dollan*! Tawdry trinkets used for fun, heed my words and weigh a ton!" a voice called out, and suddenly he found himself face down on the floor. The cuffs binding his wrists felt like they actually did weigh about two-thousand pounds. Wriggling and scrabbling to get his feet under him, Dallas tried to find the leverage to lift his arms, but the cuffs were too heavy.

"Sorry, Dallas. I was worried the ropes wouldn't be enough, so I enchanted the handcuffs," Lois called down from the top of the stairs.

Rage boiled up, and Dallas roared. He was hungry. He needed to feed. Scooting around, he managed to get into a sitting position, strangely bent legs on either side of where his wrists were firmly anchored to the floor. Flexing his shoulders and back, he pulled, but the cuffs didn't budge. Flexing again, he heard tendons stretch and pop.

"Dallas, can you understand me? Try to calm down. You're going to rip off your arms." Lois stepped carefully down the stairs while watching Dallas with trepidation.

Trapped. Hungry, he whined.

"*Oh, wow. I can understand him,*" a voice said. A voice he recognized.

"*He's hungry and pissed. Tell Stanley to bring down some food,*" the voice continued.

"Stanley! Bring the steaks," Lois called out.

I'm trapped. I'm hungry.

"I know, Dallas, but you'll be okay. You're gonna get through this," Herb's tinny voice soothed.

"S-steaks are here!" Stanley announced, almost tripping on the stairs in his haste. Seeing the beast that Dallas had become, he skidded to a halt. "Whoa. Dallas, you're sc-scary looking."

The smell of raw meat hit Dallas's nose, and he howled in response.

Meat. Meat! Mine. All mine. Meat!

"Just toss one over, Stanley," Herb advised.

Stanley lobbed a slab of meat underhand, and it landed with a wet thwack next to Dallas's pinned hands. Hunching forward, he grabbed it in his muzzle and scarfed it down.

More. More meat.

"Keep 'em coming, Stanley," Herb said. As hunk after hunk of meat landed near Dallas and was immediately gobbled up, Herb continued to talk in a soothing tone.

"There you go, bud. There you go. Feeling a little better now?"

"Yes," Dallas grunted, the word coming out as a satisfied woof. He actually was starting to feel much better. The all-consuming hunger that seemed to infuse every fiber of his being was subsiding like a slow tide. It occurred to him that he actually felt like himself. Well, a larger, furrier, hungrier, and slightly more ornery version of himself, but still.

"I'm me. I'm still me," he woofed and chuffed. "I'm still here. The wolf is here too, but I think I can handle it."

Herb related his message to Lois and Stanley. Stan clapped his hands enthusiastically while Lois was more contemplative.

"It's not that different from what happened with Herb, I guess. He was acting on instinct at first, but started to learn to control himself.

Maybe the same is true for werewolves, or at least for you." Tapping her lower lip with her finger, she reached a decision.

"We trust you, Dallas. We trust you to keep control and not kill us. I'm going to lift the enchantment from the handcuffs. Is that a good idea?"

"Yes! God, yes. Get these damn things off'a me. It's like being in the stockades," Dallas growled.

"Herb…?" Lois asked.

"Oh, uh, yeah, sorry. He said yes, we can trust him. Or at least, close enough." Herb said.

Lois closed her eyes, wove her hands through an intricate series of gestures, and spoke another odd assortment of vowels and consonants. Suddenly, the enchanted one-ton cuffs weighed nothing more than novelty store cuffs. Overjoyed, Dallas stood and flung his arms wide, shattering the links that had bound him a moment before. Sliding a thick, clawed digit inside first one, then the other cuff, he popped them off easy as snapping the tab on a beer can.

Freedom felt good, and Dallas let loose a joyful howl in celebration. Seeing Lois and Stanley take hasty steps back, he dropped down to his haunches, shook his head, and licked his chops.

"Thanks," he woofed. "I totally get that you had to be prepared, but it feels really, really good to have those off."

As Herb translated, Dallas tried to explain what he was feeling.

"I really do feel pretty okay. I mean, like normal. Things look funny, and I can hear and smell damn near everything, but not in a weird way. Does that make sense?"

When Herb translated, Lois nodded. "I suppose. This is who you are now. I'm just glad it's you. If the wolf was in control, I imagine it would be a different story."

Dallas bobbed his head in agreement. "Oh, the wolf's there. Right there. It wants things, too. Like more of that steak and to be outside with the moon. You think we could head up and chat in the backyard? Kinda going crazy down here."

Soon the two humans, werewolf, and vampire in a can were sitting in a loose circle in Dallas's back yard. A silvery globe hung overhead, bathing them in reflected light and casting watery shadows. Lois was scratching Dallas's ear while Stanley and Herb debated what the moon had to do with any of this.

"It's b-because Khonsu wanted a dog," Stanley explained.

"Khonsu?" Lois asked, raising an eyebrow.

"Sure. He was the Egyptian moon god. He always wanted a dog, so he g-got a great big one, a wolf. B-but that wolf howled and made a racket every night, so Ra, the sun god, he got m-mad. Being the sun god's a lot of work, believe you me. Ra wasn't getting enough sleep because of that wolf dog, so he told Khonsu to shut that d-dog up or he'd t-take it away. Khonsu told Ra to shove it, and they fought and fought and are fighting still. Usually, Ra's winning 'cause he's the s-sun god, you know. Pretty tough, that sun. But Khonsu, he gets the upper hand, and that moon gets b-big and full, and for a few nights he gets to have his d-dog back."

Lois clapped appreciatively. "Not bad, Stanley. Where did you learn that?"

Stanley blushed. "Oh, I was reading some old books. Society research, you know. We g-gotta be reading all sorts of books. I don't know if that's really what h-happened, though," he confessed. "It just sounded good."

"Well, it's as good a theory as any, I suppose. You like that one, Dallas?" she asked, shifting her hand to ruffle the fur on his head.

"Yep. Good story, Stan," Dallas chuffed. "Almost as good as the one where you went back inside the house and got me another steak."

Herb laughed and translated, sending Stanley on his way.

"Only t-two left, Dallas," Stanley said when he returned. "That gonna be enough, you think? I mean, you ate five already."

Dallas thought about it as he munched happily on the chewy meat. He'd always figured that werewolves just wanted to run around and kill people. It was a pleasant surprise to realize that they were mostly just really, really hungry.

Can't fault a guy for getting a bit crabby when he's got a hankering, he decided. *Hell, once I practically punched out a Girl Scout when she was taking too long to make change for a box of Thin Mints.*

"I guess," Dallas said, woofing in a tone that implied he'd get by. "How much longer do I have before I'm human again?"

"Moon sets in about two more hours," Herb answered.

"That's okay," Dallas said. "Kinda nice sitting back here with you guys."

"A wolf, a witch, a vampire, and Stan, sitting under the stars," Lois wondered out loud, looking up at an unfathomable sky. "Funny how things work out."

Funny indeed, thought Dallas, circling Lois so she could more easily scratch his other ear. *Funny indeed.*

Chapter 32

THREE WEEKS QUIETLY SLIPPED by. With no solid plan for how to handle the new normal they'd been thrust into, they had decided to keep a low profile until Dan's disappearance blew over. Lois and Dallas worked while Stanley did whatever it was Stanley did to pass the days. It was so completely normal that Dallas was almost able to forget the fact that things were anything but normal. Almost, until the Sasquatch showed up.

Lois had brought Herb over. The three were discussing whether Slow Johnson would let him be an honorary team member in the winter bowling league when there was a gentle tapping at the front door.

"That'll be Stanley. Took him long enough," Dallas grumbled. "Guy's got one job, get me food, and he turns it into a three-hour excursion. Must've had the list upside down."

With a proper ass-chewing queued up for Stanley, Dallas opened the door and prepared to unload. The tirade got stuck about halfway between his lungs and his lips when he realized he was staring at a gigantic furry stomach. Looking down, he saw two tree-trunk legs extending to the ground, terminating in the biggest feet he had ever seen. Shifting his head in the other direction, his eyes travelled up and up and up across a broad, hairy torso, impossibly wide shoulders, and finally, to a wide mouthed, wide nosed, wide browed simian face looking down at him with two large, brown eyes.

"HELPUH," the wide mouth uttered.

Dallas screamed in shock and followed the scream with three quick jabs into the creature's stomach.

"Where the hell did you come from? There ain't no gorillas in Wisconsin! Lois, grab Herb and run! I'll hold it off."

Feet dancing, Dallas fired punch after punch at the leviathan standing on his front stoop.

"You probably didn't realize,"

Punch. Jab, jab, punch.

"That you knocked on the wrong goddamn door."

Shift and duck, jab, jab, punch!

"This here ain't just the home of a goddamn hero,"

Duck and weave, punch, punch.

"but the home of a bona fide monster hunter!"

Despite the flurry of blows, the monster simply stood passively until Dallas finally wound down and stopped swinging.

"Turds on toast. You're a tough one, aren't ya?" he wheezed, doubling over with his hands on his knees.

A hand the size of an extra large skillet reached up and rubbed at the belly Dallas had just used for an impromptu punching bag.

"OWWEE," it said in the same low, loud voice. "HELPUH."

"Oh, I'll help you, alright. I'll help you pack up that huge monster ass and ship it straight back to whatever hell you crawled out of. You might be big, but I've taken down bigger. Damn right, I have. Well, maybe not literally. You are pretty big, but what I mean is, I've tangled with five, six guys at once, you know? Add all that up, and I'm sure they were as big combined as you are all by yourself. Bigger. Hell, yeah, lots bigger. So you got a choice, buddy. Walk those huge feet right outta here, or there's gonna be hell to pay."

"NO. HELPUH. SCARED."

Dallas cracked his knuckles and settled back into a boxing stance. "Oh, you better be scared. You better be,"

"Dallas! Stop," Lois interjected. "Leave him alone."

Incredulous, he spun to face Lois. "I told you to grab Herby and run for it! Geez, woman. I'm trying to watch out for you, keep you safe. That's hard to do," he explained slowly, "if you don't listen."

Lois rolled her eyes. "He's not trying to hurt us. God, look at him! If he wanted to cause trouble, I don't think there's anything we could do to stop him. Now why don't you stop posturing and ask him why he needs help instead of hitting him?"

"Oh, it's a 'him,' now, is it? And how would you know that, little miss know-it-all?"

Lois pointed. Dallas followed the direction of her finger and whistled.

"Oh. Right."

Stepping past Dallas, Lois looked up into the thing's liquid eyes. She sighed and asked, almost bashfully, "You're a Sasquatch, right? Like Bigfoot?" Childlike wonder lit up her face. "Are you him?"

What looked suspiciously like a smile worked its way across the broad, simian face.

"NO." A finger went up and scratched a temple. "CLAN. SAME. HE OLD. ME YOUNG."

Lois giggled like a schoolgirl on a merry-go-round, but Dallas simply stared. Not only was the eight-foot tall gorilla talking, but, if he was following the conversation properly, was also related to Bigfoot. The Bigfoot.

"But that can't be," he muttered. "Bigfoots don't exist."

The Sasquatch waved happily, face still split with a grin showing wide, smooth teeth.

"You said, 'help,'" Lois said. "Help with what? Why are you scared?"

"HUNTER. CLOSE. HURTUH…" the next word sounded like a boulder rolling down a cliff.

"That was his name, in his tongue," Herb chimed in.

He's right, Dallas thought. *I understood him too.*

The realization jarred another not-too-distant memory. When they'd tracked down the boo hag, it had spoken to Dallas and said some kind of confusing things. Now, though, the pieces were falling into place. No one else had commented on their conversation. It had spoken directly to Dallas, something about being one of its own.

She knew I was a werewolf, or at least a monster like she was, and she talked to me.

"I think monsters all speak monster," he said, awed by the possibilities. "I mean, there was this boo hag,"

"MOLLY," the Sasquatch said, smile fading.

"What? Oh. Crap. Um, sorry? I didn't, I mean, she was eating people's breath…" Dallas faltered and started to pluck at a speck of something on his shirt. "Anyway, she talked to me. I didn't get what she was talking about, but I understood her, and I don't think anyone else even knew she was talking."

Lois nodded her acceptance, then looked up at the Sasquatch. "Is there another name we can call you? A human name, maybe?"

The Sasquatch frowned and scratched its temple again. It pursed its lips and clucked its tongue experimentally.

"KU- KU," it started. "KEVIN." The smile returned in full force, complete with crinkled eyes and a tongue as big as a size nine sneaker sticking out between its teeth.

"Kevin," Lois repeated, smiling back. "I like that. It's a nice name. You're safe here, Kevin," she continued with a loaded look at Dallas. "No one else is going to hit you, and I'm sorry Dallas did in the first place. He's a jerk."

"Hey, come on! I thought I was helping!" Dallas protested. "I didn't know he was a friendly Bigfoot. I thought he was a giant killer gorilla." Dallas looked from Lois to Herb-in-a-can and back. "Right? I mean, look at him. Scary gorilla!"

"And now you know he's not, and next time maybe you'll take a minute to find out before you start swinging," Lois chided. "Anyway, he won't hit you again, Kevin. You said 'owee.' Did Dallas hurt you?"

"NO. BAD FOODUH." Again, the pause followed by a frown, which Dallas was starting to associate with deep thought. "POI-SONUH."

As Kevin said the word, a rumbling fart like the world's biggest whoopee cushion split the air.

"Oh my g-god! Whaaaah. I was right b-behind you!" Stanley's voice cried out from somewhere on the other side of the Sasquatch. "And my m-mouth was open. Oh, man. It t-tastes like old cat food."

Squeezing around Kevin's bulk, Stanley made his way into the house.

"Hello Mr. Sasquatch. I'm Stanley. P-please don't fart on me again."

"SORRY. BAD FOODUH."

Lois took Kevin's massive hand and patted it gently. "It's okay. We'll see if we can help you feel better. If you come inside, can you be careful? Not break things?"

Kevin nodded his head and, without further invitation, ducked, turned, and slid in through the open door. Dallas, Lois, and Stanley all stepped out of the way and continued to back into the living room as the Sasquatch stepped carefully inside. The ceiling of the rambler was only eight feet high, so Kevin dipped his head a little to accommodate his height.

"THERE?" he asked politely, pointing to an empty corner.

Lois looked at Dallas for permission.

"What? Oh, sure. Yeah, make yourself comfy. Um. Do you drink beer?"

Chapter 33

With Dallas and Herb's help, Kevin was able to share his tale. He had passed near Trappersville a few weeks before, heading for his clan's usual winter lair. Unfortunately, he was tracked. Being young, he wasn't as good as other Sasquatch at staying clear of humans.

"CLUMSY," he said bashfully.

Whoever the tracker was, they had apparently tricked the young Sasquatch by leaving muffins in the woods. Kevin loved muffins, especially blueberry. The first few that he stumbled across were fine, so when the next one smelled funny, he ate it anyway.

"YUCKY," Kevin grimaced, rubbing his stomach again. "MAKE KEVIN SLEEPY."

The hunter came for him the next night. He probably assumed the Sasquatch would be unconscious. Instead, Kevin was having what Dallas decided must've been an epic bowel movement and was luckily downwind from the approaching hunter. Since every Sasquatch knows to flee whenever a human is close, Kevin did just that. Fearing for his clan's safety, he returned the way he came from instead of continuing on. Tracked by a hunter, exhausted from running, and sick with poison, Kevin finally decided to seek help.

"You poor thing!" Lois gasped. "And you're still sick?"

Kevin nodded unhappily.

"That'd be the Society, all right," Dallas said. "They packed up and left in a hurry during my werewolf weekend because Colton got wind of a Sasquatch up in the Michigan U.P. He made it seem like they just wanted to see it, though. I mean, no one's ever really seen one, so I figured they got excited and wanted to check it out."

Lois spun to glare at Dallas.

"You see? He wasn't hurting anyone, but your little Society friends tried to kill him anyway."

Dallas held up his hands in defense. "Not my fault! They're an ancient order of monster hunters. You can't just expect them to suddenly get all kumbaya and start passing out hugs when a mythical eight-foot tall gorilla shows up."

Lois sighed, but didn't press the matter. Grabbing a notepad and pen from her purse, she began scribbling.

"Stanley, I know you just came from the store, but would you mind heading back? Here's a list of things that might help Kevin's stomach feel better. While you're out, I'll go back to my place and see if I can find a healing spell. Dallas, you and Herb stay here and keep Kevin company. Talk to him or watch a little T.V."

"I don't know what Bigfoots watch," Dallas protested.

"*Animal Planet?*" Herb suggested.

"DIFF'RENT STROKESUH."

"*Or... Diff'rent Strokes.*"

"Fine," Dallas sighed. "You and Stanley go do stuff, and I'll babysit the vamp-in-a-can and Baby Huey. Busted up blower fans. Just when everything was going so well," Dallas complained. Being a werewolf wasn't at all what he expected. Cracking a fresh beer, he reclined on the couch and tried to make conversation with Kevin.

"So I don't get it. You said you hide from humans, but you speak English, eat muffins, and watch *Diff'rent Strokes*. I might not be the sharpest number two in the pencil box, but that don't figure."

Kevin shrugged. He had sidled closer to the couch and was busy sliding Herb back and forth across the table with a thick finger while Herb made *weeee* noises.

"MUFFINS GOODUH. SHOW GOODUH," he explained.

Dallas didn't let up. "But you knocked on my door. If you're so scared of humans, why come here?"

"YOU LIKE MEUH," Kevin explained after letting Herb's can slide to a stop.

"Here we go again. Look, I might be... whatever the hell I am now. Werewolf, whatever. That don't mean I just turned in my 'human' card. I'm still human, too. I mean, look at me!"

Kevin obliged, his sad, brown eyes looking deep into Dallas's own.

"It's gotta be harder for you than it was for me," Herb said softly. *"I mean, I got turned, and suddenly every day was different. You get to be almost human for like twenty-seven days out of thirty. But Dallas, you have to accept that you aren't human. Not anymore."*

Dallas looked down at his hands and studied them for a while. Skin, knuckles, nails, and fingerprints, all the requisite parts to be considered human hands. Completely normal, completely human, except that just below the skin, something else ran through his veins.

"I know, Herb," he sighed. "I know."

Chapter 34

"**T**HIS STINKS OF RANDALL," Dallas complained. "I don't think Colton and Aletia are the sort to use dirty tricks. They confront stuff head-on. Randall, though. He's a sneaky little shit. If it ain't a taser, or taking a cheap shot with a paintball gun when your eyes are closed, he's dropping poisoned muffins in the woods. What a jerk."

Lois had made some herbal tea for Kevin, explaining that, combined with a simple healing spell, it would make him feel much better. While she tended to the ailing Sasquatch, Dallas, Herb, and Stanley tried to figure out a plan.

"M-maybe we poison him back. You know, get some brats from Cecil's, soak 'em in the castor oil, and leave 'em out in the t-trees." Stanley rubbed his hands in an earnest but ineffective attempt to look devious.

"Sure, Stanley, because I know I would definitely stop and eat a random bratwurst I found lying in the woods." Dallas sniffed. "Next."

"I say we keep it simple. If he's been tracking Kevin, he should be getting close. Why don't we just wait, jump him when he shows up, and, um," Herb faltered. *"Tell him to leave Kevin alone?"* he finished lamely.

Dallas interlaced his fingers, stretched his arms, and bent his hands back, thick knuckles popping as he stretched.

"I like parts one and two, but I'm going to make a minor adjustment to part three and add a part four. We tell him to leave all of us alone. If he argues, I'll beat the holy crap out of him. That's what we'll do."

"And Colton? Aletia? If Randall's on Kevin's trail, his friends won't be far behind," Lois pointed out.

"So? There's three of them. There's five of us." Dallas looked at Stanley. "Four of us." He looked at the little can holding Herb. "Three." He shrugged. "Okay, three of us, but Kevin there is frickin' huge. That's advantage monsters, right?"

Kevin shook his head while trying not to spill the tea cup he held gingerly in his massive hand.

"NO FIGHTUH."

Dallas threw his hands up, exasperated. Of course, the four-hundred pound gorilla would be a pacifist. Why could nothing ever be smooth?

"Uh, guys? I don't mean to be a downer, but we don't really have any more time to plan. Randall's here."

Dallas sprang to the window.

"Where?"

"Well, not here, here. Maybe a mile, mile and a half away, approaching from the north. It's about as far away as I can see, but it's definitely him. He's on his moped and is heading this direction."

"You think he knows Kevin is here, or is he just coming to talk to me?" Dallas wondered out loud. "Okay. Decision time. Lois, grab

Herb and Stanley, and head to the basement. Kevin, you, um. Crap. I dunno. Where do you hide a giant gorilla?"

"Garage?" Lois asked. "Do you have a tarp or something?"

"Good plan. Kevin, you head to the garage and hide under a tarp. Everyone else, get downstairs."

While everyone hurried to their respective hiding spots, Dallas did his best to undo Lois's cleaning fit and make his place look like a messy bachelor pad again. Soon, his sensitive ears heard the high-pitched whine of a two-stroke engine. Herb was right. Randall was definitely heading his way.

Flipping on the television, he cracked another beer and settled onto the couch, doing his best to portray a casual nonchalance that was at complete odds with what he was actually feeling. The telltale sputter of the moped's engine crescendoed in his driveway and then stopped. A moment later, boots crunched on the gravel, and a hand rapped on his front door. A quick sniff put a final nail in the mystery. Cheap hair gel, mild B.O., a whiff of bacon. Definitely Randall.

Dallas opened the door, feigning surprise.

"Randall! Buddy! What are you doing here? Gonna try and tase me again?"

"Dallas," Randall said by way of greeting. "Not a social call."

Dallas held the door for the other man and walked into the kitchen to grab a fresh beer. When he returned, Randall had pulled a chair up to the table.

"How's that werewolf situation?" he asked without preamble.

"You drove all the way from wherever the hell you were to ask me about that? Geez, Randall. One of these days, I'm gonna teach you about that crazy thing they call a phone."

"You didn't answer the question. What's the status on the were-wolf? Still a problem, or were the Hero of Trappersville and his stuttering sidekick actually able to do something all by themselves?"

Dallas crossed his arms across his broad chest. "Werewolf situation is fine, thanks for asking. Now why don't you answer my question? What the hell are you doing here, Randall? Doesn't seem like you to run off by yourself. I think you'd find the experience of not having your nose all the way up Colton's ass too scary."

Randall stood abruptly, knocking over the chair, and went chest to chest with Dallas.

"Where do you get off?" he stammered, face going red.

"Bedroom, normally, but I confess I've rubbed a few out in the shower," Dallas said with a grin.

Randall smirked. "Whatever. Look, Colton and Aletia will be this way soon enough. I went ahead because that 'squatch we were tracking doubled-back this way. I hit town yesterday and started looking into things." He sized Dallas up for a moment before continuing.

"Let's just say some of the things I looked into don't add up to you taking care of that werewolf problem."

The knife was out before Dallas could blink. He did blink, though, and when he was done, the knife was still there.

"And there's 'squatch scat in your yard. So now I got a real conundrum. I don't think the werewolf situation has been handled, and now I'm starting to think the newbie is getting cozy with another monster. Makes me nervous, and when I get nervous, I tend to cut things," he finished menacingly.

Dallas was shocked. "Kevin! You shit in my yard? Not cool, dude. Not cool."

The door to the attached garage cracked open, and a massive head partially covered by a grease-stained tarp peeked in.

"WHAT'CHOO TALKING 'BOUT, DALLAS?"

Randall's jaw dropped. His eyes shifted in disbelief from Dallas to the Sasquatch and back, the knife following.

"I knew it. I frickin' knew it," he gasped. "Why would anyone harbor a monster, unless that someone is a monster too? Something stinks in Denver, that's what I say. So you got exactly three seconds to start explaining before I gut you like a fish."

"I'm a werewolf," Dallas stated matter-of-factly. "And that there Sasquatch in my garage is Kevin. Oh, and there's a witch and a vampire in a beer can in my basement."

This time it was Randall who blinked, which was all the opening Dallas needed. His hand lashed out and knocked the knife aside. A fist followed, catching Randall under the chin. The blow sent the hunter reeling into the table. Closing in, Dallas was caught off guard by a low kick, and he tumbled to the side.

Randall pounced and landed heavily on top of Dallas, driving the knife downward. Dallas managed to grab Randall's wrist and deflect the blow, but the blade still slid down the side of his shoulder, opening a bright line of red across his skin and a barrel of rage in his stomach.

Thrusting his hips and twisting, Dallas flipped Randall onto his side. Still lying on the ground, he drove a knee up and landed it squarely in Randall's groin.

"Urgh," Randall gasped in pain while simultaneously boxing Dallas's ear with his free hand. The blow was hard enough to stun Dallas, giving Randall time to squirm away and regain his feet. Dallas was quick to follow, and the two men squared off for round two.

"I knew you were trouble from the start," Randall growled. "Told Colton, too. I think having Tia around all the time is making him soft."

Dallas barked out a laugh. "Aletia might be guilty of many things, but making a guy soft ain't one."

Launching a series of jabs, Dallas drove the attack and forced Randall backward into the small kitchen. The knife flashed and flashed again, always close to finding skin but never quite connecting.

"Your little toy ain't doing you much good, huh?" Dallas joked between punches.

"Yeah? How's that shoulder feel?" Randall countered.

Dallas stopped swinging. Relaxing his posture, he looked at the bloody fabric of his sliced flannel. Reaching across, he poked experimentally and pulled the fabric open to expose the skin.

"I've had paper cuts that were worse," he commented. "So I guess I can't complain."

Randall set his shoulders and dropped back into a half-crouch.

"You won't be alive long enough to complain," he said, and attacked.

Dallas and Randall had tangled a time or two, and Dallas thought he had the man's measure. Reality sank in quickly, though. Randall really was a tough son of a bitch and actually had been holding back. Now that he knew Dallas was a werewolf, Randall was in full hunter mode and fought like a man possessed. Despite his increased speed and strength, Dallas found it harder and harder to block the man's attacks. The knife found his stomach and scored a fresh, bloody line across his flesh. Randall's other fist and feet connected so many times Dallas was starting to lose count. As the tide of the fight swung, Dallas was driven back into the living room. He wasn't accustomed to losing a fight and was starting to get a tad concerned when a beer can hit Randall square in the forehead.

"Banzai!" Herb yelled as his can connected.

Dallas didn't hesitate. Springing forward, he side-stepped Randall and grabbed his knife hand. Swinging his leg back, he caught Randall behind the knees and knocked his feet out from under him. Pivoting, Dallas bent Randall's arm and fell forward, his full two hundred and ten pounds driving the knife down like a sledgehammer. He felt the blade scrape a rib and plunge straight into Randall's heart.

Randall gave a surprised yelp and was still. Dallas fell to the side panting and stared at the blood welling up around the knife's handle and soaking Randall's shirt. When he looked up, he saw Lois standing across the room, a look of revulsion on her face.

"Can you try not killing people for a change?" she asked, staring at the dead hunter.

Herb's tinny voice broke the ensuing silence.

"Well, I've always felt people should do what they're good at. Now, could I get a little help here? My can's getting a little worse for wear, and I think we've found my new body."

Chapter 35

DALLAS HAD NEVER SEEN Lois look so nervous. It had taken a few days for Stanley to help her gather the necessary ingredients, which was longer than she wanted. The Society and the next full moon were both getting closer by the minute. Lois worried that if they didn't get it done right that night, she'd have her hands full with werewolf Dallas and people trying to kill werewolf Dallas. Also, each passing day meant Randall was getting more and more dead.

"He's in the freezer. What's the worry?" Dallas had asked.

Lois squeezed the bridge of her nose, frustration plain in the gesture. "The longer the host body is dead, the harder it is for the soul to take hold. If that wasn't an issue, I could've dug up any old body for Herb. It's supposed to be a freshly dead body. I just hope we're doing this soon enough."

Following her instructions, Dallas and Kevin cleared a patch of earth in his backyard and dug a shallow grave. Night had pulled its dark curtain across the horizon by the time they were done, adding to Lois's concerns. Since Herb was a vampire, he had to be safely back before the sun rose. It'd be a cruel joke indeed to resurrect him, only to watch the poor guy burn in the morning sun.

"How long do you think it will take?" Dallas had asked, earning a terse reply that it would take as long as it would take, and could he please just be a good dog and do what he was told? He shelved the rest of his questions and followed her list of preparations.

Soon, a folding table held a small collection of herbs, the heavy book of spells she'd shown him, and Dallas's electric crock pot. A bright orange extension cord snaked its way back to the outdoor outlet. It had taken him close to half an hour to scrub the chili and goulash grime from the inside, but Lois had demanded that it be spotless. While Dallas was up to his elbows in dish soap, Kevin and Stanley had painstakingly recreated the intricate pattern Dallas had seen on Lois's coffee table. When they had finished, a strange latticework crossed over and around the shallow grave like a six-foot wide dreamcatcher made of salt and colored sands.

Preparations finally complete, the witch, werewolf, Sasquatch and alien abductee stood in a circle around the grave containing Randall's corpse. An air of expectation made the already quiet evening seem unnaturally silent.

Lois gently set the Milwaukee's Best can that held Herb in the center of the pattern directly above the corpse that rested below.

"Are you sure about this, Herb?" she asked. "I mean, I think I can do it. It's just that, well, if I screw something up, I have no idea what will happen."

Even though he sounded like a busted little transistor radio, Dallas was touched by the genuine emotion he heard in Herb's reply.

"Lois, you're the most amazing person I've ever known. From the first day I saw you walk into Ronnie's, I knew you were special. I love you no matter what, but I'm really not worried. You're going to do great."

Heavy tears welled up in Dallas's eye. His ignorance had sent his best friend to an early grave, broken the heart of a wonderful woman, and thrown him into a sixty-proof quagmire of guilt. Now, though, there was a chance that the things he had broken could be made whole.

"He's right, Lois. Randall's just another beer can. You did it once. You can do it again," Dallas said, voice gruff with uncharacteristic emotion. Stanley's head bobbed in agreement, and Kevin gave a hearty thumbs up. Lois took a deep breath and nodded. Then things got weird.

First, she raised her arms up over her head. Tipping her head back, she looked up at the darkening sky. Her eyes shifted back and forth like she was imploring each and every awakening star to fall so she could wish for luck. The moon had already risen, its pale, cratered face a silent witness to the events far below. Dallas's eyes traced along the dark sliver on its edge, a sickle shadow holding the wolf at bay. He could feel the moon in his bones and for a moment understood why entire oceans would rise and fall at its whim. Maybe Stanley had the right of it. Maybe that strange orb really was a god holding an invisible leash looped around Dallas's neck. It gave him a strange sense of comfort. The thought of being inexorably tied to the whims of some ancient god was better than having his life turned inside out by a hunk of dead rock endlessly floating through space.

Coming out of his reverie, he returned his attention to Lois. Her arms were still raised, and her head was still tilted toward the night sky, but her eyes were now closed, and her lips were moving. Even with his preternatural hearing, Dallas couldn't make out any words. Listening harder, he realized he couldn't hear anything except the sound of his own breath. Even that sounded impossibly distant.

For what seemed like an eternity, that was all there was. The soft sighs of his far-away breath and Lois, statuesque in the starlight and silhouetted by the moon. All of creation seemed focused on those two things. Then a new sound emerged, a meandering hum so low in tone that Dallas wondered if purely human ears would even register it. The hum seemed to come from all around him, but some part of him recognized its source. When he looked at Kevin, he saw the mild-mannered Sasquatch smiling and swaying gently from side to side.

Lois's eyes opened as she noticed too. Her lips continued to move through their silent mantra, but a gentle smile pulled at the corners, and the worry that had furrowed her brow started to dispel. Without warning, Stanley began humming as well, a surprisingly sweet alto that caught the cadence of Kevin's tune and complemented it. The two threads, deep melody and lilting harmony, unraveled the surrounding silence. It was haunting and beautiful, thawing parts of Dallas he'd never known were frozen, shining light onto the parts he'd never known were shrouded in shadow. It was also, he realized, incomplete.

He took hold of his self-consciousness and set it aside. Softly clearing his throat, Dallas added his own song to theirs. At first, his wordless tenor ran against the grain of the tune. Soon though, he found his song moving along with Kevin's and Stanley's, the hopeful harmony weaving a warm blanket around the group.

Lois's arms seemed to gather up the song and pull it close to her chest. Holding it there, it radiated warmth and vitality. A softly glowing, shapeless pillow of life. Slowly, so slowly, she opened her arms.

The radiance dispersed, rolled down across the fresh grave, and sank into the upturned earth.

Lois turned to look from Dallas to Stanley and finally, to Kevin. "Thank you. Truly, from the bottom of my heart, thank you."

Her hands wove an intricate pattern while she spoke softly. "*Suthlan mo kalpussen ra.* Life, we affirm you and celebrate you with song. Be here with me, be strong in me, be mine to hold, and mine to give."

Turning her attention to the crock pot, she dipped a finger in the simmering water and brought it to her lips. With a satisfied nod, she added pinches of spice and clumps of herbs to the water and stirred it gently with an old wooden spoon. The resulting smell exploded in Dallas's nose and coated his throat, causing him to gag. Stanley started to wheeze, and even implacable Kevin chuffed. Only Lois seemed unaffected as her voice slashed out, each syllable a harsh challenge.

"*Rathu pronsetha dur. Shum taren. Koth!*" she cried. "Death, we refute you. Your place is not here, your time is not now. Be mine to scatter and mine to banish."

A wailing moan rose up. A thousand haunted, empty voices cried out from the depths of the afterlife, a mournful chorus of loss and ruin. Lois opened the heavy book. While reading aloud from a marked page, she stirred the contents of the crock pot. Each thrust and pull of the wooden spoon formed a counter-rhythm to her voice. As Lois spoke and stirred, stirred and spoke, a heavy steam boiled up. Shapeless at first, it stretched and coalesced into a hundred different forms, thickening and clinging to the spoon's handle like a heavy syrup. Still, the myriad voices wailed and cried, becoming louder and louder as Lois pushed and pulled at the heavy liquid.

Suddenly, Lois pulled the spoon free and threw it to the ground. Grasping each side of the pot, she tried to lift it. For a long moment, she strained, gritting her teeth, flexing her arms, stretching her back, but the pot wouldn't move.

"It's too much!" she sobbed. "I can't do it. I can't!"

Not understanding what was happening, but knowing what was needed, Dallas strode forward. Meeting Lois's frantic eyes, he took her hands away and placed his own on the sides of the familiar old crock pot.

Damn strange bucket of chili, he thought, watching the heavy liquid heave and roil of its own accord.

"What do I do?" he yelled.

"It has to be poured on the grave," Lois shouted back, her voice barely audible over the tornado of wails and moans whirling around them.

Well, that's easy enough, he reasoned, grasping the sides of the pot and lifting.

A memory of the World's Strongest Man contest popped into his mind. Dallas, Herb, and Stanley sat around the T.V., watching mountains of muscle on two legs flip tractor tires, toss logs, and pull airplanes. If only this were as easy as that. Trying to move the crock pot was like trying to shot put a boulder. Dallas heard his tendons creak and teeth grind. He felt tiny fractures form in the crock pot's molded plastic sides where his fingers and palms pressed. Despite his Herculean effort, the pot didn't budge.

"Can we skip this part?" he asked loudly, only to see Lois shake her head madly back and forth.

Well, crappers. When a thing needs doin', you just gotta do it. Even if it sucks.

The moon, so close to full, inundated Dallas with its cold avalanche of reflected light. He opened himself up to it and let its strange power soak through him. Feet spread, he squatted down and wrapped his arms around the pot. Commanding each and every muscle he had to stop being such a pussy and man up, he lifted.

Inch by unforgiving inch, the crock pot raised up from the T.V. tray. Dallas arched his back and flexed his legs. A foot shuffled forward, followed by another. Step by painful step, each one leaving a deep impression in the soft earth, Dallas moved forward until a voice cried,

"Now! Dump it now!"

A final heave, and the crock pot tilted forward. The viscous liquid poured forth and burned the grass when it hit the ground. Pulled by unseen forces, it followed and filled in the intricate pattern until the entire criss-crossing shape was full of churning, black liquid. Dallas felt the crock pot go suddenly and amazingly weightless as the final drop spilled free. The shift was so sudden, he stumbled backward and landed on his rear.

The voices reached a crescendo as they formed an invisible tornado above the grave. Spinning with a violence that threatened to tear the whole of Wisconsin apart, they centered above the small can of Milwaukee's Best and dove down, down, down.

The silence that followed was so complete that Dallas feared he'd gone deaf. Looking around in a panic, he was relieved to hear Kevin whimper and Stanley sob.

"Is it over?" Stanley begged. "P-please say it's over."

"SCARYUH," Kevin added, huddled into a giant, furry ball.

Dallas looked to Lois. She knelt at the edge of the pattern, face expressionless as she watched the strange liquid bubble and churn.

"Almost," she finally whispered. At the sound of her voice, the liquid suddenly sucked straight down into the dirt like a giant drop of water on a drought-starved field. Everyone held their breath and waited for whatever was supposed to come next.

When the hand pushed up from beneath the dirt, Lois gave an involuntary sob of relief. When the next hand pushed its way up, Dallas and Lois sobbed in unison. Soon, two forearms were free, followed by two elbows. The arms squirmed and reached and finally found the leverage to push a head free. A dark haired, widow's peaked head with milky eyes and a mud covered goatee.

Randall's reanimated corpse pushed itself inch by muddy inch from his grave. His torso cleared the ground, followed by methodically churning legs. His mouth stretched, and a moan poured out, a solitary version of the wails that had rocked the countryside a few moments before.

"Shit!" Dallas yelled. "Zombie! Zombie! Get me a hockey stick! It's a frickin' Randall zombie!" Scrabbling to his feet, he readied himself to confront the new monster as it rose up and shuffled a step forward.

Kevin sobbed and made for the trees, his heavy feet thumping the ground. Stanley started screaming and ran back and forth, waving his hands in a panic.

"I don't got a hockey stick! I don't got a hockey stick," he cried in a manic voice.

Dallas cursed as the zombie took another shambling step forward. "Fire poker, tent pole, whatever. Just get me something pointy!"

"No!" Lois yelled as she ran toward Dallas. "Get the beer can. Get Herb! We need to make it drink Herb!"

Dallas looked at her incredulously, but the look on her face convinced him that while she might be bat-shit crazy, she was one-hundred percent sincere. Jumping inside the pattern, he scooped up Herb in one hand and grabbed zombie-Randall's neck with the other. Muddy clawed fingers raked at his face, but Dallas ignored them and bent the head back. With a loud victory cry, he shoved the beer can up to the zombie's mouth.

Randall tried to twist his head, moans and wails becoming more frantic, but Dallas held the can holding Herb firmly to Randall's lips. A milky white smoke poured out and down the zombie's throat. Suddenly, Randall went lax in Dallas's grip. When a cold, muddy hand reached up and grabbed Dallas's own, he yelped but refused to let go.

A suckling sound reached his ears. Randall was now actively drinking the smoke, guzzling it down with a series of hungry gulps. Dallas felt the cold flesh gripping his own shift its fingers around the beer can. As Dallas released Randall's throat and stepped back, the zombie stood on its own, can of Milwaukee's Best tipped up as yard after yard of milky smoke poured down into its mouth.

What happened next was the strangest thing Dallas thought a pair of looking balls could ever witness. Randall's skin started to ripple, his arms started to vibrate, his legs started to twitch. His face stretched and contracted. The scraggly hairs of a goatee shriveled and wilted. In their place, a reddish five o'clock shadow spread like peach fuzz over rounding cheeks and a softening chin. Freckles popped out across a once sharp nose turned not-quite-bulbous, and the dark widow's peak pulled back to a less severe hairline defined by brown hair turning a familiar, rusty red.

Herb Knudsen raised the empty can high above his head and smiled, his long fangs glinting in the light of the moon.

"Best beer in the whole world, and that's a fact."

Chapter 36

DALLAS, STANLEY, LOIS, AND Herb sat in Dallas's living room, each one lost deep in their own thoughts. No one spoke, but it wasn't an uncomfortable quiet.

After Herb's return, Lois had wrapped the reincarnated vampire up in a hug so fierce, Herb complained about her trying to squeeze him to death right after he'd come back. When she finally released him, Stanley took her place. Blubbering sobs wracked his wiry frame as he clung to his friend. Herb patted him on the back affectionately, muttered nothings, and told Stanley everything was fine, just fine, and thanked him for being such a great friend.

Then it was Dallas's turn. He knew he was supposed to say something, do something, but couldn't for the life of him figure out what. So finally, he just stuck out a hand.

"Welcome back, buddy. I'm sorry about everything, but I'm damn glad you're back."

"Me, too," Herb replied, grasping the offered hand. "Me, too."

Now the four sat in a loose circle, Dallas and Stanley drinking a couple of beers while Herb and Lois drank in each other's closeness.

When Dallas spoke, he asked the question everyone was thinking while trying equally hard to not think.

"So," he started. "Now what?"

Herb looked up from Lois's eyes. "I suppose maybe I could go back to work at Ronnie's. You know, explain everything and see if I could pick up the night shift again."

"The K-king Pins are back together!" Stanley yammered. "We'll get back in the league and w-win the tourney again." His smile magnified when Herb offered a hearty thumbs up.

"We should go find Kevin, too," Herb suggested. "I'll bet he'd love bowling. Might be hard to find big enough shoes, though."

Dallas looked at Lois.

I reckon it's my job to burst the bubble? he thought.

When Lois dropped her eyes and turned her head away, he knew the answer.

"Sorry, compadres. I'm not sure a happy ending is part of this particular massage. Herb, the sheriff still thinks you're guilty of all those murders. Like it or not, they're right, too. The first guy, definitely, and even if you could prove that Helen did the other girl and those frat boys in before frying herself, you'd be an accomplice, at least."

Pounding a fist on his knee, Dallas continued the litany of their misfortunes.

"Eventually, someone's going to notice Fancy Dan's gone missing. I think we covered our tracks, but even the smallest clue puts me squarely in the 'Trappersville's Most Wanted' category. Local law enforcement aside, there are also a couple of folks in particular that are going to come looking for Randall. What do we do when the Society shows up?"

The quiet returned, but this time it wasn't nearly as comfortable as before. When no one spoke, Dallas raised his voice again.

"I think Kevin had the right idea. We should run. All of us. We can head up to Michigan, or even Canada. Fake our deaths here, maybe, and get a fresh start with new identities."

Stanley brightened. "Oh, yeah. Like in *Murder, She Wrote*, season eleven, episode fifteen. *T-twice Dead.* You know, when everyone thinks Max is dead?"

"Uh, sure. Yeah, I suppose just like that," Dallas conceded, attempting to prevent Stanley from describing not just the entire episode, but also the ones before and after to provide context.

"So? What do you think? Pack tonight, tie up loose ends tomorrow, and hit the road?" he asked.

Lois shook her head. "Even if we did want to run, the sun rises in a couple of hours, and tomorrow night's the full moon, remember? Herb can't travel during the day, and how far could you get tomorrow night before you turn?"

Her good point did a pretty solid job of ruining his already not-so-great mood.

"Well? What's Plan B?" he asked, exasperated. "Ride out the weekend, hope the Society doesn't pop in, and then blow this Popsicle stand in a few days? Risky, but maybe the better way to go."

"Guys, we can just stay here. In Trappersville. No need to run, no need to hide. You're forgetting an important detail. I," Herb said, dramatically, "can whammy people."

Lois lit up like a Christmas tree, and Stanley clapped.

"Th-that's right!" he crowed. "You can whammy 'em. Ronnie and the sheriff and the guys at b-bowling and Rhonda and Jasper and P-pam and Stein and,"

"Okay, Stanley! We get it, already." Dallas cut in. "Well, Herb? You think you got the juice to whammy half the town?"

Herb sat back with a thoughtful look in his eyes. "I dunno. I suppose, if I could get them in one or two at a time."

"I can help with a spell," Lois added. "Like, a temporary amnesia spell. We get a bunch of folks together. I cast the spell, and then Herb can work the crowd and whammy them." Her eyes pleaded with Dallas. "It could work. We could stay, and everything could be okay again."

Suddenly, Dallas found himself at the center of three sets of imploring eyes, all seeking his approval.

Well? What would the harm be? We're just erasing a couple hundred folks' memories and replacing them. That ain't so bad, is it? Hell, I bet the government does it every day.

"Deal. Lois does the witchy stuff, Herb does the whammy stuff, and we stay. Trappersville is our home, after all. Even if we don't all quite fit the mold, we still belong here as much as the next monster. That doesn't solve the Society problem though. I mean, I guess there's a chance we could catch Colton and Aletia off-guard and whammy them, too, but something tells me they won't be that easy to take down."

And do I really want to mind-bend Aletia? he wondered. The townsfolk were one thing, but messing with Tia's memories gave Dallas a bad feeling.

"If they show up," Lois started.

"When," Dallas interjected.

"Fine. When they show up, I guess we'll just have to deal," she finished. "But tonight I don't want to think about it. Let's just let tonight be tonight. Okay?"

Pushing down his rising anxiety, Dallas raised his beer. "I'll drink to that," he toasted.

After Herb, Lois, and Stanley had all left, Dallas lay awake in bed for a long time. Tonight was tonight, but tomorrow he'd be a werewolf again. He just hoped that Colton and Aletia were taking the scenic route.

Chapter 37

"**B**UENOS DIAS, STRANGER."

Dallas stood in his boxer shorts, mouth agape.

"Aletia? What are you doing here?"

She slid up to him, placed one palm on his bare chest, and the other some place much more intimate.

"Oh," she pouted. "And here I thought you'd be happy to see me." Kissing his still open mouth, she looked up into his wide eyes.

"You are happy to see me, aren't you?"

Dallas tried to recover, failed miserably, and tried again.

"What? Oh, yeah. Yes! I just, I... well, I thought you guys were 'squatch hunting up in Canada or something. I just wasn't expecting you. Here. Today."

On the morning of the night that I turn into a goddamn werewolf, he thought.

Aletia slid past him into his living room and settled into the couch.

"We were. Trail went cold, so we split up. Colton and I continued north, and Randall circled back in case we missed something. We thought he'd swing through town and check in with you. Guess not, huh?"

"Who?" Dallas fumbled. "Oh, right. Randall. Ah, no. Nope. Haven't seen him since you guys left town. A, you know, month ago."

Aletia rolled her eyes. "El es un idiota. We told him to come to you for help. Don't feel bad though. He knows you're a good hunter. He just takes a while to warm up to newbies. Especially when the newbie happens to be tall, dark, handsome, and pretty much naked," she added with a wink.

Still standing in the open doorway and wearing nothing but a pair of boxers and a look bordering on panic, Dallas tried to think of what to say. When Aletia stood up, slipped off her jacket, pulled her tee-shirt over her head, and slid her skin-tight jeans down to the floor, he decided that saying things wasn't really necessary at that exact moment in time. Closing the door, he let Aletia tackle him.

Later, Dallas lay on his back with Aletia's head pillowed on his outstretched arm. While her hand traced lazy circles on his stomach and her foot rubbed playfully against his, he watched the slow creep of a ray of sunlight across the far wall. Like a countdown timer to the end of the world, the sun tracked west across the sky with the full moon nipping at its heels.

"Mmmmm," she moaned. "That's more like it. Just promise me you don't greet all the girls this way."

"Just you, babe. Just you," he sighed.

Her fingers stopped their listless doodles, and she propped herself up on an elbow.

"Que pasa? You seem a little far away. Are you okay?" she asked, eyes searching his face.

Turning his head, he looked into her dark eyes. Breathing in the scent of her, basking in the warmth of her, he tried again to think of what he could do, what he could say, how he could explain any of the things that had happened the past month and have her not instantly shoot him with a silver bullet.

"You never told me why you joined the Society," he finally said. "What made you want to do it?"

Aletia lay back on the mattress, situating the sheet across her waist and folding her hands carefully on her stomach. For a few moments she just lay there, eyes staring past the ceiling far into her past.

"You have a right to know, and I don't want you thinking I'm hiding things from you. It's just not that easy to talk about, you know? And I'm not entirely sure where to start."

"Maybe at the beginning?" Dallas suggested softly.

"Maybe after breakfast," she replied with a smile. "I'm starving."

When Dallas stepped into Ronnie's, he wasn't expecting to see Lois. As the waitress and Aletia locked eyes, the air practically crackled with mutual hostility.

Dallas grit his teeth in frustration. He'd been certain Lois would be with Herb, not working.

Except it's the daytime, dummy. Herb's sleeping.

Hastening to avoid a replay of their first encounter, he grabbed Aletia's arm and whispered urgently, "Just give me a second to explain."

The momentary warmth he'd felt walking in from the cool October air froze under the hunter's icy stare, but she held her tongue. Walking her over to a booth as far from the other patrons as possible, he sat and studiously picked up a menu.

"One," Aletia said, voice edged with frost.

"Really? I mean, it's good, but not a lot of food. Just eggs and hash browns. I usually go for the number three myself, unless I'm in the mood for eggs benedict," Dallas commented, all innocence.

"No, it's been one second. Now explain."

Mentally slapping himself in the forehead, Dallas tried on his most disarming smile, the one he usually reserved for girls that asked when he'd last been tested for STDs.

"I told you. Lois and I talked, and that witchy stuff was just a phase. I set her straight, and we're all good. No need to make a scene."

Aletia looked less than convinced, but didn't challenge him. Heaving a huge mental sigh, Dallas tried to figure out what to do. Colton hadn't popped up yet, but he had to be in town. To make matters worse, there was a big full moon on deck to ruin his charade. But did it really have to be a charade? There was no denying that he and Aletia had something. Maybe if he just talked to her, told her the truth, she'd understand. It had worked for Herb and Lois in a weird kind of way, hadn't it?

It's not like I'm always a werewolf. Just a few days a month. No reason for that to spoil a good thing, right?

Before he could put any more thought into the matter, Lois arrived at their table.

"Hi Dallas, and um. Dallas's friend. I don't think we were properly introduced the first time we met. I'm Lois," she offered, holding her order pad and wearing a smile that almost masked her panic, but not quite.

"Aletia," the hunter said with a thinly painted smile of her own. "Dallas said you two talked over a few things after we... met. I'm glad to hear you've moved past your experimental phase."

Lois laughed a high, brittle laugh. "Oh. Right. Yeah. Gosh, I just feel so silly about the whole thing. Dallas, though. He's such a great guy. Really helped."

Gulping, Lois tapped her pen nervously on her notepad. "So, um. You two ready to order?"

While Aletia dictated her order in a tone crispier than burnt hash browns, Dallas tried to ignore the gallon of water under each armpit. He also tried to ignore his hunger. Over the past few weeks, he'd been consuming a staggering amount of food. Now, sitting in Ronnie's with the smell of meat all around him, the unnaturalness of his hunger became glaringly apparent. He didn't want the number three or the eggs benedict. He wanted everything on the menu.

"Dallas?" Lois asked.

"Oh, yeah. Me. Um."

Better keep it light. Restraint, old boy. Show some restraint, and you'll get through this just fine.

"I'll get the ham and eggs, steak and eggs, both with hash browns and white toast nice and soggy, a side of sausage links, and a short stack of pancakes. And, um. Bacon. Two sides," he rattled off.

Aletia and Lois just stared. Realizing his definition of 'light' might be a bit heavier than it should be, he buried his face in the menu to hide his blush.

"Hungry," he managed by way of explanation.

After Lois had walked off to place their orders, Aletia raised an eyebrow.

"Guess you worked up an appetite this morning," she commented coyly. "You okay with me taking credit for that?"

Relief flooding through him, he grabbed the offered life preserver and winked.

"Absolutely. You certainly know how to help a guy burn calories."

While waiting for their food, Aletia talked a bit about their trek north following the Sasquatch. Dallas peppered in questions about whether Canadians always ate their French fries with gravy and if she was going to start ending all of her questions with 'eh.' The tension that had thickened the air when they first arrived slowly eased, and Dallas let himself believe, if just for a moment, that there was nothing to worry about. It was a short-lived fantasy, though. When their food arrived, Aletia grabbed Lois's wrist as she set down a plate.

"Do I need to worry about what's in this?" she snapped, glaring up at Lois.

Lois yanked her hand back and huffed. Using Dallas's fork, she speared a hunk of eggs off of Aletia's plate, stuffed it in her mouth, and chewed pointedly.

"One-hundred percent *spell*-free eggs. Enjoy your breakfast," she shot back before stomping off to the kitchen.

"Was that really necessary?" Dallas asked. "I said there was nothing to worry about."

Aletia grimaced uncomfortably. "Lo siento, Dallas. What can I say? I have trust issues." She took a bite and chewed thoughtfully. "At least the food is good here."

Chapter 38

BACK AT DALLAS'S PLACE, the two relaxed on the couch. Aletia patted her stomach appreciatively and groaned with pleasure.

"That really was a good breakfast," she sighed. "Sometimes, we end up in towns where the best thing to eat is the leather belt you brought with. Not Ronnie's, though. I can see why it's famous. Yummy and filling." Poking Dallas in the stomach, she added, "Por Dios, you must be stuffed. Even Colton doesn't eat that much."

"Oh, yeah. Well, man's gotta eat and um, yeah. I'm fit to burst," he laughed, inwardly praying that he'd get a chance to grab some more food when she wasn't looking. "Speaking of Colton, where's he at? If you're here, he can't be far behind, right?"

"Poking around town. He was going to try and track down Randall. We didn't get a chance to teach you everything, but Society members have a sort of secret code. We're pretty good about leaving info and clues for other hunters. If Randall came this way, Colton will turn up sign of him soon enough. We're going to rendezvous at the cabin later tonight. Plenty of time for us to enjoy ourselves until then. That is, if you aren't too full," she offered, stretching her legs across his lap.

Dallas wasn't too full by any stretch of the imagination, and he wanted to enjoy himself. He really, really did. Unfortunately, he also really wanted to come clean. He'd tell her he was a werewolf, that it happened by accident, and that it was only for a few days a month. Otherwise, he was completely human. No big deal, right? She'd understand, and everything would be okay.

"Aletia," he started after rubbing his sweaty palms on his pants. "We should probably, you know. Talk about a few things."

She sighed, nodding her head.

"Yeah, you're right. I can't put it off forever. Grab me a beer, and I'll tell you why I joined the Society."

While it wasn't exactly the topic Dallas had in mind, he figured it'd be a good place to start. When Dallas returned with the beer, Aletia wasn't nearly as relaxed as she'd been a minute before. Instead of stretching languidly across the cushions, she sat up straight, feet firmly planted on the floor, and hands on her thighs. Taking the beer, she took a long, introspective drink and began her story.

"I grew up in southern Mexico, but moved to Oregon when I was thirteen. Papa was a professor, and he'd accepted a position teaching international studies at Southern Oregon University. I was sixteen years old when he ended up in the hospital. The doctors told mom it was a dog bite or maybe a coyote. He'd been teaching a night course and was attacked in the parking lot after class. A couple of his students found him and called an ambulance. The entire way to the hospital, Papa was raving, completamente loco. First, he swore he'd been attacked by a giant wolf. Then he said it was just a really hairy crazy guy. The doctors doped him up with sedatives, but they weren't working. He was still raving when we got there. I remember watching him and thinking it was the scariest thing in the world. I hadn't seen anything yet."

Aletia took another drink of beer, giving Dallas's whirling mind a second to catch up.

Her dad was bit by a werewolf? What are the frickin' odds?

He didn't have much time to ponder the implications, though, because Aletia wasn't done.

"Papa spent one night in the hospital. Just one. The next morning, Mama and I showed up, and he was fine. Completely, totally fine. The bite that a night before looked like it was bare centimeters from ripping his arm off at the elbow was just a lightly puckered scar. His mania was gone, and he was cool as a cucumber. When Mama asked him about being attacked, he shrugged and said he really couldn't remember the details that well and that the doctors were probably right. Just a dog. Maybe a coyote. He didn't have rabies, and since his wound wasn't as bad as they thought..."

For a moment, Aletia stared at her beer can. A sharp laugh escaped her lips.

"Wasn't as bad. Increíble. That was the understatement of the century, but I was the only one that seemed concerned about that point. He was discharged, and we all went home. About a month later, I was making out with my boyfriend Jason in the back of his Pontiac and starting to freak out about being out past curfew. It was such a beautiful night, though. Completamente romántica, with a full moon and everything. Eventually, I convinced him that I really should go home. When we got to my house, we found the parts of Mama that Papa hadn't eaten. I was holding Mama's head in my hands when Papa attacked. Jason managed to fight Papa off, and we ran. The local high school was nearby, so we hid in the equipment shed."

Aletia sighed and sat quietly. Dallas was about to ask what happened next when she took a deliberate breath, shook her head, and continued.

"Jason showed me the bite on his shoulder, and I did the best I could to clean it and bandage it. He raved and ranted all night. The next day, he was fine. That night, when the full moon rose again, I was ready. I cut off his head with a gas-powered hedge trimmer and then hunted down Papa. It was a hard fight, but I won."

Aletia's eyes stared hard at the floor. "I killed them. When I was sixteen years old, I killed my boyfriend and my father with a hedge trimmer."

Aletia finished her beer and set the can carefully on the coffee table.

"Need another?" Dallas asked quietly.

Aletia shook her head as a yawn stretched her full lips in a wide 'O.'

"No. I can barely keep my eyes open."

Fidgeting, Dallas asked, "So what did you do? After your dad, I mean." Seeing tears well up in her eyes, he backpedaled. "Never mind, it doesn't matter."

Wiping ineffectually at the tears, she sighed.

"It's okay. I promised you the story, so you're getting the whole story. To answer your question, I ran. Since I had nowhere to go, I came back. I knew that no one would believe that Papa and Jason were werewolves, so I hid. For close to a month, I slept huddled in alleyways, ate out of dumpsters, and tried to find the courage to kill myself. It was just dumb luck that the Society had sent a new hunter to investigate the possible werewolf attacks. Even luckier that Colton found me, ragged and half-mad, and had the heart and the patience to clean me up and straighten me out."

Another yawn pulled her out of her story for a moment. Dallas took advantage of the ensuing quiet to give a slow whistle.

"Aletia, I'm so sorry. I can't imagine what that must've been like."

She looked up and wiped ineffectively at the tear tracks streaking down her cheeks.

"I think you can, mi amor." She placed a hand on his cheek. At first, he thought he was feeling the tears on her fingers. As her thumb stroked his skin, he realized she was pushing away his own.

Hand sliding down his face, her arm fell back to her side. Confused, Dallas watched her eyelids droop and close. She settled back heavily into the couch cushions, and her chin dropped down toward her chest. A moment passed, and she was sound asleep.

"Aletia?" he asked, gently shaking her arm. "Hey Tia? You okay?"

"Geez. That took long enough," a familiar voice said, scaring the crap out of Dallas.

Leaping from the couch, he spun to see Lois's face poking in through the front door.

"I lied about the eggs," she explained with a shrug.

Stomping over, he yanked the door open and loomed over Lois.

"You cast a spell on her? Balls on a badger! Why in the hell would you cast a spell on her?"

In response, Lois shoved a finger into his chest.

"Why in the hell would you bring your murdering girlfriend to Ronnie's? Why in the hell would you bring her anywhere? Why in the hell aren't you doing everything in your power to get her out of here? Or warning me and Herb so *we* can get the hell out of here?"

"I was going to tell her the truth," he sputtered in response to her fury. "About me. I think she'll understand. Like you and Herb, you know? Me and Tia, maybe we can work it out."

For the second time in as many minutes, an unexpected voice scared the crap out of Dallas.

"No. You won't," Colton said, and then everything went dark.

Chapter 39

D ALLAS CAME TO AND was instantly annoyed.

What good is having super hearing if these guys can keep sneaking up on me?

Wits coalescing around that particular thought, he decided to give himself a pass. He had been thoroughly distracted by Lois's arrival and not really paying attention to much else.

Lois! Oh, crappers, did he get Lois, too?

Turning his head, he was overcome with nausea and suddenly gave back most of his breakfast. Long after the contents of his stomach had been artlessly deposited on the floor beside him, Dallas continued to dry heave.

"Hang in there, Dallas," he heard Lois say, her voice as raw as his throat felt. "I think it's a side effect of whatever he used to knock us out. It should pass in a minute or two."

Thank god she's okay, he thought. *Except she's here, which means she's probably not gonna be okay.*

Opening his eyes again, he saw Lois bound and slumped against a nearby wall. At least she still had her clothes on. Dallas wasn't so lucky. He'd been stripped down to his boxers. A quick look around confirmed what he'd already smelled. They were in the cabin in the woods. Colton and Aletia were nowhere to be seen. Just him and Lois, tied in heavy coils of sturdy rope.

"Feels like a class-five hangover. Lucky for me, I've had worse. Gimme a sec, and I'll be right as rain," Dallas grumbled. Taking a series of deep breaths, he shoved his brain into 'ya gotta work, even if you'd rather curl up and die' mode.

"Okay. I'm good," he said after a throaty belch. "What happened back there? How'd he get the drop on us, and why am I in my birthday suit?"

Lois shrugged, or at least tried to. Her restraints didn't leave a lot for freedom of movement.

"Your buddy Colton is a professional monster hunter. Guess he had a few tricks up his sleeve we weren't expecting. As for the you being almost naked part, I have no idea. I'd ask him, but they took off about fifteen minutes ago in his truck. God, I really hope Stanley and Herb are okay."

Dallas groaned. Nothing, not a single thing, was going as planned. It really pissed him off, even though there wasn't much of a plan to begin with. Shifting his posture, he started to flex against the ropes.

"Well, nothing to worry about. Big D is here, and we know from recent experience that a few ropes aren't a problem. Colton might think he knows what's what, but he doesn't know jack about old Dallas."

Squirming and flexing, Dallas let himself get caught up in his building rant. It felt good to finally have an outlet for the simmering rage.

"What Colton didn't bank on was that nothing—nothing!—can keep this wolf down. Not a sneak attack or a sucker punch or

taking my clothes and sure as badger shit not a bunch of ro...
aaaaaaAAAAARRRRGGHH!"

The pain scorched deep across his skin and caused him to contort
and flop over on his side. Unfortunately, that just made things worse.
It was like someone had set the ropes on fire. Gasping in shock, he tried
to figure out just what the hell was happening.

"Dallas! Stop! There's a padlocked silver chain wound in with your
ropes. I can see it now. You must've pushed it up against your skin. Try
to stop moving. See if you can get the ropes between you and the silver
again," she advised.

He heard her, but it was really hard to concentrate on her words.
The pain scoring his arms and chest turned his brain into a whimpering pile of jelly. Flopping like a beached bluegill, he twisted and shook,
every movement a dance of agony.

Calm down! Get a hold of yourself, he thought frantically.

By sheer force of will, he stilled his spasms and tremors until he
lay completely still. He could feel each link of silver burning into his
flesh, but by opening himself up to the pain, he was able to accept it
and move past it. After a few deep, controlled breaths, the burning
felt more like nuked Cheez Whiz on his skin instead of molten lava.
Moving gingerly, he shifted his center of gravity and pushed himself
back into a sitting position. Once upright, he started to shrug his
shoulders and wiggle his arms. As he'd hoped, the silver chain wasn't
bound tight like the ropes. They must've figured the pain of contact
with his skin would be enough to keep him in line.

Damn near did, too, except that I'm a frickin' badass, he thought,
his grimace becoming a rictus grin.

As he shifted and hitched his shoulders, the looser links of silver slipped over the coils of rope. When the various sections left his skin, the burning sensation abruptly stopped. After a minute or so, Dallas felt less like a flame broiled Whopper and more like a really pissed off guy tied up and dumped in a busted down cabin in the woods.

"Aaaahhhh," he sighed in relief. "Better. Much better, except I don't think I'll be busting the ropes anytime soon. Sorry, but our escape plan now hinges exclusively on you. Time to do something witchy!"

"Can't," Lois replied tersely.

"Whadaya mean? Don't you have, I don't know, like a, 'Tony Danza was the boss, turn these ropes to dental floss,' spell or something?"

Lois shook her head sadly. "I tried a few spells. There aren't many that can be done just with words. Most need some type of gesture or special herbs or artifacts. There are a few though, and I tried every one I know. Nothing happened. I'm guessing the ropes they used on me are enchanted."

"So we're stuck," Dallas muttered in frustration. "Fan-frickin-tas-tic."

"What do you think they'll do, Dallas? I mean, they wouldn't just kill us right here, would they?"

Dallas levelled a look at Lois that conveyed his utter helplessness. "I think that's exactly what they'll do. And lucky us, we won't have to wait around long for the fun. I can hear Colton's truck."

Dallas's sensitive ears had picked up the telltale rumble of the old pickup truck. Soon, it was loud enough for Lois to hear, and they both looked anxiously toward the cabin's door. When the truck arrived, Dallas's ears picked up another noise, the sound of Stanley's scared and stuttering voice. A moment later, Colton shoved Stanley roughly into the cabin. Kicking out his legs, he dumped Stanley down next to Lois.

"The gang's all here," Colton announced. "Come on in, Tia. Let's get this sorted out."

Dallas turned to watch Aletia walk through the door. Every muscle was tensed, and the look she gave him could've set ice water to an instant boil.

"Si, Dallas," she said, voice brittle with barely contained anger. "Let's talk. Where to start? With you lying to me? Or with you having your bruja girlfriend cast a sleeping spell on me?"

"She's not my girlfriend!" Dallas protested. "I told you, she's my buddy Herb's girlfriend. There's nothing going on with me and Lois!"

If he hadn't been naked, tied up, pissed off, and scared stupid, he might've thought Lois and Aletia rolling their eyes in unison was a bit funny. Instead, it just tipped his scared-to-pissed ratio a little further toward pissed.

"What? It's true. Lois, tell her. You and Herb are a thing. We're just friends."

"Herb? El vampiro muerto?" Aletia asked in shock. "Girl, you've got some serious issues if you still consider yourself romantically involved with a pile of ash."

Before Lois could say anything back, Colton cleared his throat.

"Let's all just take it down a notch, and Stanley, please stop. Your crying is one of the weirdest sounds I've ever heard. You sound like a baby seal with a nasty head cold."

Stanley choked back his sobs and managed to get them down to scared whimpers. Nodding with satisfaction, Colton continued.

"Thanks, Stanley. Much appreciated. Now, Dallas. There seems to be a bit of a conflict of interests here. You're a member of the Society. Ancient order of monster hunters, if you recall. You also, by my reckoning, aided and abetted a Sasquatch, are actively consorting with a witch, and murdered one of your sworn brethren. On top of all that, you're a werewolf."

"We're not consorting! Tits on a tortoise. What do I have to do to convince you guys me and Lois ain't a thing? Tia, you're the only girl I want, believe me."

Aletia looked away, and Colton laughed a sharp, mirthless laugh.

"Of all the things I just said... Okay, Dallas. Let me spell it out in crayon for you. Consorting means associating with. As in, you're hanging out with a witch, not tying-to-a-stake-and-burning a witch. A definite no-no by most *human* standards. That really gets us to the heart of the problem, though. You aren't human."

Dallas glowered. "What tipped you off? Did I forget to hide the flea powder?"

A bullet appeared in Colton's hand as if by magic. Stepping forward, he pressed it into Dallas's bare shoulder. Dallas cried out in pain and twisted to try and get away from the burning metal.

"Well, there's a nice bit of proof. Although honestly, Randall told me. Well, not directly. Aletia said she told you how the Society has a system for leaving messages for other hunters. Randall was many things, but first and foremost, he was a damn good hunter. It didn't take long to find his trail and turn up some interesting tidbits about you."

Pulling the lump of silver away from Dallas's shoulder, Colton squatted down on his heels and searched Dallas's face.

"I'm guessing you killed him, otherwise he'd be here instead of you. Really wish you hadn't, but that'll happen. No one said being a hunter was the safest way to spend your time. I also know you two weren't exactly sweet on each other. What I can't wrap my mind around is why you were planning to kill Aletia. If you'd shifted, I'd get it. One can't expect a monster to behave humanely. But for you and the witch to lure her in like you did today and knock her out so you could have her as a late-night snack after the moon rose..." Colton looked up at Aletia and back to Dallas, genuine amazement plain in his face.

"Dammit, Dallas," he snapped, voice thick with sudden emotion. "That girl thinks the world of you."

"Thought," Aletia corrected. "Won't make that mistake again."

Dallas's eyes went wide. "What the hell? You think I planned this? Aletia, I would never hurt you. I wanted to tell you what I was. I was going to tell you, and the spell wasn't my idea," he added with a dark glance at Lois. "But you gotta believe me. I thought that if I told you I was a werewolf, maybe... I don't know. Maybe you'd understand, and we could, you know. Figure something out because I think the world of you, too," he finished.

For a long moment, Aletia and Dallas looked into each other's eyes. For a long moment, Dallas knew that everything would be okay. The moment abruptly ended when Aletia turned back to Colton and said, "How long 'til moonrise so I can cut his head off?"

Chapter 40

*L*ET ME OUT. *I need to be out. Let me out.*

Dallas fidgeted, shifted, squirmed. He could feel the moon coming. He felt it in his molars, in his toes, in each and every follicle on each and every square inch of skin. The sun was a fading orange light pushing shadows down the walls and across the floor. Every second, the shadows lengthened, deepened, and took back what was rightfully theirs inch by slow inch.

The impending full moon filled his brain. It was a strange thought, one that Dallas had to work his mind around more than a few times. Since forever, the full moon was just a thing. Nothing special, nothing worth getting all excited about. Not once in his life had he ever stopped to consider the coming of the moon. The opening kickoff for a big game, sure. Fourth of July or New Year's Eve, sure. The Trappersville Men's Bowling Tournament, abso-frickin-lutely. But the full moon? Who cared? Who would upend their entire life in preparation for that?

Werewolves, Dallas thought woefully. *Lucky us.*

Sitting on the cabin floor, he took small solace in the fact that it wasn't a worry he'd have after tonight. Aletia had produced something that could either be pegged as a short sword or really long knife. It was slender, double-edged, and reeked of silver. As the final seconds of his life ticked away, he knew with a cold certainty that the moon would rise, he'd turn, Aletia would separate his big, wolfy head from his thick, wolfy neck, and it'd be so-long Dallas.

Strangely, he wasn't worried about dying. What worried him were the distinctive smells coming from outside the cabin. Fresh-cut wood, saw dust, gasoline. He knew that the obstacles and fake monsters he'd trained with were being converted into kindling for a nice, toasty bonfire. Colton and Aletia hadn't been shy about their plans. After he turned and was put down, Lois would be burned at the stake.

When Colton had articulated the simple plan, Dallas had gone into a rage. The burning strands of silver woven in with his ropes kept his rage contained, but only exhaustion had finally brought it to a seething end. Panting, he managed to ask about Stanley.

"We'll have to see," Colton had said without a hint of rancor. "Honestly, he doesn't really have a lot of value as a member of the Society. Sorry, Stanley."

In response, Stanley had erupted into a fresh round of sobs. Shaking his head, Colton continued.

"The trouble is, he's human. We're not murderers, so we're not going to kill him, but he is mixed up with the wrong crowd. We'll have to figure out some way to set him back on the right path."

"Lois is human," Dallas had grunted.

Colton clicked his tongue and wagged a finger in response.

"No, Lois is a witch. That's different. Speaking of, I'd best get the fire pit ready."

Out. I need to be out. Let me out.

The shadows won. Every scrap of sunlight wiped away, the new-born night filled the small cabin. Heart racing, muscles tensed, Dallas felt the change coming, felt it crawling and carving its way through the dark straight for him.

"Colton!" Aletia called out. "It's starting."

As if given permission by her words, Dallas felt the now-familiar pain in his gut. A pitchfork twisting his intestines like spaghetti noodles, a jackhammer in his stomach, a wolf clawing its way from the inside out. Dallas writhed in agony as the change shoved its way through him. As he stretched and contorted and swelled, the ropes that bound him creaked, and the silver chain burned hard against his skin.

Wracked with waved after wave of agony, his convulsions grew more violent. Flailing and slamming his way around the floor, he bucked and kicked and banged his head against the wooden boards. Muzzle stretched unnaturally wide and lengthening teeth bared, he screamed and spat, cursed and howled.

Out! Let me out!

"Colton!" he heard Aletia yell again.

"Got it," Colton yelled back as he burst in through the cabin door. "We'll wait until he's fully turned, then I'll hold him down."

Aletia. No! Please, no! You don't have to do this!

Dallas tried to speak, but even if his altered mouth could still make human words, the pain of the change and the burning silver would only allow sounds of anguish and torment. When the change finished, the number of separate agonies quickly dwindled until the only suffering left was the burning silver twined with a deep sadness. Dallas ceased his thrashing and lay still. His eyes roamed and finally found

Aletia. A soft moan escaped his lips, and his yellowed claws scratched feebly at the floor.

Please. Please don't, a small, frightened part of him whimpered. *I love you. I love you.*

Colton stepped in front of Aletia. He held a long pole with a metal semi-circle at the end that reeked of silver. When he jabbed it down across Dallas's neck, it burned with such ferocity that Dallas couldn't even draw a breath. Every muscle went rigid, and he tasted blood where his jaws clamped down on his tongue. Eyes wide, he saw Aletia step closer and raise the long knife.

I'm sorry, he thought. *For all of it. Herb, Lois, Dan, Randall, Aletia. I'm sorry. I'm so goddamn sorry.*

When the bowling ball hit Colton in the chest, it knocked him back with such force that he flew a good ten feet across the cabin.

"Strike!" Herb cried.

Suddenly free of the silver collar, Dallas twisted on impulse and felt the silver blade's tip score a deep cut across the back of his shoulders. Aletia had time to swear and pull the blade free from the wooden floorboard before a blurred shadow knocked her aside.

Dallas was still trying to figure out just what the hell was happening when Herb materialized at his side.

"Sorry to cut it so close," Herb said. "I knew Lois was in trouble, but I couldn't leave the house until sundown. Also, I lost a little time trying to decide if I should drive here or run."

Dallas grunted.

"Well, I couldn't find Lois's keys, so I ran."

Another grunt, this one edged with frustration.

"Right. One sec, fuzzy buddy," Herb replied while grasping the ropes that bound Dallas tight. Stretching them taut, the ropes split. Next, Herb snapped the padlock and carefully unwound the silver chain.

"Okey doke. That oughta do it," Herb proclaimed with satisfaction.

Dallas rose up to his full height and howled. Stretching his limbs and craning his neck, he reveled in his newfound freedom. Heavy, lumbering steps carried him to where the roof had caved in. Looking up at the newly risen moon, he opened his muzzle to howl again.

"I understand, but now's not really the best time for moonlight serenades," Herb advised. "Can you hold them off while I get Lois and Stanley?"

Turning, Dallas looked at his unexpected savior. Vampire Herb practically glowed in his altered vision. Shocks of red hair jutted in every direction, eyes shone with an inner radiance, and long, pearlescent fangs glowed in the moonlight. His bowling jersey billowed dramatically like a red-trimmed cloak in the wind. Seeing him made Dallas's heart swell. Nodding his massive head, he stomped over to where Colton lay massaging his chest and trying to regain his breath.

Squatting down, he brought his bared teeth to within inches of Colton's face. Nostrils snuffed as a deep growl rumbled up from inside, and saliva dripped from his muzzle onto the front of the man's shirt.

You're meat. Nothing but meat, and I'm hungry, Dallas said, words coming out as menacing chuffs.

The shot split the air, leaving a painful ringing in Dallas's ears and a burning hole in his gut. Staggering back, he saw Colton raise the pistol and ready a second shot. Dallas batted the gun aside and leaned in to bite off the man's arm when a fresh pain erupted in his shoulder.

With a roar, he twisted to pull the knife free and turned to confront the new threat. Aletia crouched a few feet behind him, a second knife in her hand. Her calculating eyes shifted restlessly from Dallas to Colton to the silver short sword a few yards away. He saw the decision in her eyes, grabbed Colton, and pulled him in a quick arc just as the knife flew from Aletia's hand. This time, it was Colton screaming in pain as the knife buried itself in the back of his shoulder.

"Dammit, Aletia!" he cursed.

"What?" she shot back. "He's faster than I expected."

Dallas shoved Colton aside, and the three combatants squared off. Colton grunted and strained as he reached for the knife while Aletia took slow, deliberate steps toward the silver sword. Dallas watched them both carefully, trying to quell the maelstrom raging inside.

Kill, the beast demanded.

No, he shoved back.

Colton pulled the knife free and dropped into a half-crouch. Still, Dallas watched, his inner struggle freezing his muscles with indecision.

"I got 'em, Dallas!" Herb yelled, triumphant. "C'mon. Let's go!"

He cocked his head and saw Herb standing protectively in front of Lois and Stanley, the trio inching their way toward the door.

"You're not going anywhere," Colton growled back. "You're dead. You're all dead."

Dallas stepped sideways and placed himself squarely between Aletia and the silver sword.

No, he woofed with finality. *This ends here, now.*

"Dallas says it's over," Herb translated. "We don't want any trouble. We just want to live our lives. Why can't you people understand that?"

Aletia glared at Herb. "So you're the vampiro boyfriend, huh? Everyone said you were toast. Another lie from your werewolf pal. Where've you been hiding all this time?"

"Dallas didn't lie to you. He killed me. I was dead," Herb explained. "But Lois brought me back."

"Why?" Aletia questioned, aghast. "What possible reason could you have to bring back a vampiro?"

Love, Dallas grunted.

"Love," Herb translated.

"Love," Lois agreed. "And despite all of Dallas's not inconsiderable faults, he really does love you, Aletia. That has to be worth something, right?"

Aletia looked at the hairy, hulking monster Dallas had become with the rising of the full moon. Dropping to his haunches, he offered a soft whine and playful bark. Despite Colton's curses and objections, Aletia reached out a hand, fingers trembling, and Dallas accepted the invitation. Snuffling her palm with his wide nose, he dipped his head and positioned an ear directly beneath her fingers.

"You've got to be kidding me," she whispered, fingers twitching in a hesitant scratch. "Are you really in there, Dallas?"

I'm here, he woofed.

"He's here," Herb said. "It's Dallas. I mean, not like the old Dallas, but you know, people change."

"You aren't people!" Colton screamed, brandishing a crucifix and lunging at Herb. As the vampire hissed and recoiled, Colton dove, rolled, and came up with the silver sword. He pivoted and brought his arm down in a wide, desperate arc.

Dallas felt the blade sink deep into his hairy shoulder, cutting through skin, muscle, and the thin shred of control he had on the wolf inside. A clawed hand shot out, and Colton's neck erupted in a spray of red. Heavy jaws clamped down on the man's head and crushed his skull. Colton's body convulsed, its spasms turning the spurts of blood into geysers.

"Colton!" Aletia cried. "Dallas! No!"

Her voice cut deeper than the silver blade, all the way to Dallas's heart. Dropping the very dead Colton, he turned his gore-soaked face to look at Aletia.

"He was right, he was right." Aletia's eyes brimmed with terror and fury, and her voice trembled. "You aren't people. You're monsters. Damn monsters."

Giving Dallas a final, long look, she turned and sprinted for the door.

Herb moved to chase her, but Dallas pulled him back and shook his head.

It was over.

The Final Chapter

WHERE DO WEREWOLVES GO when they don't want to cause any more pain?

Dallas climbed a small rise and looked down on the trees below. Northern Michigan's Huron Mountains were a rugged change from Wisconsin's gentle hills and temperate forests. The oaks, hickories, maples, and beech he was more accustomed to had given way to pines and spruces. The hardwood trees were still there, remaining leaves burning gold, orange, and red in the setting sun, but more and more the rocky landscape was covered in blue and green firs. It was breathtaking in its loneliness.

Aletia had been right, and so he had run. Herb, Lois, and Stanley had called after him, begging him to stop. Herb even gave chase, but Dallas was a creature of the woods. Long lopes sped him through the trees at a speed even Herb couldn't match. Soon, their cries no longer reached his sensitive ears. Still, Dallas ran, each bounding stride carrying him further and further away from his friends and his home.

I'm a monster, he had howled again and again. *A goddamn monster.* The full moon agreed, and so he ran.

When the setting moon finally released its hold on him, his human legs continued to push him northeast, further and further into the wilderness. When exhaustion finally claimed him, he curled up in the leaves under a broad-limbed elm and cried until he slept. The full moon turned him again that night, so he hunted. The following morning, he woke next to the eviscerated corpse of a stag. Drying blood and bits of entrails covered the ground, each piece of torn flesh a gory reminder of Dan and Colton and what Dallas had become. The sun had trekked halfway across the sky before he was able to look away and continue on.

Dallas figured he'd head east across Michigan's Upper Peninsula until he reached Sault Ste. Marie. From there, he could jump the Canadian border and lose himself in southern Ontario. There were easier ways to hike across Michigan, but he forced himself far up into the mountains. With any luck, he'd fall off a cliff or get eaten by a bear. At the very least, he'd be far away from anyone else.

Now, two weeks into the wilderness, he stood staring at the deep, wide forest. The quiet landscape offered little distraction and allowed his thoughts to find their stubborn way back to Aletia. He knew she was out there somewhere, rounding up the Society and planning an all-out assault on Trappersville. He only hoped Lois, Herb, and Stanley would be long gone before then.

Thinking of his friends brought a flood of unbidden memories. Drinking and playing pool with the guys. Lois's first day on the job at Ronnie's when she bent over to refill his coffee and he got a peek down her shirt. Seeing Deloris for the first time at the dealership, freshly washed and only six miles on the odometer. Hauling Herb up onto the bar to give the big toast after the bowling tourney. So many moments, so many normal, human moments.

"All gone now, I suppose," he said out loud. If the forest below had a different opinion, it kept it to itself.

He only had two more weeks until the next full moon. When it came, he wanted to be as far away from civilization as possible. With a heavy sigh, Dallas set his shoulders and headed down the far side of the hill toward the waiting trees.

He hiked during the day and slept beneath the stars at night. He drank from streams and snare-trapped rabbits and squirrels for food. He got wet when it rained, cold when the season's first snow came down, and warmed himself on a wide rock when the sun returned. As the days passed, the man that was Dallas: lover, brawler, champion bowler, professional beer drinker, recreational pool hustler, HVAC repairman, member of the Society, and Hero of Trappersville fell away piece by piece. Lost among the sticks and leaves and moss-covered rocks, they left only a shell of a man. Inside that shell, the wolf waited for the next full moon.

• • • • • • • • •

AUTHOR'S NOTE

Dallas tried his darndest to do the right thing. With that and a buck fifty, you can buy a pop. What will happen to the poor werewolf? What will happen to the friends he left behind?

321

The adventure continues in **Undead Cheesehead**. A zombie apocalypse is overtaking Trappersville, and it's up to Stanley to stop it. He can't do it alone, though. Sure, Lois and Herb will help, but they'll need Dallas, too. If that isn't enough, Stanley will have to be twice the man he is. Or three times. Maybe even four...

· · · · ● · ● · ● · · ·

If you like paranormal comedy, sign up for my once-a-month newsletter, **The Paranomedy Pint**, and get a **FREE short story!** Each month, I share a great book to read, a fun show to watch, a tasty drink to drink, and a little paranormal weirdness, too.

· · · · · ● · ● · ● · · ·

THE END

Did you have fun?

I HAD A HECK of a good time writing this book. If you enjoyed reading it, I hope you'll take a moment to share a rating or even a review! Ratings and reviews for authors are like tips for bartenders. We love 'em. They also help others who stumble across the book decide if they should give it a try.

Use these QR codes to easily post a review on your preferred site(s):

Jerry is the Worst

When I wrote my first book, *Wisconsin Vamp,* I didn't want Herb to know how he'd been turned. I also wanted him to be far from where vampires would normally be found. The challenge became: how to turn some schlub in rural Wisconsin into a vampire without having a vampire bite him.

I don't know how it works for other authors, but inspiration for me isn't like a lightning strike. It's more like a recall notice for my car's seat belt buckle that the manufacturer sends periodic postcards about. I get a nudge here, a nudge there. Eventually—finally—all those nudges from the universe turn into inspiration.

In this case, the first nudge was rewatching *Interview with the Vampire* and wondering about Claudia's transformation. The next nudge came a few years later when I watched the 2004 Russian film *Night Watch* by Timur Bekmambetov and Laeta Kalogridis. If you haven't seen it, put it on your list. Fantastic urban fantasy. I won't bore you with a synopsis here, but I do want to mention one element:

the Gloom. It's a dimension that supernatural creatures can travel through and draw strength from.

It's also full of mosquitos.

I saw that movie and loved the idea of mosquitos as tiny vampires. So, there I was, thinking about schlubs becoming vampires and vampire mosquitoes. How Herb would become a vampire was slowly taking shape. All I needed was a way to get a vampire mosquito to northern Wisconsin and have it bite a line cook. The next nudge was circa 2010 when the news was full of stories about bed bugs invading New York City. Every time I traveled, I was terrified of what I'd inadvertently bring home.

Lightning finally struck, and Jerry, the traveling paper salesman, was born.

When I started *Wisconsin Vamp,* I didn't plan on writing a series. By the end, though, I knew I wanted to keep going. Dallas and Stanley were too fun to simply have as side characters in a book. They needed their own adventures. I also really liked Jerry. The poor guy that inadvertently kicked off Herb's trials and travails struck me as a comedic device. He became an elemental force. Chaos incarnate. The personification of just how wonderfully random the universe can be. Sending Jerry around the country and infesting his luggage with supernatural bed bugs tickled my funny bone, so I gave him a rotten boss and bought him a plane ticket to Illinois.

Where will he go next? What new disasters will he inadvertently cause?

Don't just sit there wondering. Read *Undead Cheesehead* and find out!

A Bit About Scott

People say you should write what you know. That's damned good advice, so Scott writes about ordinary Midwesterners making an extraordinary mess of things. Hey, if the flannel fits...

Oh, one more thing. "Ordinary" totally includes vampires, werewolves, zombies, witches, shapeshifters, aliens and more!

Find Scott on:

www.swbauthorblog.wordpress.com

www.facebook.com/swbuthor

www.instagram.com/swbauthor

www.goodreads.com/swbauthor

www.bookbub.com/authors/scott-burtness

and in bars and bowling alleys up in the Midwest.

FREE Short Story

Get *Five Stars*, a FREE demonic horror comedy short story, when you sign up for **The Paranomedy Pint**, Scott's once-a-month email featuring a great book to read, a fun show to watch, something terrific to drink, and a little paranormal weirdness to enjoy!!

Beer-Fueled Urban Fantasy by Scott Burtness

THE MISADVENTURES OF A PARANORMAL
POST-RELATIONSHIP PERSONAL EFFECTS
REPOSSESSION SPECIALIST

An Oracle Walks into a Bar

A Scarecrow Wins an Award

A Siren Sings Her Heart Out

MONSTERS IN THE MIDWEST

Wisconsin Vamp

Northwoods Wolfman

Undead Cheesehead

Monsters in the Midwest: The Complete Trilogy

Bjørn Again: A Monsters in the Midwest short story

SCOTT BURTNESS

ODDS 'n' ENDS

A is for All the Monsters We Can't Stand: A Hilarious Monster-Themed Coloring Book for Grownups

Story and poems by Scott Burtness | Illustrations by Harold Torres